Hailey Edwards writes about questionable applications of otherwise perfectly good magic, the transformative power of love, the family you choose for yourself, and blowing stuff up. Not necessarily all at once. That could get messy. She lives in Alabama with her husband, their daughter, and a herd of dachshunds.

Visit her website at www.haileyedwards.net

By *Hailey Edwards*

The Foundling Series

Bayou Born
Bone Driven
Death Knell

DEATH KNELL

Hailey Edwards

piatkus

PIATKUS

First published in Great Britain in 2018 by Piatkus

1 3 5 7 9 10 8 6 4 2

Copyright © Hailey Edwards 2018

The moral right of the author has been asserted.

A CIP catalogue record for this book
is available from the British Library.

ISBN 978-0-349-41709-7

Typeset in Goudy by M Rules
Printed and bound in Great Britain by
Clays Ltd, Elcograf S.p.A.

Papers used by Piatkus are from well-managed forests
and other responsible sources.

Piatkus
An imprint of
Little, Brown Book Group
Carmelite House
50 Victoria Embankment
London EC4Y 0DZ

An Hachette UK Company
www.hachette.co.uk

www.littlebrown.co.uk

For Oliver Doodlesworth and
Charles Beanington.

*The only thing better than having
one corgi is having two.*

CHAPTER ONE

———◦◦◦———

Balmy air slid over my skin, the tickle that of mosquito legs as they made their selection from the buffet that was my bare thigh. The buzzing drone pulled me from sleep as I swatted at my ear. The air conditioner I installed yesterday with help from Miller hummed in its mount over the bed, but my private Antarctica had turned downright Floridian thanks to the door a nighttime visitor had left open.

Sunlight pierced the backs of my eyelids and erased the muzziness from sleep. I almost knocked over the precarious stack of romance novels cluttering my nightstand when I reached for the bottle I had shoved to the farthest edge to make room for more books. As I sipped the lukewarm water, my vision cleared, and once I identified the culprit, I huffed out a laugh.

A dragon tail wrapped my ankle four times, its sliver-white scales iridescent in the dawn. The slender tip tickled the arch in my foot when I moved, and its scales fanned when I traced a scallop with my fingertip. The sleek length hung off the end of the king-size bed, snaked across the floor, then slithered out of sight.

I swung my legs over the side of the mattress and stretched until my spine popped like bubble wrap under a zealous thumb, then followed the serpentine path winding before me.

Beyond the threshold, sprawled across the deck, the rest of the dragon lazed in dappled light the way a housecat might bask in a sunny rectangle on the carpet. With one crimson eye slitted, he watched my approach, the edge of his lips curling to expose knifelike teeth in sharp amusement.

An inquiring noise rose in the dragon's throat, a polite inquiry about how well I had slept.

"You do realize—" I yawned wide, jaw cracking, "—I can't afford to air condition the entire swamp."

I regretted the words as soon as I tasted them. They savored of Aunt Nancy. They called to mind a bright red door on a tidy cottage that now sat empty. They reminded me of a beanpole of a woman with dark skin and warm, brown eyes. *We're air conditioning the whole neighborhood standing here like this.*

Never again would she fuss about cooling costs, and that was Famine's fault, and War's fault, and mine.

The dragon, catching the drift of my thoughts, lifted his closest wing in an invitation to join him.

Affection was so much easier between us this way. I understood the dragon better than the man he sometimes pretended to be.

A firm yank on my ankle brought me stumbling closer and put me in range of his membranous wings. The heavy wrist nearest me smacked against the backs of my knees, and my legs crumpled. He caught me in a clawed hand then lowered me gently onto the planks by his side. The treacherous wing lifted again, and this time the dragon arched the ridged line above his eye in a silent dare.

"Bully," I groused, reclining against his sun-warmed hide. I pretended not to love the silken drape of his wing across my shoulders, or its comforting weight, but I did, and I doubted he was fooled. "I'm still mad at you." I plucked at the tank top Portia had loaned me to sleep in after I accepted the hard truth that no AC in the bunkhouse meant no long-sleeve pajamas for me. "You woke me up early on the last day of my vacation."

Vacation was not the right word, but we all pretended it fit anyway.

His massive paw flexed against the wood, lightly scratching, a cat sharpening his claws.

"You could have just asked." We had played this game before, almost every morning for the past week. "You do have a voice."

Judders along his side alerted me to the fact the dragon was laughing at me.

"I swear to God, I will end you if you try any funny business." I gripped his wing joint at the wrist and swung onto his back, digging in my heels to keep my seat while reaching up and scratching behind the rounded tabs of his ears and the fringe of mane that itched worse in this humidity. "I mean it this time."

"That's what you said last time," Santiago drawled from the murky water. "And the time before that."

The urge to cover my arms prickled in my palms, but Santiago was coterie. That meant, even if he didn't like me much, he was safe. Still, old habits died hard, and exposing the intricate rose-gold lines banding me from wrist to shoulder required a courage I had never tested before coming to live at the bunkhouse with the others. The sight comforted them, connected us, but it had alienated me from other humans.

Humans.

As if I wasn't one any longer.

As if I ever had been.

"I expected him to go up." I glowered at Santiago while raking my fingers through silky fur. "Not down."

"The first time maybe," he allowed. "What about all the rest?"

The dragon perked his ears for my answer, but I wasn't about to admit the light that sparked in Cole's eyes when he suckered me onto his back then dove into the swamp was worth picking duckweed out of my teeth every single time.

A peculiar sting along my spine, the sensation of eyes on the point where the two halves of the rose-gold *rukav* joined at my nape, had me ready to shout a warning to Santiago. Only our uninvited guest wasn't my sister, War, but my new partner, Adam Wu.

Instinct warned me to hold still, even if it meant exposing the full design spreading over my shoulders and across my back to him.

Golden-brown eyes steeped in eternal knowledge stared at me across a pier that felt too small all of a sudden. The black hair he kept trimmed in an undercut was slicked back with the same precision that defined him. Built tall and lean, he made his simple black suit look good. The clean lines and quality fabric whispered rather than screamed *money* so long as you didn't notice the shoes, the watch, or the belt. His predatory elegance as he crossed the dock made me wonder at how humans ever imagined him to be one of them.

Water rippled on my periphery as Santiago made his exit.

Chicken.

Wu couldn't still be pissed about that trip to New York. Probably. Maybe.

"The picture of domestic bliss." His sardonic grin drew my attention to the fullness of his upper lip, and its redness. Plucking it was a nervous habit of his, and I had zero intentions of cluing him in to his one damning tell. "How charming."

"Wu," I said, and damn if I didn't sound a little bit glad to see him. "I didn't expect you until tomorrow."

"There's been an incident." His gaze slid down my arms in an intimate caress. "Your vacation is over."

Again, the urge to cover myself sent fine tremors racing down my arms, but I squared my shoulders and faced him head-on, refusing to show weakness.

A warning rumble poured through the air between us as the dragon grasped what the fascination in Wu's eyes meant. He bared fangs longer than my hand and hissed, his pink tongue ribboning between his teeth. Unspooling his tail from my ankle, he cracked the stinging tip against the dock a half inch from the toe of Wu's fancy shoes, daring him to step closer.

"Control him," Wu said, sounding bored, though I noticed he didn't move, "or I will."

Cold blossomed in my heart, each beat pumping icy rage through my bloodstream. "You can try."

"Perhaps one day," he countered, like this was a negotiation, "but not today."

A tickle down my arm spooked me, and I almost toppled off the dragon when I twisted away from the unexpected contact. Above me, a boxy tom with midnight fur dangled a gray shawl from his jaws. The muted color reminded me of the downy fur on the baby field mice Thom brought me yesterday. For breakfast.

Murmuring my thanks as he cocooned me, I swung my leg over the dragon's side and slid until my feet hit the wood.

A heartbeat, half that, and Cole stood beside me dressed in his White Horse uniform. Murder glinted in his eyes where they fixed on Wu's vulnerable neck, and his lip quivered, his throat working like he already tasted hot blood pouring down his parched throat. "Who are you to look upon her?"

"I apologize," Wu said, not sounding contrite in the least. "I overstepped."

Cole trembled with barely leashed fury. "The *rukav* is for our eyes only."

Our, he said.

But what I heard was *mine*.

"Let it go." I fit my palm between the slabs of his muscular shoulder blades. "There's no harm done."

Chest heaving, Cole turned his back on Wu, a deliberate insult, and captured my hand in his. He lowered his head until he buried his nose behind my ear. He filled his lungs, and his shoulders eased a fraction. His soft lips caressed my skin when he growled, low and possessive, "Show no one your markings."

The coterie was an extension of me, of us, and I understood he wasn't excluding them but outsiders. "You don't have to tell me twice."

But I kind of wished he would if it meant keeping his mouth on me.

This much, at least, had changed between us during my time at the bunkhouse. His knowing I wanted to be his while not making demands that he be mine in return was soothing a broken thing in him that needed to heal before we could be more than simmering potential.

I could wait for him. I *would* wait. For as long as it took. Forever if we had that long.

"We have company," I murmured with reluctance.

"Wu is not company," he countered, straightening. "He's a nuisance."

"Play nice." I drummed my fingers on his left pectoral, right over his heart. "We need him."

"All I need is . . ." His teeth clacked together, biting off the sentiment with a vicious snarl he aimed inward. "You're right."

His fingers uncurled from mine. "We do." Head down, he eased from under the weight of my palm. "For now."

Ignoring the raw ache when he withdrew, I trained my gaze on Wu, knowing he had heard every word and noted how Cole's swift urge to possess had dwindled to regret for wanting in the first place. Facing him was harder than it should have been after that. "Have a seat."

A wrought iron table and chair set anchored the far end of the pier, its heft meant to accommodate Cole. Wu and I sat. Cole positioned himself behind me, his right hand on my right shoulder. His gentle caress sought out the raised grooves beneath my skin before settling inside the gold-rimmed aureoles as if each ring had been fitted to his fingertips. The significance was lost on me, but Wu hid his clenched fists in his lap.

A yowl shot my attention up to the mossy-green umbrella, my contribution to the patio set, and I glared as Thom perched on the decorative pineapple finial, casting his cat-shaped shadow over Wu's face.

"So, Wu." I eyed the wobbling umbrella with apprehension. "What brings you all the way out here?"

"A corpse washed up in Vicksburg."

"Okay." I crossed my legs and leaned back in my chair, mentally adding purchasing seat cushions to my to-do list. The metal was digging into my tailbone. "Charun?"

"No." He mirrored my position. "Human."

"Okay," I said again, eager for him to get to the point. "What does that have to do with anything?"

Bodies washed up on shores all the time. The NSB wouldn't care about one more without good reason.

"The corpse was still twitching."

"You mean the person." A frown tightened my brow. "The person was still twitching."

"No, it wasn't alive."

And that, my friends, was the sound of the other shoe dropping. Or was it?

War had burned me once with her games already, but I couldn't afford to ignore events that might be portents of Death breaching. One last player on the board was all it took to kick start this round of Armageddon, and I aimed to win.

Cole trailed a scarred knuckle down my nape, the gesture absentminded, until he snagged a sweaty curl he wrapped around his finger. "Is this the first?"

"No." Wu forced his hands flat on his thighs. "The first in our jurisdiction, yes."

"This couldn't wait until morning?" I smashed a mosquito on my wrist above the heavy leather bracelet I wore, the one Cole had given to me. "You couldn't have called first?"

"I was in the neighborhood."

"Who were you visiting?" I snorted. "The frogs or the gators?"

"Perhaps I missed you." He squinted into the sun, making it impossible to read his expression. "It's been seven days, and you haven't texted once."

Unable to decide if he meant it, I dithered on my response until Cole stepped in to fill the silence.

"She's been in mourning." His palm wrapped my nape. "She needed time to heal."

Heal implied the festering wound in my chest where I preserved the memories of Aunt Nancy and Uncle Harold could be flushed clean with a squirt of peroxide, slathered over with antibiotic ointment, and bandaged until scar tissue formed. Maybe, for someone else, that might have been possible.

For me? Not so much.

I picked the scabs, relished the sting, and refreshed my blood vow to avenge them whatever the cost.

"You did too," I reminded Wu. "Famine almost killed you."

A negligent shrug rolled through his shoulders. "Hazards of the job."

"You look much better than the last time I saw you." A flush kissed my cheeks when I remembered that damn teddy bear and its assless chaps snuggled up against his side when I visited his room at the charun medical facility. "The break was good for both of us."

The slow grin spreading across his face told me he had clued in to what I was thinking, and he chuckled.

Cole shifted his weight, sensing the undercurrents in our conversation but unsure what had caused the ripples that left me smelling embarrassed and Wu looking smug.

The coterie was aware I had visited Wu after sitting with my dad, who was being kept in a medically induced coma while they purged the toxic cocktail of charun venom Famine had been dosing him with since the night War took him captive. But I might have glossed over the BDSM plush the florist sent in place of the giant rubber ducky I had ordered to keep the peace.

"What brought you out here?" I set our conversation back on its tracks. "Specifically?"

Wu cut his eyes in the direction of the bedroom I was borrowing. From Cole. A sleek garment bag with a designer label hung from a rusted nail. How it got there, I had no clue. His hands had been empty when I greeted him. Or so I'd thought. But I had been otherwise occupied when he arrived. Maybe Wu had been watching us for longer than he let on. "I brought your new uniform."

A knot formed in my throat at the reminder I would never wear my Canton Police Department uniform again, and I couldn't swallow past it. "Not more spandex, I hope."

His thumb smoothed the upper arch of his lip. "Not this time."

"Hmm." Curious as a cat, I stalked over to inspect his offering. The zipper parted beneath my hand, and I thumbed through the hangers one by one. The bag held one outfit in triplicate. I almost laughed. "Wow. We really are the men in black. Only with demons instead of aliens." I thought about the fact the charun came from other terrenes, other worlds. "Or maybe not."

The contents included three tailored pairs of black slacks and three fitted blazers to match them. Three black leather belts hung down in front of three pressed shirts, the bright white offering the only pop of color to my new wardrobe.

"Check under the bag," Wu instructed in a tone that screamed *but wait—there's more!*

A box emblazoned with *Lucchese* winked up at me. Without cracking it open, I guessed it contained supple leather boots that fit the theme. "What?" I shook the box. "Only one pair?"

Ignoring my snark, he flicked his wrist again. "No, not that one."

A second box huddled behind the first as though designer labels intimidated it as much as they did me.

"Hello, lovely." The hard-shell plastic case gave away its contents. "You bought me a gun." I lifted the case by the molded handle and flipped the tabs. "A Glock 19." I lifted the gun out of the foam and tested its grip. "She's a skosh smaller than my 22." I had an emotional attachment to the 22 after carrying one for four years, but it had been department issue. I didn't miss the extra length or weight offhand, but a trip to the range would earn or lose my trust. "Concealed carry?"

"That's the idea," he said dryly. "There's a shoulder holster in the bottom of the garment bag."

"Do all new recruits get the same welcome package?" I appraised my haul. "Or am I special?"

"You're my partner." He savored the word *my* like it was his favorite flavor. "You're also cadre." The reminder of my lineage sobered him and me both. "There's no one like you on this terrene or any other, Luce Boudreau."

The sentiment, while sweet, was not what I wanted to hear. "Kapoor mentioned an Otillian on the taskforce."

The lure of a charun from Otilla, like me, who might have answers to all my questions about where I came from, who I was to those people, was his favorite bait.

"I have limited interactions with the taskforce," he said, which neither confirmed nor denied the claim.

I bit the inside of my cheek until I tasted blood to keep my questions bottled up for later. He was always more forthcoming when we were alone. Asking him around the coterie put Portia, Maggie, and me in danger of testosterone poisoning.

"Do I get a company car," I joked to prove I had moved on, "or do I drive the Bronco to work?"

"I'll pick you up this week. Your car hasn't been delivered yet."

A splash alerted me to Santiago's reemergence. He flattened his forearms on the pier and hauled himself out of the water. He sat there dripping wet, feet in the swamp, and grinned at Wu. "What he means is they haven't had time to install the surveillance they want placed on your vehicle."

Seeing no reason to deny what we all knew to be true, Wu shrugged. "That too."

"No one has mentioned where work actually is," I pointed out. "Where do I report?"

"To me," Wu said, too smug for his own good.

"Vicksburg is about an hour away." Santiago reclined across the planks, crossed his ankles then linked his hands behind his head. "I assume you'll have Luce home in time for dinner?"

Predatory stillness swept through Cole and triggered a cascade of shivers down my spine, but it wasn't a fear response.

"It depends on our initial findings." Wu let his gaze linger on me. "We might spend a night in the city."

"That won't be necessary," I cut him off before Cole sprouted a tail and strangled Wu with it. "It's close enough we can drive down again the next day if we have unanswered questions."

"Or we could all go," Miller suggested as he clomped down the pier with bags of takeout strung down his arms. "It's a short trip." He glanced over his shoulder at Maggie—or Portia—who carried a tray of drinks. "They're getting restless. Getting them away from Canton, even overnight, would help."

As always, my heart pinched when I set eyes on Portia, and it was her. The swagger wasn't Maggie's graceful stride, and the cocked hip when she stopped was wrong too. Despite the fact I was looking at Maggie's body, I saw no trace of my best friend in there.

"Luce," they whispered, voice breaking as Mags took the wheel.

"Sorry," I murmured, hating my guilt had dragged her to the surface. "I was just wondering if he's right. Are you guys up for a road trip?"

"Yes," Maggie breathed. "We're bored out of our minds."

Town was out of the question for them unless they pulled on a ballcap and shades then rode in the back of the SUVs behind darkly tinted windows. Maggie was still an open missing persons case for the FBI, which meant Portia had to remain scarce too unless we wanted to answer some tough questions.

"You heard the lady," I told Wu. "Looks like we're talking a family vacation to Vicksburg."

My new partner sighed, his weary resignation music to my ears.

"I will allow this." He stood, the heavy chair legs scraping, and crossed to me. "For you."

"Aww, shucks." I beamed up at him. "Thanks, partner."

"You grasp the implications." Gold sparkled in the depths of his brown eyes. "Are you prepared?"

To face the final cadre member? To face Death?

"Yes." Fingers twitching at my side, I recalled the glide of Uncle Harold's blood, hot and slick, on my skin the night Famine blew her cover, and I blasted a hole through my uncle's gut. "I am."

Death had already come at me, after all. I was eager to return the favor.

CHAPTER TWO

Jean Ashford smelled about as good as you might expect for a bloated corpse that had been submerged in water for several days before washing ashore. The features were feminine, yet indistinct due to swelling and discoloration. Seams where flesh had split or been sliced by floating debris made the cause of death impossible to pin down at first glance. Hungry fish hadn't helped things, either.

I hated morgues, the neatness of people shelved for later perusal, but most cops felt the same.

Reminding myself I wasn't a cop anymore didn't help, and neither did my partner's cool detachment.

This was a human, and I was the only person in the room who cared what happened to those.

"What's this?" A box of blue nitrile gloves sat on the counter beside me. I snapped one on and turned the victim's hand palm-up on the table. "Looks like she put up a fight. There's skin under her nails."

Wu made no comment.

"This makes no sense. She was a floater." I picked at her nailbeds. "This tissue should be as decomposed as the rest of her, but there's fresh blood smearing her fingertips." I repositioned her hand how I'd found it, a small courtesy that didn't matter to her either way. "What aren't you telling me?"

"You could fill this room with things I'm not telling you," Wu mused. "Perhaps the entire building."

"That's so comforting. I can't imagine why you didn't have a partner until now."

"I didn't have one, because I didn't want one." His grin was slight, pointed. "I want you."

"Mmm-hmm." Conquest on a choke chain was what he wanted. He was settling for me. For now. To entertain the notion he meant anything else was ludicrous. "Her injuries are otherwise consistent with a drowning death. There are no peculiar markings or indications she was a host."

"That's what makes this interesting."

I cocked an impatient eyebrow and waited for him to enlighten me. Even in the early days, Rixton hadn't been this insufferable as a training officer.

Rixton.

God, I missed him.

"Touch her. Skin to skin." Wu waited. "Go on."

"I hope you brought some antibac with you." I snapped off the glove and pressed a single bare finger to her shoulder. Her eyes opened, milky and vacant. Her mouth gaped open, her lips forming words, but no sound emerged. I yelped and jumped back three feet, flinging my hand like it was on fire instead of just cold. "What the hell, Wu?"

Slowly, her eyelids sank lower until her matted lashes rested on her cheeks.

"I was curious." He touched her in the same spot. Nothing happened. "I wondered if the corpse would relay its message to any charun or only to you."

I worked through what he wasn't saying. "Is this proof Death has breached?"

"There are other charun who can control the dead," he allowed. "That's why it was important to get you here as soon as possible to test my theory." He gestured toward her. "Try again. This time maintain contact."

Skin crawling, I did as he directed. Nothing happened. "Well, that was anticlimactic."

"This body isn't fresh enough. The vocal cords are too degraded." He glared at poor Jean with a snarled-up lip. "We're done here."

Fresh. Like produce. *Ugh.* A little sympathy for the dead wouldn't kill him.

"Well?" I glared on my way to wash up in the basin near the exit. "Does this mean Death is here or not?"

"I'm not sure," he said after a minute.

I said what he must be thinking. "War pulled this stunt with Famine. She made us think Famine was on the prowl, but we had no hard evidence she had breached until it was too late."

"Has Santiago mentioned any disturbance in the breach site to you?"

Santiago had sunk a Doppler something or other in Cypress Swamp, where I first surfaced. The idea was he could track disturbances in the water and notify us of a possible breach, but he hadn't said a word. Since he wasn't the quiet type, that meant he had nothing to share.

"No." I dried my hands. "I'll ask when we get back to the hotel. He might want to check his equipment to be sure." I kept my distance from the body on the tray. "Any other surprises?"

He dared me with a cocked eyebrow. "Where would the fun be in telling you?"

We walked out together, past a tech who had to lock his knees to prevent himself from falling at my feet. Again. I suppressed an instinctive cringe, grimaced when I tried to smile, and kept going.

"Worship makes you uneasy." He sounded amused. "Others thrive on it."

"I don't need someone to pat my head or rub my belly every time I do something right. I prefer constructive criticism to brown-nosing."

"I'll keep that in mind."

"Where to next?" We stepped out into the sun, and I filled my lungs with sweet, fresh air. "The river?"

"The river," he agreed. "We need to determine if the corpse was raised there or elsewhere."

We drove downtown to a park that promised Mississippi River views, walked the curving sidewalk until we hit a scenic overlook, then climbed down to the water. The police department had left a small flag stuck in the ground to mark where the corpse had been found. We picked our way there until it became obvious there was no point in being careful. The scene had been trampled, any evidence destroyed.

"Three teenagers found her," Wu explained before I could bitch about how we knew to do things right in Canton. "The scene was trampled prior to the arrival of the authorities."

Oh. Well then. My apologies to the uniforms of Vicksburg. "What's in the report?"

"One of the boys, a Jay Lambert, saw a woman struggling against the current and dove in to save her. He hauled her onto the shore to impress his would-be girlfriend, and that's when the screaming started."

"I bet." Poor kids. I can only imagine the boy's horror at what he'd rescued. "Anyone question them?"

"The local police." Wu's tone implied that interacting with humans was a waste of everyone's time. "The corpse scratched him during the altercation. The girlfriend was concerned about him turning into a zombie. The police, thanks to one of our agents, didn't take samples of what is clearly the boy's skin and blood beneath the victim's nails. They told him he was scratched by a tree limb."

Tree limbs are prickly boogers, but not many twigs wrestle with their saviors. "He bought that?"

Wu stared down his nose at me. "He wasn't given a choice."

Good luck with that. Teens weren't as gullible as most people thought. And they recorded *everything.* "I assume you've secured his phone and those of his friends."

"We're missing one." His lips flattened. "The best friend claims he dropped his in the river helping Lambert to shore, but cell phone records show activity after the fact." His annoyance was plain. "We'll secure it soon enough. He won't be able to resist accessing the footage for long."

Social media conditioning made that a promise. The kid would strike while the iron was hot to snag his fifteen seconds of fame. The scratches brought up another question. "Is contagion a concern?"

"Despite the human fascination with their own demise, there are no transmutable zombie viruses."

"So the kid will be okay?"

"We had our doctors examine him."

Putting my faith in their doctors—in any doctors—was hard, but these were the same white coats handling Dad's care. I had to believe that meant they were the best. Otherwise, I might be tempted to let Conquest slip her leash the next time I visited him.

"All right." We walked the riverbank, searching for clues. "Tell me about the other cases."

"There have been two. One in Louisiana and one in Tennessee."

I thought about that. "Both places the Mississippi River travels."

"Yes." He gazed across the water. "No attempt was made to conceal their identities. The bodies belong to local missing persons."

"Any other connections? Gender? Race? Charun affiliations?"

"None we have determined. The discovery of Jean Ashford might help with that."

"You don't sound convinced." We reached an incline that required more climbing than I was dressed to do without ruining my fancy new suit. "What's your theory? You must have one."

"Death might be trying to contact you. Why reanimate a corpse if not to deliver a message?" His expression tightened. "The membrane between worlds is worn thin over the seal, but she's no Conquest. She can't slip in and then leave. She would have to communicate via a surrogate."

Who needed passé stationery when you could just murder one of the locals? "She has people on this terrene who would help?"

"Each member of the cadre has her loyal followers, as you've seen. Charun loyal to Otillian rule, if not to the individual embodiments."

"How would they figure out the timing, though? Her contact would have to know when Famine breached to be certain when it was Death's turn." Only an intermediary who had contacts within a coterie or the NSB could monitor the situation that closely. "Do you think she could have asked War to bring an emissary through with her?"

Allowances had been made for Famine, so why not Death too?

"It's possible," he conceded. "Most coteries won't leave their master. Most of Death's coterie can't leave her."

"Something tells me I'm not going to like this." I braced myself. "Why not?"

"Unlike War, Death doesn't birth her coterie. She raises them. Her spiritual energy animates them."

"They have to be in close range, or they drop like the puppets they are. Gotcha." I kicked a rock into the water. "Either Death is closer than we think, or her proxy is that powerful."

"We might understand better if we heard the message."

A knot formed in my gut. "Are you really telling me a corpse is going to open its mouth and speak to me?"

Wrinkles gathered across Wu's forehead. "Weren't you listening to me earlier?"

"I thought you were being metaphorical."

Relay its message through clues on its person or—hell, I don't know. Not sit up and talk.

"Your touch animated the corpse. Why key it to you if not to tell you something?"

"I'm really wishing I was an only child right now."

"With any luck," Wu said, "you soon will be."

We returned to the hotel after our excursion to regroup. Up in our suite, Wu passed me the case files on the other victims, which he'd had couriered over while we were off corpse-whispering, and I settled in on the plush sectional to read.

Wu had secured us a suite with four bedrooms, a generous living space, and a fully functional kitchen. It was luxurious by anyone's standards and ridiculous compared to mine. But Portia and Maggie lit up like twin Christmas trees when they spotted the jacuzzi tub in their room, and I didn't have the heart to grumble about the excess.

Miller plopped down next to me sometime later, and I took a break to let my eyes rest.

"Where is everyone?" I lifted my phone to check for messages but found none. "I haven't seen any of you guys since breakfast."

"Cole is meeting a local contact, and Thom is working a case." He pulled my feet onto his lap to give himself more room. "Santiago is out with Portia and Maggie."

"You left them alone with him?" I wrinkled my nose. "He's such a party pooper. Why didn't you go?"

Miller glanced away, his fingers tracing the design embossed on my boots. "Portia invited Santiago."

The two were good friends, so that made sense. What didn't track was why Miller let it get to him when their closeness had never bothered him before. "What did Maggie say?"

"She said it was fine."

"But you wanted to go," I guessed. *With her.*

He didn't answer since living at the bunkhouse had brought us—and our secrets—closer.

"Maggie was engaged," I said gently. "She loved Justin very much. She's not thinking romantic thoughts about Santiago—" *or anyone else,* "—if that's what worries you."

"I don't want her in that way," he rushed out on a single breath. "Not exactly." He looked devastated. "She's human."

"Explain *not exactly* to me." I set aside the file to give him my full attention. "You're allowed to want, Miller."

"I don't want Portia." A flush stained his cheeks. "I never have."

I took a stab in the dark. "The combination of Portia and Maggie is doing something for you. She's just enough charun to hit your radar, and just enough Maggie to make it different."

"Yes," he exhaled on a gust of relief.

Since we were confiding in each other, I told him, "Wu explained the mating urge is all instinct for charun, that biology determines whether a pair stays together or switches partners." I held my breath. "He claims charun don't love the way humans do."

"He's right," Miller agreed, cracking my heart. "Charun are more primal than humans. We don't process emotion in the same range they do. Love is . . . complex. I don't fully understand its scope." He hesitated. "That doesn't mean we don't have an equivalent."

Behind my ribs, my heart gave a painful lurch. "Is it more or less?"

"More," he said without hesitation. "We are longer-lived, and we enter into bonds mindful that we're choosing life partners for the mortal equivalent of eternity. There is no greater honor than to bond with a mate, and there is no breaking one after it's set. Even if you fall out of . . . love . . . it remains."

A sick feeling twisted my gut. "Are Cole and I . . . ?"

"Ask him." Miller softened his voice. "When you're ready to understand, ask him."

I rubbed the skin above my breastbone. "What if I don't want to know?"

"You do." He brushed his knuckle down my cheek. "Or you wouldn't have brought it up."

"Damn logic." I forced a laugh.

"Luce." He hesitated before saying, "He was never this way with her."

Tears sprang to my eyes, and I blinked them away. "Thanks."

"You deserve to know that he sees you for who you are and not what you once were."

I reached over and squeezed his hand, marveling at the comfort in that small touch. "I know all of Maggie's favorite movies. I might be persuaded to provide a list if you help me out with a problem."

Miller ducked his head, pink creeping up his throat before he cleared it. "How can I be of assistance?"

CHAPTER THREE

———◆———

I was curled up on the couch, typing up a report for Kapoor on our initial findings, when the TV clicked on. I started at the sound but then smiled as Cole sank down beside me. He pulled my legs onto his lap then coasted his fingers down the grooves pressed into my boots. I had the oddest impression he was subconsciously mimicking Miller, layering his scent over the other male's, and it turned the center of my chest to warm goo.

"There's something you ought to see." He turned up the volume. "The local news just caught wind of it."

An anchorwoman onscreen stood outside the local hospital, her face grave. " ... Jay Lambert was discovered foaming at the mouth and mumbling incoherently. If you think his name sounds familiar, it's because he was the boy who heroically dove into the Mississippi River, only to realize the woman he meant to save had already drowned."

"Your informant has the inside track on this?"

"According to her, six other local teens have also suffered epileptic fits. All friends of his."

"I've got to call Wu, see if he's heard." I rubbed my face. "This kind of heat is just what we don't need."

Laugh at zombie viruses, eh? He wouldn't be grinning after he heard this news.

"I've got Santiago researching who discovered the previous victims and who they interacted with afterward. We ought to have an idea if this is an isolated incident soon."

"With our luck?" I laughed. "What are the odds?"

Cole awarded me the point then went quiet. "I bumped into Santiago and Portia at the Mesa Grill."

Mmm. I could go for some steak and chicken fajitas right about now. A sizzling platter of onions and peppers, fresh pico de gallo and sour cream with fresh tortillas to wrap it all up in. "You met your contact at a restaurant?"

"You expected a back alley?"

Honestly? "Yes."

"We operate a legit business. There's no reason for cloak and dagger." He shrugged. "Most of the time."

Forcing my growly stomach on the backburner, I zeroed in on the topic change. "Was Maggie enjoying herself?"

"She wasn't present. That's why I mentioned it. The girls are getting better at trading off so they both enjoy new experiences, but that didn't happen here." He squeezed my ankles. "Santiago intimidates her. I'm sure the way Portia acts around him doesn't help matters. When they're alone with him, she sleeps."

"Maggie prefers Miller."

"Yes," he said, looking at me. "Most females do."

"Miller is good friend material." I held out my hand, still amazed when he meshed our fingers. "Besides, if I can stomach your clandestine meetings at Mesa Grill with a hot charuness, then you can deal with Miller being my friend."

"How do you know Lorelei is hot?"

"Ugh. Even her name is sexy." I flicked a hand to encompass the room. "I have yet to meet an unattractive charun. Some have made poor host choices, true, but otherwise . . . I'm thinking you guys are vain."

"And you?" His gaze slid over my face. "What about your beauty?"

"I can't remember wishing myself like this, if that's what you mean." I flushed to the tips of my toes. "I was a kid. Who can even tell then? I was all elbows and knees with twigs and mud in my hair."

Vanity might be encoded in charun DNA. Pretty sure made life easier. That was an ugly fact. But I had avoided mirrors and reflected surfaces all my life. The disconnect between what I saw and who I was had lessened with the understanding that *dissociative* wasn't a strong enough word for my condition. Two fully realized people shared this body, and neither of them wanted to let go of the wheel.

"The first time I saw your chosen form," he said gruffly, "I knew you would only grow lovelier with age. I hadn't doubted it. Beauty is a weapon, and Conquest wields it mercilessly, but watching you mature into the woman you are now was . . . " An expression that never settled into one emotion flittered across his face. "I wasn't prepared for the experience."

"You watched me grow up." All those years I could have known him, known them, wasted. Except that might have cost me my aunt and uncle even sooner, injured my father worse, lost me Rixton and my job before I learned either of them well. No, I couldn't regret keeping the two halves of my life separate for as long as it lasted.

"You're allowed to have mixed feelings about that."

"All I have are mixed feelings."

About *me*. That's what he meant, and who could blame him?

"I should shower." I tugged on my legs, but he refused to let go. "I smell like morgue."

"I hurt you." He cradled the side of my face in his palm. "It's not my intention."

"I know." I gripped his bare wrist, and the metal warmed beneath my palm. "I don't hold it against you."

A shuddering exhale tripped over his lips when I caressed the scar tissue with my thumb. "Luce . . . "

The door swung open so hard it smacked the wall and bounced. Cole and I broke apart, and this time he let me put my feet on the floor.

"We're back," Portia called, arms spread wide, shopping bags hanging from her wrists. "Today was perfect, so perfect I bought everyone gifts." She plopped down between Cole and me. "Here's one for you." She passed him a box of condoms. "And one for you." She winked as she passed me a handful of fabric. "I would ask you to model, but Cole gets so territorial. It's hot—don't get me wrong—but I doubt he wants the guys to get an eyeful of your *assets*."

A strangled noise caught in my throat as I detangled my gift. "Dental floss. You shouldn't have."

Portia lifted the black lace teddy by its gossamer straps and held it aloft for all to admire.

It was beautiful, and it was highly inappropriate. No wonder she liked it.

"Oh, come on." She elbowed Cole in the side. "It's only a matter of time, and we all know it." She wrinkled her nose then hooked her thumb in his direction. "Has anyone ever told you—?"

"Yes." I groaned, covering my face with my hands since the

teddy was no help. "You can all smell my dirty thoughts. I got it. You really don't have to keep reminding me."

"Well, yes." She snorted. "But I was going to ask— Has anyone ever told you how he smells around you?"

Cole released a warning rumble that Portia was quick to ignore.

"No." I slowly peeked at her through my fingers.

"He gave you his room at the bunkhouse, Luce. He wants you in his bed. That's why he put you there."

I opened my mouth to point out there wasn't a sixth bedroom, and his was the largest.

Almost like they had built it expecting us to share.

Oh.

Oh.

"He's kicking out possessive pheromones that make the guys' eyes water." She batted her lashes at Cole. "It's enough to make a girl go into heat."

"That's enough, Portia."

"She deserves to know where she stands with you," she protested.

"It's all right." I stood and stretched. "I know where I stand with him."

Her eyes rounded. "You do?"

His narrowed. "You do?"

"Yes," I told them. "Anywhere he wants me."

The shocked expression wreathing her face was worth it. I turned on my heel and sauntered into the bedroom I had claimed with the expectation Cole would share it with me. I went to the bathroom and cranked up the hot water. When I reentered the bedroom to root through my luggage for pajamas, I bounced off his chest.

"*Oof.*"

He caught me by my upper arms and swept his hands down to capture mine. "You deserve more."

"I don't deserve what I have," I said truthfully. How he stomached touching me at all was a miracle given all that Conquest had done to him. "I'll take what I can get."

His fingers traced my knuckles. "It's not right."

A vice clamped over my heart, twisting closed until the pinch was unbearable.

"I didn't date much, and only part of that was because I was a curiosity and not a real person to most guys. But the other reason is I never wanted them. There was no spark, no desire. I figured I was too broken by the events that left me in the swamp to have those urges."

"And then you met me," he supplied with a hint of a smile.

"I met you," I agreed, "and I realized it wasn't that I didn't have those same desires. I just wanted . . . "

"Me."

"You," I rasped.

He nodded as if it made perfect sense to him that I would only want him to the exclusion of everyone else, and that worried me. There were ties between us I kept tripping over, but he wasn't in any rush to point out how those strings connected.

Ask him.

Ask why wanting him hurts so damn much.

But I was terrified what our connection meant about the one he shared with Conquest.

Bawk-bawk.

Guess Santiago wasn't the only chicken in our coterie.

After casting me a lingering glance over his shoulder, he left. As much as I wanted to invite him to join me, I didn't. I wasn't sure he would say yes, and with my heart still tender, I couldn't handle him saying no.

CHAPTER FOUR

Wu was waiting for me on my bed when I stepped out of the shower. That was my first hint Cole had left the building. Otherwise, my partner wouldn't have looked quite so chill where he sat beside my clothes. Kissing my *me* time goodbye, I gathered my pajamas and hit the bathroom to make myself comfortable.

Once I had detangled my hair, I squared off against Wu. "We need to visit Jay Lambert in the hospital."

Wu bestowed a patient look on me. "No."

Winding up for the fight, I growled, "He had some type of reaction—"

"Do you have access to his medical records?"

"No." I bit out my answer.

"Then how can you know the boy hasn't suffered a seizure like this before?"

"I don't know that. That's why we should visit him, chat up his doctor, and find out."

"Under what pretext?" Wu lounged on the mattress, legs crossed, files spread across his lap. "A follow-up to his heroic efforts to save a dead woman from drowning?"

"Sure, if that gets us in." It even skated the edge of truth. "I don't get it. Why are you fighting me?"

Santiago entered the room with a tablet balanced on one palm and a small kit tucked under his arm.

"Your focus is in the wrong place." He tapped the display, grunted at what it showed him, then pinched the screen. "You're bristling at a potential threat to a single human boy while your partner here is thinking globally."

"Six other local teens have been affected," I protested. "Cole's informant passed it on."

Santiago paused before shaking off his hesitation. "You're still using the wrong scale."

"I'm doing what I was brought here to do. I'm working the case I was given." I palmed a case file then shook it until all the papers slid across the floor. "Hmm. That's weird."

"You acting one apple short of a cobbler?" Santiago snorted. "Not all that weird."

"No," I said flatly, nudging the papers with my toe. "I don't see a passport. All I see is a receipt for a hotel in Vicksburg, Mississippi. It's almost like our case is *here*, and not out there."

The world could wait. This couldn't. Better to investigate a potentially infectious charun-borne disease now than let it blossom into a full-blown epidemic later.

"I won't fight you on this." Wu ignored both the mess and the mess-maker. "The corpse brought us here, not the boy. Or his friends. We're leaving tomorrow. There's nothing to do but wait until another body is discovered. We have other pressing matters in need of our attention."

Teeth grinding, I forced out, "Such as?"

"Sariah is asking for you." He had baited his line well and hooked me in one. "We believe she's ready to cut a deal."

War's firstborn, my niece, and the architect of my uncle's demise. Sariah wasn't my favorite person. The only cuts I wanted to deal her involved a knife at her throat.

Huh. I couldn't tell if the thought belonged to me or Conquest. That was probably not a great sign.

"Where is she being held?" I hadn't asked, and I didn't particularly want to know now.

"A secure facility," Wu said, and Santiago snickered behind him.

Intel on the cadre I expected to be doled out on an as-needed basis, so smacking face-first into this wall didn't bother me. "Is this the same secure facility where Famine is contained?"

"I'm not at liberty to divulge that information."

"You're a dirty liar, Wu." I jabbed him in the chest with my finger. "Who do you report to? Who is above you?"

Jaw flexing, he offered me no answers, and that was answer enough.

"You can show yourself out." I left the papers where they had fallen. "I'll pick this up tomorrow."

Wu rose stiffly, smoothed his clothes, and exited the room without another word.

"Here you go." Santiago plopped down next to me and offered his tablet. "Lambert's medical records."

"You are something else," I told him, eagerly scanning the history of an otherwise healthy young man. "I'm glad you're on my team."

"Stop it," he drawled. "I'm blushing."

"Lambert is clean." Vindication had me grinning like a fiend. "You know what that means?"

"Hmm. Let me guess." He reclaimed his tablet and wiped off my fingerprints. "We're paying him a visit."

"Got it in one."

"There's something else." He hit YouTube and cued up a video. "This went live ten minutes ago."

Already having a hunch what to expect, I wasn't shocked to learn one of the teens had filmed what they thought was a heroic rescue at the time. The clip cut out halfway through, but I didn't need to see more. "Your feed is stuck."

"No, it's not." He huffed in affront. "It's been erased."

"How did you erase it when I was sitting right here beside you the whole time?"

"Magic," he deadpanned. "The hard part will be rooting out all the copies. Social media is a plague, and teens spread it like fleas on rats."

"You can contain the situation?" Lambert and his cohorts had no chance of survival otherwise.

"Yeah, yeah," he grumped. "We caught it early. I can fix this."

Left unsaid was the real threat that if he hadn't been so damn good at what he does, it might have been unfixable. "Thanks."

"Let me put on shoes." Ignoring my appreciation, he stood. "I'll give Cole a heads-up."

Asking where Cole was still lit a fire under Santiago, though less now than in the beginning. I suspected he had given up on the inevitability of Cole and me, and he was tired of enforcing rules we were hellbent on breaking. Too bad neither of them had handed me a copy. I might not be so hot to smash them if I had an idea of why they existed in the first place. But Santiago would donate a kidney—if he had one—before giving me his reasons.

"Give me ten." *Goodbye, pajamas.* After I dressed, I cleaned up my mess. After all, it wasn't the paperwork's fault that Wu was an asshat. Santiago returned, tossing his keys then plucking them out of the air. "You're in a good mood."

"Wu doesn't want you to visit the hospital." He shrugged. "That means I think it's a dandy idea."

"Simple as that, huh?" We didn't pass anyone in the halls or on the elevator ride down. The rest of the coterie was still out and about on their individual business. Wu might have retreated to his room, but I doubted it. "Did you and Portia have a good time?"

He grunted rather than admit he enjoyed her company. "Maggie chose not to be present."

Thinking on what Cole said, I offered, "Maybe you intimidate her."

"Maybe." He cut his eyes toward me as we hit the parking lot. "Or maybe she was pouting because Miller didn't go."

The barb struck home, and he knew it, which meant he knew Miller had a—crush wasn't the right word, interest maybe?—in Maggie.

"Or maybe you're being a prick because you're not used to sharing Portia, and now you've got to deal with having a part-time bestie."

He tripped over the curb. "Bestie?"

"Best friend. As in the thing that Portia is to you."

"We aren't humans," he sneered. "We don't paint each other's toenails or book spa days together."

"Mmm-hmm."

"I tell her every time her ass looks fat in jeans. I laugh every time food gets stuck in her teeth." We reached the SUV, and he popped the locks. "And one time she gave me a magazine with hairstyles and let me pick hers. I had the stylist shave her bald. She cried when she saw, and I filmed the whole thing."

And it ate at him. It must if he had a prepared list of small cruelties lined up in his head, ready to fling out like a defense against anyone who challenged what he felt for her.

"Forget I said anything." I threw up my hands. "Clearly I misread the situation."

"Hell yes, you did."

The drive to the hospital was short thanks to Santiago working out his aggression on our fellow motorists. The upside was, if Wu had spotted us leaving and got suspicious, there was no way he could have tailed us without planting trackers on the SUVs. And Santiago swept for those and added each one he found to his collection for later dissection.

With a purposeful stride, I headed toward the front desk. Santiago almost popped my arm out of the socket yanking me back.

"What the hell?" I wrenched free of his grip. "What was that for?"

"You can't waltz up there and demand his room number," he condescended to me. "You have no authority." I opened my mouth to contradict him, and he shushed me. "No authority they would recognize."

"What's the plan?" I folded my arms across my chest. "You've got one, or you wouldn't have come."

"I'm going to hack their system." He settled into a chair in the waiting room, removed a tablet from his pack, and passed me a dollar. "Go buy me a Coke. This is thirsty work."

"Anything else?" I packed as much sarcasm into the question as it would hold.

"I wouldn't say no to crackers, but I'm light on cash." He shook his head. "Who carries paper bills anymore? Honestly? It's ridiculous. Tattoo barcodes on our wrists or implant chips in our palms. Much more effective."

Much more invasive too. "I thought you were anti-chip."

"I'm anti-NSB tracking my bowel movements. A cashier's chip would be—"

"Just as simple to track. Each of your transactions would be catalogued through your bank and the merchants' banks. Anyone could peek at your receipts and know which shops and restaurants you frequent or if you're traveling."

"That Coke ain't getting itself," he grumbled, sinking into his work.

Poor baby. I hated to burst his bubble. Actually, no. I didn't. The occasional pop was good for his ego.

Leaving him to his subterfuge, I scouted the ground floor in search of a vending machine. This hospital was as sterile as every other one I had ever visited. The smell was the same too, like someone canned the air in old hospitals then sprayed it like air freshener in new facilities.

Eventually, I stumbled across a cafeteria. It would have to do. It was a nice one. Meant to be shared with patients' family members. Parents and spouses were easy to pick out. Full plates and empty eyes. Even without the scrubs, staffers were just as easy to spot. They laughed, read books, or played on their phones while shoveling in food. You could look at them and hear the clock ticking on their breaks.

Gooseflesh tickled my spine when I pictured Dad sitting in a place like this, waiting on me to be released any one of the dozen times I'd been admitted for testing after he found me. Neither of us talked much about those stays. Not about the clinical trials for drugs without names, not about the surgeries that removed samples of the metal from under my skin, and not about how he was the only thing that had saved me from being turned into a bonified lab rat.

Shaking off those super-pleasant memories, I approached the cashier and paid for a fountain drink. They were out of Coke, so I stabbed the button one flavor down. After backtracking through the facility, I stood over him, waiting. When he ignored me, I sat the cup on the screen of the tablet braced across his knees. That got his attention, and the rumble pumping through his chest as he clenched the Styrofoam turned heads in the lobby.

"Ah-ah." I tapped the end of his nose. "Behave."

"Did you just . . . ?" Jaw slack, he rubbed the end of his nose. "You *booped* me."

"You deserved it." I sank down beside him. "Did you get what we need?"

"Ten minutes ago," he groused, hunching his shoulders like I might boop him when he least expected.

"We were barely here ten minutes ago."

"I was digging through their records earlier, remember?" He made a disgusted noise when he took a sip of his drink. "This is not Coke."

"You're telling me you knew Lambert's room number when we walked through the door, but you're just now getting around to telling me?"

"I was thirsty," he enunciated clearly.

While he had one hand full of tablet and the other wrapped around his drink, I very slowly reached between us and pressed the tip of my index finger against the end of his nose.

Boop.

"I will end you," he snarled.

"Hey," I joked, "that's my line."

Proving he had zero sense of humor, Santiago didn't even crack a grin.

In grumpy silence, we crossed the lobby and rode the elevator up to the fifth floor. He indicated Lambert's room then took up position outside the door. I entered, eyes adjusting to the darkness. The teen slept flat on his back, his skin ashen but for the multitude of tattoos sleeving his arms.

Tubes and cords snaked out his pierced nose and mouth to

slither across his bed. Equipment hummed and beeped in a steady rhythm, and beside him, a machine breathed quietly for him. His seizures must have been more severe than the news reported. Conversation was out of the question.

Part of me wondered if Wu had known about his condition, if that was why he had dismissed the idea of interviewing Lambert out of hand. He couched it as a waste of time, that anything a human had to say was banal, but I didn't believe he was so close-minded. But it wasn't like I could call him out without admitting I'd done exactly what he told me not to do in coming here.

On a sigh, I exited the room and brushed past Santiago. "Let's go."

"That was a quick interview." He caught up and kept pace. "He asleep?"

"He's intubated." I smacked the down button on the elevator hard enough to sting my palm. "I can't question him."

"You can always try the next time you're in the city."

That sounded almost ... nice. I narrowed my eyes on him. "What do you mean 'next time'?"

"Portia and Maggie are staying here in Vicksburg for a few days while you and Wu go visit Sariah."

"Okay." I cut him a look. "You're staying behind too?"

"Miller and I volunteered to keep an eye on them, yes."

The ride down left my stomach hovering up around my ears. It had to be that and not the question burning a hole through my tongue. "Thom's working a case. Will that keep him here? Or will he have to return to Canton?"

Santiago, as usual, saw right through me. "Cole will remain here. His contact has information we need, but she's skittish. She knows you're here. She knows you traveled together. She's not going to dial down her paranoia until she can get him alone."

The hit landed, and I exhaled like his words had been a fist to my solar plexus. "So I go alone."

While Cole stayed here and cozied up to his contact, who he had been buttering up since we arrived.

"Sometimes I really hate you," I murmured to Santiago's back.

"Sometimes I do too," he said and kept walking.

The worst thing about Santiago was not his cruelty but his honesty. What he said wouldn't hurt half as much if it was a lie. He had an uncanny knack for seeing the smallness in a person and exploiting it. Cole wasn't mine. I had no claim on him. What he did with his time, and who he did it with, was none of my business. But Santiago knew I wanted it to be. And that's why he made certain I understood it wasn't, and that might never change.

CHAPTER FIVE

———◆———

Cole didn't return to the hotel that night, or if he did slip in, he didn't make it back to our suite. To say I woke on the wrong side of the bed was too mild for the snit brewing in me. I felt turned inside out, like I was a suit put on wrong. I missed Cole like an amputated limb, and the sensation only worsened when I emerged from the bedroom to find the rest of the coterie looking anywhere other than at me.

Santiago lounged on the couch, buried under three tablets, a laptop, and a phone. Miller sat in an accent chair too small for his height and held a book in his hands. It wasn't upside down, nothing so obvious, but his eyes kept straying from the words to the blonde staring out the floor-to-ceiling windows.

The longing I glimpsed there made me grateful when a knock on the door announced Wu's arrival.

"Come in." I didn't have to raise my voice. His hearing was phenomenal, the same as the others'. "I have clothes to last another twenty-four hours," I told him when the door opened.

"After that, we've got to stop long enough for me to hit a dry cleaner."

Wu crossed to me and waited until I gave him my full attention. "I was curt with you yesterday."

"You did seem to have your tighty-whities in a bunch," I allowed.

"I'm not used to having a partner to gut-check myself against, but I am trying." His peace offering was a chai latte and an everything-but-the-kitchen-sink bagel. "Have patience with me."

"You're bribing me." I confiscated said contraband. "I like it."

His smile was a hesitant thing that made me think he was being earnest. "Am I forgiven?"

A sip of the latte made me sigh happily. "Bribe me again around noon, and I'll give you my answer."

"Are you leaving?" Maggie turned from the window. "When will you be back?"

I set down my goodies, crossed to her, and wrapped my arms around her. "Yes, and soon."

Hugs used to be awkward affairs. They still required coordination on my part to make sure everything fit where it ought to go. Casual affection was getting easier, but I still had a ways to go before it came naturally.

Balance was required to maintain a healthy coterie. I was learning that, remembering it maybe, and it reminded me of being a kid. When Dad planted his food plots for deer in the spring, I would help myself to his wildflower seeds. I sat in the grass cupping the small kernels in my palm for hours on end, hoping one of the birds interested in us might trust me enough to land. None ever did. I had to hope my odds were higher with the coterie than the wild cardinals.

Chin propped on my shoulder, she whispered, "Miller is staying?"

"Yes," I promised her. "He's staying. Santiago too."

"Okay." She withdrew, nodding to herself or maybe to Portia. "That works."

"You'll be fine." I willed her to believe me. "Both of you. Call if you need anything or if you just want to talk."

"We have your number." After a quick glance at Miller, their gazes connecting and snagging, she turned back to the window. "Be careful, Lucey-goosey."

"That goes double for you, Magpie."

I caught Wu staring at us when I turned and gathered my things. "Problem?"

"No," he said thoughtfully. "Have you said all your goodbyes?"

"The others won't take long," I promised. "Santiago, don't be an ass." I sipped my latte and burned my tongue. "Miller, don't let him be an ass." I raised my eyebrows at Wu. "Good enough?"

"Yes." His gaze touched on each door in the suite. "Good enough."

We exited together and stepped on the elevator. The doors rolled almost shut before a broad palm speared through the gap and pried them open. Cole stood in the hall. A short woman with black hair cascading to her waist stood behind him. Her coloring reminded me of Santiago, but she read about as predatory as a baby bunny to me. Granted, my charun power scale was skewed thanks to the coterie and Wu, but I sensed none of that killer instinct in this woman.

I didn't like finding them together, him wearing yesterday's clothes, so early in the morning.

What Santiago implied—that she couldn't wait to have him all to herself—I liked even less.

Hands framing the doors, forcing them wide, Cole asked, "You were just going to leave?"

"All signs point to yes." I met the woman's wide-eyed stare, and she flinched. Huddling closer to Cole, she hid behind his back. "You weren't here."

"I had business to attend."

"So I see." I flicked my gaze to her then back to him. "You should probably get back to it."

Faster than I could track, he fisted the front of my shirt and hauled me from the elevator, slapping the button to close the doors for good measure. Cole loomed over me, his favorite trick, but I kicked my head back to hold his stare. Where I had expected anger, his meltwater eyes glimmered with ... amusement. He was laughing at me.

"You don't know who she is, what she is, or why she's here." He flattened his palm against my sternum, a tiny smile forming. "You're also growling."

There was nothing human in the noise reverberating through me, and that ought to worry me more than it did, but only Cole brought out these instincts in me. "I'm not a morning person."

He buried his face at the point where my neck met my shoulder and inhaled, filling his lungs, pressing our chests together. "You're jealous."

"You're not mine." I gasped when his hot breath hit my skin. "I don't get to be jealous."

"Luce," he breathed my name. "How could I want anyone else?"

That list stretched longer than I was tall, starting with how Conquest had slaughtered his people and razed his homeland and ending with the fact she had enslaved him and hauled him from his world and beyond.

No, that wasn't right. It ended with the bone-deep fear that despite all those things, he might view me as a watered-down version of her, an echo of what drew them together in the first place.

As much as *my* name on his lips warmed me, I had to get out the words. "You're free to choose someone—"

"No."

"Cole—"

"No." He straightened enough to put us at eye level. "You're mine."

"I want to be." I sagged against him, the wind taken from my sails. "Yours."

"Call me when you finish." The rhythmic vibrations through his chest melted my knees. "I'll keep my phone on me."

"You're purring," the woman, who I had forgotten, yelped and stumbled back.

An instant of blinding rage that she had heard, that she might have *felt*, clouded my vision.

I sucked in oxygen then blasted it through parted lips. The urge to rake my claws down her face eased. A skosh. Not much, but enough.

This would be the other side effect of coterie bonding. The touch aversion they were healing had gone deeper, unlocking facets of my inner charun. Mostly my protective streak where they were concerned and my possessive urges toward Cole.

I wasn't convinced it was an improvement, but it was done. There was no going back. If we had any hope of me learning to tap into the power at my core, this was a firm step down that path.

"Okay?" Cole asked, understanding how close I was to losing my temper all over his *informant*.

"Yes," I hissed, words more difficult to form when I was this riled.

"This is the difference between you and her." He drew a scarred knuckle across my jaw. "You're fighting your instincts. You're choosing to walk away and leave me here when you could order me to follow. You're giving me my freedom and trusting me to honor you with it."

I wrapped my hands around his wrist as far as they would go. "I don't own you."

The reverence in his expression shifted into a bittersweetness I could almost taste.

"Yes, you do." He took my hand and placed it over his heart. "For the first time since my world fell, I'm proud of that fact."

"Go take care of your business," I told Cole, and this time I sounded like myself, not petulant or scorned or seconds away from committing homicide. I nudged him back so I could step around him. "I'll call with an update as soon as I put the visit to Sariah behind me."

Cole leaned over and mashed the down button on the elevator. "I'll wait with you."

"That's okay." I pivoted on my heel and started walking. "I'll take the stairs."

Better I pound the steps to cool my temper than his informant's pretty face.

CHAPTER SIX

———◆———

We flew commercial, which surprised me. I would have thought the taskforce kept its operatives separate from the general population, but apparently not. Wu explained the private jet and, more often, helicopters, were deployed only during missions. Not for the sake of comfort or expedience.

For once, I didn't mind being flown. The ride was much smoother via machine than charun.

Our ultimate destination was Butte, Montana. I had never been this far west, and the scenery was breathtaking. Right up to the point when the plane landed, we got shepherded into a waiting SUV, and Wu blindfolded me.

In hindsight, I should have expected something along those lines. I had no doubt he wouldn't have clued me in at all if he could have avoided it, but plane tickets and check-ins made it impossible for him to conceal our location entirely.

"How very cloak and dagger of you." I mourned the loss of my view more than anything. "How far . . ." I let the sentence trail into nothing. "You can't tell me. It would give me a means of pinpointing the location."

"I do regret the necessity."

"I bet," I grumbled. "What do you think I'm going to do? Storm the castle and free Famine and Sariah?" A kernel of anger flared at the insinuation. "I helped put them there. The last thing I want is either of them to escape."

"The cadre plays a long game," he said calmly. "I know you well enough to believe you would never betray humanity for the sake of your sisters, but the others know only what previous cadres have taught them."

Having met two out of Conquest's three siblings, I couldn't fault them for being wary. "I understand. That doesn't mean I have to like it."

"There's too much at stake to make allowances." He exhaled into the quiet. "We've never held the advantage over the cadre, and that's thanks to you."

"Let me guess." I sighed. "It makes them even more suspicious of me."

"No Otillian has ever aligned with a foreign terrene, and none—in all our histories—has betrayed her cadre."

"You keep using *betrayal* like it's going to wound me. I chose my side. I'm loyal to my people." The cadre had singled out my human family and brutalized them. "The cadre aren't my kin. I don't know them, and what I do know about them only cements my belief this is the right course."

"Forgive me." Apology lingered in his tone. "I don't mean to needle you. It's ... difficult ... even after having spent time with you, to believe you're genuine. It's like praying for rain during a centuries-long drought. You convince yourself the first drop must have been your imagination, that salvation can't be at hand."

An uncomfortable weight settled on my shoulders. I shifted on my seat, but it didn't budge. "I'm no savior."

"Yes," he said, his elegant fingers draping over mine in a brief caress, "you are."

The curious intimacy of being alone and blindfolded with Wu raised chills down my arms.

"That would make the coterie my disciples." I forced a laugh. "I can picture the murals from here."

"There were murals, statues, on other terrenes." Leather creaked beside me as he withdrew to his side of the car. "Evidence trickled through to this one. Small shrines, pieces of art older than civilization. The cadre is worshipped in Otilla. They're revered throughout many of the lower terrenes, their appearance viewed as a blessing."

The almost clinical recitation had me wondering. "Have you ever left this terrene?"

Wu let the question hang for a few minutes, so long I almost forgot what I had asked him when his voice startled me to attention.

"Not since I arrived," he said softly. "I was a small boy then."

"Your father brought you here." Wu claimed to be following in his footsteps, so it fit. "What about your mother?"

This time the quiet stretched longer, and there was no end to it.

As I settled back against the seat and dozed, I sensed his eyes on me. Whenever I lowered my defenses around him, it made him twitchy. Last time I blamed my willingness to nap in his presence on Thom having my back. The truth was more along the lines that I believed if Wu wanted to do me harm, he would give me the courtesy of stabbing me in the chest and not in the back.

After all, hunts are more satisfying when prey knows it's been cornered.

*

Fingers sliding through my hair woke me. I jolted awake and clamped my hands over wrists too thin to be Cole's. A punch of fear kicked my heart into high gear, but the blindfold slid down my nose to reveal Wu's face—much too close to mine.

"We're here," he said, not fighting back. "You can release me now."

"I'm not used to being touched." I let him go. "It's not my favorite thing."

Coterie was the exception.

Flecks of gold sparkled in his eyes. "The others touch you."

Busted.

"The others are coterie." I kept from wiping my hands on my pants, but barely. It wasn't that touching Wu offended me. It was ... Honestly, I'm not sure what it was. All I could do was chalk it up to the biological changes I was undergoing and make a mental note to ask Cole what it meant when I called him later. "It's different when they touch me."

"Comforting?" His gaze dropped to my lap, to my hands. "You're changing."

There was no use denying what he would discover soon enough. "Yes."

"Interesting." He opened his door and slid out, then offered me his hand. "We're late."

Avoiding his touch would validate whatever he wanted proven, so I took his hand, ignored the wrongness, and let him guide me out of the car. The sensation was no worse than before, when humans touched me. I could deal with discomfort if it wiped the smirk off his face.

The vastness of the space we had entered swamped me, and I wobbled on my feet. "Where are we?"

"Officially, the facility's location and name are classified." A smirk twisted his lips. "Unofficially, we call this place The Hole.

It's where charun who are too valuable to be killed—or who can't be killed—are tossed and forgotten."

"I'm guessing Sariah falls into the former category." A feral pleasure swept through me when I recalled, "She bled like a stuck pig. I couldn't take her down, but a member of my coterie could have finished what I started."

"You really are changing," he murmured, and it didn't sound like a judgment.

The cavernous room where we stood appeared to be a docking bay/parking lot/checkpoint. Rows of vehicles filled one corner while semis with fading chain store logos backed against walls stood waiting to receive whatever passed for cargo around here.

Against the back wall, carved into the rock, was a guard shack manned with six armed men. They snapped to attention when Wu got within a few yards, their gazes reverent. One's knee kept buckling as if he were fighting the overwhelming urge to kneel.

To borrow from Wu, *Interesting*.

"Thank you for your service," he told them and pressed his clenched fist over his heart. "You do your people proud."

His praise caused their chests to swell, their eyes to brighten, and their chins to jut. It was clear that they knew him and respected him. But what could have drawn Wu here often enough for the guards to be so familiar with him? Perhaps there were more interesting inmates besides Sariah that warranted his attention. Famine, for example.

"This is Luce Boudreau." Wu gave them a moment to digest this, and the glow on their faces locked down as their gazes fell to me. "She is mine."

"I'm his partner," I clarified.

The guys looked ready to faint when I rebuffed Wu's claim of ownership, and the one with the shaky leg almost collapsed in his shock.

A commotion near the rear had me skimming their heads for the source. They parted to reveal an older woman, late fifties or early sixties, with snow-white hair and obsidian eyes that fastened on Wu.

"Adam," she purred, the effect not sensuous but distortive. "You kept me waiting, *chala*."

"Apologies, *heri*." He bowed at the waist. "Luce's coterie was reluctant to part with her."

"I doubt that." The woman fastened her eerie focus on me. "What slave wishes for its master's oversight?"

A hot flush raced up my nape. "I'm not their master."

"Consider Miller," Wu all but whispered, and I understood what I said to have been wrong in their eyes.

The NSB wanted to know I had ironclad control over my people, Miller in particular. The old woman was baiting me. She wanted to trap me. And I was locking the door behind myself.

Eyes the flat black of a shark's, she studied me. "You were saying?"

"My coterie is well in hand," I grated from between clenched teeth.

Her soft laugh told me she didn't buy my change of heart for a hot minute, but she let it pass. "Come."

She led the way past the guard shack into a wide tunnel twice my height. Wu fell into step beside me, his knuckles brushing mine to catch my attention. Or annoy me. Letting him know his touch bothered me had been a mistake. But he simply looked at me as if asking *Are you all right?* without risking the acoustics revealing our conversation to our guide.

I plastered on a fake smile and mouthed, *"Just peachy."*

If the point of entry hadn't driven home the fact we were underground—*far* underground—then the trek even deeper into the earth made it clear they had spared no expense in creating a prison worthy of holding cataclysmic inmates.

Butte, Montana, was an old mining town. This facility must have started life as a warren of mine shafts. The remoteness of the area, combined with a head start on excavating, must have added to the appeal. For all I knew, some mineral in the walls acted as charun kryptonite. There was no point in asking when they wouldn't tell me, so I saved my breath.

The incline leveled off about the time my pulse started jumping in response to the steady drop in temperature and the oppressive weight of so much rock overhead. The tunnel spit us out into a circular tower identical to what human prison guards used to keep watch over mundane inmates.

Upon our arrival, the dozen officers present snapped their heels together and saluted. I wasn't sure, at first, if the respect was meant for the woman or for Wu. But Wu returned their salute, and they resumed their duties.

I cut my eyes toward him, the question in them clear. *Who are you really?*

He pretended not to understand and gestured for me to follow the woman into an elevator rated for cargo, which had me questioning exactly what types of charun they kept sequestered here. We could have spread our arms to either side and not brushed fingertips, but Wu stood close enough for his body heat to warm me.

The smug bastard was getting his money's worth out of his claim on me.

The room we exited into was a hub. Doors lined the curved walls, leading to who knows where. The woman took the direct route—the door in front of us—and it opened onto a white room with a box in the middle. *Hello, sensory deprivation.* The lack of color in the empty room made it difficult to guess the size of the cube, but I decided it was a twelve by twelve solitary confinement cell by the time we walked up to the clear door that stretched a head taller than Wu. Within, Sariah lounged on a cot bolted to the wall.

"Auntie." She beamed at me. "You came."

The woman beside me curled her lip, but I couldn't tell which of us it was meant for. "I'll leave you to it." She hesitated before Wu, her head bent. "Your father sends his regards."

Whatever manner of beast lurked beneath his skin rose to the surface and stared out, his eyes blazing gold, and his multi-layered voice hit me with the force of an uppercut when he snarled at her, "Leave us."

The woman staggered back, clutching her head, palms glued to her ears. "Yes, my lord."

That's what it sounded like she said, but it couldn't have been. My ears must have still been ringing.

She left before I could ask her to repeat herself, and Wu was gazing at me with such naked hunger I had to break our staring contest first. Had the look simply been desire, I could have dealt with that. Had it been a craving for flesh, well, I could have compartmentalized that too. The same way I did for Miller. But I wasn't sure what the look meant, and I didn't like the way it made my nape sting like ants were marching down my spine. The sensation reminded me too much of my birthday, of Ezra, and I shivered.

During those long years of wondering who and what I was, those annual calls from Ezra had sustained me. His voice banished the ache in my bones, cleared my head, kept me from bursting out of the skin Wu was so eager to peel away and look beneath. "You're not what you pretend to be," Sariah mused in his direction. "You must fit right in, eh?"

Happy to ignore Wu while he wrapped himself in faux humanity again, I glowered at her. "What do you want, Sariah?"

"World peace," she deadpanned.

"Cute." I turned on my heel and started back toward the exit. "Have fun with that."

"Wait." She slapped her palms against the plexiglass. "Just—wait."

Heaving a dramatic sigh, I paused within reach of the door. "You've got thirty seconds. Make them count."

"Get me out of here."

I shook my head. "I don't have that kind of power."

"He does." A growl entered her voice. "They worship him like a god around here." She must have shifted her focus onto Wu. "Why is that? Who are you? *What* are you?"

"Adam Wu," he said, his power a faint echo.

"Yeah. Right." Sariah scoffed. "And I'm the Easter bunny."

"Fifteen seconds," I called. "Can you hurry this up? We skipped lunch, and I'm starving."

"I'll give you something of equal value," she blurted. "I'll give you the location of War's coterie."

Slowly, I turned to face her. "Why would you do that?"

"I want out."

"That's it?" I approached her cell. "You're willing to roll over on War to save your own hide?"

"She would do the same to me." A frown gathered on her brow. "She *has* done the same."

Knowing Sariah had survived because she was a stone-cold pragmatist cast in her mother's mold was one thing, but watching her thought process in action drove home how very broken their coterie must be to produce such a child. "Do you think she's noticed you're missing yet?"

"Doubtful." She considered that. "I wasn't scheduled to check in with her for another month."

"Famine was captured. She must know that by now." There could be no hiding Uncle Harold's death. The cover story

Kapoor cooked up about a B&E gone wrong made all the papers. Paired with Aunt Nancy's death, the story had been too juicy for the vultures to let lie. They were still picking those bones clean. "You were the one in charge of cleaning up after her. Don't you think War will summon you to get answers about Famine's whereabouts?"

"She'll assume I've gone underground." A snort escaped her. "And I have." She ducked her head, swallowed. "She'll know I won't answer any summons from her. Not after I lost Famine. She was my responsibility, and I failed. Only a fool would come when Mother called under such circumstances, and I haven't lived this long by being stupid."

Here was War's pride and joy, her heir, and yet Sariah would turn on a dime if it meant her freedom. With a sociopath like War for a mother, Sariah's ability to sacrifice family to further her own agenda might very well be the reason she was so beloved by her parents. "What about your father? You're not worried she'll send him to hunt you down?"

"No." Her lips twisted into an ugly smile. "Father would never lower himself to perform such an errand."

"Your father won't help you." It wasn't a question but an observation.

"I'm his firstborn but . . . " Sariah shook her head. "Only those who help themselves survive."

Hmm. That might be the family motto, but it sounded like she wanted to be a daddy's girl. Maybe that was the relationship to exploit and not her bond with War.

"I'll have to discuss this with my partner." Wu, who hadn't moved or spoken since she addressed him directly, still wasn't quite right. "He'll set the terms." Sariah was wary of him, and that could only help our cause. "You'll have to agree to them and to cooperate when we enforce them."

"All right." Her gaze cut to Wu. "I accept."

"We haven't laid down terms," I protested.

"It doesn't matter." She turned her back on us and flopped down on her cot. "I'd agree to anything to get out of here. Do you know they pipe in Muzak? I thought elevator music was dead, but I swear I heard a synthesized version of 'MMMBop' last night."

Yes, fear a pop song from the late nineties but not the wrath of War.

Good to know our turncoat had her priorities straight.

CHAPTER SEVEN

———◆———

Sariah sprawled over the armrest, invading my *me* space, to cuddle. Teeth gritted in determination, I endured the forced contact, but it was all I could do not to peel her off and sling her across the aisle. Wu looked on, amused, but he wasn't the one with a groggy predator tucked against his side.

This time, we rated private transpo. The taskforce jet was waiting for us at a secluded airfield, and the interior was lush beyond comprehension. All buttery leather and burled wood accents. Clearly, this wasn't meant for conveying the taskforce itself but ferrying the men and women in charge of them.

No wonder they didn't want to share their toys with the riff-raff, meaning me. Whatever Wu was, he was clearly on the tier who utilized this plane often enough to be comfortable in what I assumed was his usual seat. Stocked with his favorite snacks and drinks, it had everything but his name on a plaque bolted to a headrest.

"How much tranquilizer did you give her?" I nudged Sariah a

fraction, but she was dead weight and slid right back into place. "She's drooling on my shoulder."

"I gave her enough to make this trip pleasant for all of us." He laughed at my expression. "Two out of three aren't bad odds."

Accepting my fate, I settled in for the misery of having so much contact with a person who turned into a giant gator when pissed. "Do you think we can trust her intel?"

"Yes." He passed me a bottle of water—flavored and carbonated. I rolled my eyes but accepted. "War will be proud to learn her daughter escaped on her own merit. That she sold out her mother's operation to do so is a danger of the business they're in. War will have contingency plans in place."

What a miserable way to live, unable to trust anyone. Even— if not especially—your family.

"She has created a coterie of younglings," he continued. "They're not battle-hardened like Sariah. They'll break if you apply enough pressure in the right place."

"I'm going to stop you right there and tell you that's one of my least favorite sayings." At least I wasn't on the receiving end. This time. "What difference does experience make if she rolls over as easily as the others?"

"War is paranoid. I doubt anyone suspects the full scope of her endgame. Thanases will be aware of most of the pieces. He's her mate, she would confide in him, but Sariah can guess them. She knows how her mother operates. She understands how her mind works. Her tactical thinking is an asset worth more to us than any locations she fingers. I expect her to point us toward a few active sites while hiding the ones most likely to be occupied by her mother."

"How can you trust her when you just admitted you expect her to balk at handing over the prize?"

"No, what I expect is further negotiation." In fact, he sounded

resigned to it. "She'll give us a taste, proof she's willing to cooperate, and then she'll barter what we really want to get whatever
it is she's after."

"So, you *do* think she wants more than her freedom."

Wu tried looking innocent, but it didn't fit his face well.
"Didn't I just say as much?"

Eager to prove two can play the innocence game, I asked, "So
are you going to tell me about *chala*?"

"She's Commander of—" He wiped a hand over his mouth,
plucking at his upper lip before he lowered it. "She's in charge
of The Hole."

"I got that much." I pressed my luck further. "She works for
or with your father?"

"She's one of his underlings," he allowed after a moment's
consideration. "What is it you're really asking?"

"No offense, but you lost your shit when she passed on that
message from your dad."

"Our relationship is strained." And now so was his voice. "You
mustn't view our bond through the lens of yours with your father.
A message from mine means a visit is imminent. It's a warning,
not a greeting."

From everything Wu had let slip about his dad, any father/
son bonding time would be on par with corporal punishment.
But what had Wu done to merit the sudden interest? How
had his actions in the past several weeks earned him a slap on
the wrist?

Granted, I hadn't seen him for a week when he showed up at
the bunkhouse, but seven days didn't give him much room to
cause this kind of trouble. And it was trouble. Wu hadn't lost his
cool for no good reason. The worst reaction I had ever seen from
him was a clenched jaw or fist. That vocalization technique—
that was next level pissedoffedness.

"Okay," I said, playing it off like it was no big deal, "so we brace for a visit."

The expression Wu turned on me was that of a man grasping for a lifeline. "You would stand with me against him?"

"Is that how it is?" Honest curiosity had me asking, "I'm either with him or against him?"

"Yes," he said, leaving no room for doubt. "Either you're an ally or an enemy."

Proving I can't leave well enough alone, I had to push one last time. "Which are you?"

His smile was all teeth, his voice pure silk. "What do you think?"

"I think I'm glad you're on my side." I slumped down in my seat, trying and failing to get comfortable. "Your dad can't be worse than you."

CHAPTER EIGHT

———◦◦◦———

Adam watched Luce sleep, an old habit he lacked the willpower to break. She was never more real than when she was awake, her ancient eyes blazing with righteousness. Had any Otillian ever burned brighter? Such a weapon he had forged, and he was lucky to still be here to wield her. Though, if his father had caught wind of them, he might not live to see the final battle. Not much could kill him but . . . his sire would crush him when he discovered his betrayal.

Their would-be spy was out cold. He had given Sariah twice the amount of sedative the doctor recommended. He was taking no chances with Luce's safety. Their tableau flummoxed him. It was evidence of Sariah's subconscious trust in Luce. She had writhed out of his grasp, sensing the threat to her, but she burrowed against Luce and slept as secure as a cub with its mother. Except Sariah had never known a mother's love, not in the way Luce understood parental affection.

His phone vibrated in his pocket, and the number broke him

out in a cold sweat. He rose, strolled to the rear of the cabin, and closed his eyes. "Father."

"I sensed your presence today," he said with polite interest. "Yet you did not come pay your respects."

"I had other matters to attend," he said coolly. "I apologize for not showing you due reverence."

"Sarcasm, Adam. Is that the best you have to offer?" A dangerous thread of interest wove through his words. "You are my son, my heir, my will made flesh. You ought to thank me for raising you so high."

"I am grateful." His fist clenched until his knuckles popped. "Your interest in my pursuits honors me."

"On that, we agree." His amusement portended nothing good. "You brought a guest with you. That's rare. You prefer to work alone."

"A partner." He kept playing bored. "Given the timing, I thought temporary backup might be prudent."

"The cadre's reemergence," his father supplied. "I had forgotten this was their time."

Such things were beneath his notice. His eyes were ever turned skyward. So long as the protections sandwiching Earth held, he had no reason to bother himself with what he considered a nuisance. A minor irritation. An annoyance better left to his son. Father did so enjoy delegation.

Adam was tired. So tired. Of it all.

"Three of the four have breached," Adam informed him, seeing no reason to lie. "The fourth should arrive shortly."

Eagerness coated the blade of his voice. "How many have you killed?"

"None," he admitted, knowing it would be seen as a failure.

"Do you require assistance? I am happy to oblige, my son."

He would wipe Luce and the others off the face of the planet, along with half the population, human and charun. There was no standing against his father.

A reminder that came too late.

"I have matters well in hand," he echoed Luce's earlier sentiment. "Famine has been secured as well as War's second in command."

"That I had not heard."

Adam ground his teeth. He hated delivering news to his father. He much preferred to avoid him altogether. "Testing has already commenced."

Each species of charun existing on Earth did so at his father's sufferance. The only reason species aside from theirs were allowed to live at all was because Adam had dedicated his very long life to finding ways to wipe out other breeds if the occasion called for such mass-extinction. Father tolerated no threats to his power. Not even from his son. Especially not his son.

The only species resistant to their methods were Otillian. Their chameleonic nature made them the charun equivalent of cockroaches. Impossible to kill unless you stomped on each one individually.

"This will be your second time having a cadre subject. Do have a care with this one. The last one expired before yielding acceptable results."

The thing about experimentation was it made allowances for errors, such as the syringe full of a rare venom he had injected into the carotid of the previous incarnation of Conquest to end her suffering. "Yes, Father."

What his father had never understood was the only way to maintain balance was for every predator to fall prey. Checks and balances kept an ecosystem healthy. Earth had no such equilibrium. His father had no such rival.

But his father hadn't faced off against Luce Boudreau, either.

CHAPTER NINE

———◈———

Even on a private jet, the trip from Montana to Mississippi still lasted eight hours. I slept six of them. When I woke, Wu was in an ugly mood, and I didn't try pulling him out of his funk. I didn't know him well enough to trust what I said to make things better and not worse.

There was no limo waiting for us this time. The White Horse SUV had been reclaimed too.

Sariah was alert enough to have opened her eyes, but there was no one home behind them yet. Wu dumped her in a wheelchair and pushed her to the curb.

I didn't wait for him to make arrangements. I dialed up Cole. "Can you swing a pickup for three?"

"I think I can manage," he rumbled, and it vibrated down my spine.

Headlights winked to life three rows in front of us in the parking lot, and the vehicle circled, pulling to a stop in front of us. The window lowered, and Cole leaned out, taking in our third wheel. He threw the SUV in park and exited the vehicle with a bounce in his step that had me curious.

"You're in a good mood," I observed. "What's that in your hand?"

"I had this made for you." He held out his palm, and a set of ornate handcuffs plated in rose gold rested on them. I traced the design, reminiscent of the *rukav*, and I lost the ability to speak. "I wanted to give them to you before you left, but they weren't finished yet."

Beside me, Wu snapped to attention. "Is that rosendium?"

"Yes," Cole said, not taking his eyes off me.

"You didn't have to do this." I accepted them, though. Their weight was a familiar comfort, and the fact he had commissioned the piece made them precious. Too valuable to waste on Sariah, who might ding them just to spite me. "Thank you."

"She doesn't understand." Wu dropped his gaze to Cole's wrists, one of them exposed, both inflamed. "How could you bear it?"

"What is he talking about?" The gift took on an uncertain weight in my hands. "Cole?"

Wu backed off and left Cole to his explanation.

"Rosendium is a metal produced by Otillians." He smoothed his thumb over the lowest band on my arm, the one above my wrist, and the resonance made my knees quiver. "They harvest it from their bodies and use it to bind their coterie to them."

Understanding struck with the force of a two-by-four to the face. "You let someone pry out your bands?"

"The moment you captured Famine rather than kill her, I knew the day would come when you required a means of restraining her." Determination brightened his eyes. "When you took Sariah as well . . . I had to act, to protect you."

"But at what cost?" I clasped his hand, the one with a naked wrist, and turned it gently from side to side, inspecting the ridges of skin, years' worth of scar tissue. His hatred for his bindings had carved a valley in his flesh as he picked them out, over and over. But they regrew. Whatever Conquest had done—whatever I had done—to him, it was permanent. Or it was until I decided otherwise at the very least. "You should have told me. I would have—"

"*No.*" He softened his voice. "You can barely set foot inside a hospital because of what those doctors did to you."

"That's different," I protested. "I was a child then."

"Let me do this one thing."

"Thank you," I said again, and this time I kissed each of his wrists, right over the swollen flesh.

A shuddering exhale gusted through him, and I wondered if he was affected by the gesture or the brush of my lips against his hands. Mine were sensitive. And War had shown me they were more than decorative, more than a means of subduing our coterie. She had struck hers against mine and— I had no words to describe the sensation.

One day I would work up the courage to ask Cole what else was possible, but not tonight. Not in front of Wu and Sariah. A tiny suspicion was bubbling up in me that a fraction of my previous touch aversion was thanks to humans' lack of resonance. Contact from them was a screeching discord while my coterie and I vibrated on the same frequency. Other charun were less offensive to my senses, but still discordant.

Allowing myself to compartmentalize how Cole had brutalized himself for my sake, I focused on what had been worth the sacrifice. "How do they work?"

"The metal itself is harmless, to humans and charun, unless it completes a circuit."

"That explains the design." I turned the cuffs over in my hands. "These have to connect to be effective?"

"Yes." He pointed to the keyholes. "They're double latched." He showed me how the tricky second lock functioned. "They're no more effective than standard cuffs unless you lock them on your target."

"What's with the chain?" I gave it a tug, and the links held firm, but there was something odd in the way they had been anchored to each cuff.

"The cuffs also function as bangles," a soft voice murmured from the shadows. "They will give you limited control over whoever wears them." The small woman from the hall stepped forward and drifted into Cole's shadow. Her gaze fell to his wrists, and she winced. "Handcuffs to subdue, bangles to subjugate."

A warning growl pumped through Cole, but the woman didn't shy from him.

No, I was the one who terrified her.

Jealousy failed to rouse this time, and I was glad for the reprieve. "You designed these?"

"Yes." Self-loathing made her choke on the admission. "I owed him a favor. This clears our debt."

The woman's reappearance captured Wu's interest, and he sidled up to me. "The craftsmanship is exquisite. Could you forge another pair?"

"No," she spat. "Never again." She made a sweeping gesture over her chest that came across as Catholic but couldn't be. "I have never used my talent for evil, but that—that is cursed." Her gaze latched onto mine. "He promised me you were different. He vowed you were here to save us. Please. *Please*. Destroy the cuffs after. Let them serve your purpose. Wield them with my blessing. But do not force me to live with the knowledge such a foul thing exists, and that I birthed it into this world. No one deserves to have their will stripped. These cuffs are an abomination."

"I give you my word," I said before Wu finished

voicing his protest. "I will destroy them the second I don't need them anymore."

"That's not good enough." Resolve starched her spine, and she inched away from the safety Cole provided. "When the fate of this world is decided, I want them gone."

"All right." I allowed a smile at her ferocity to bend my lips. "When the fate of this world has been decided, I will destroy the cuffs myself. Failing that, I will entrust them to someone who will carry out my wishes. You have my word."

The woman wilted on the spot as the head of steam she'd built up evaporated. "Go then, with my blessing."

Cole offered the woman a formal bow then kissed the back of her hand. "You have my gratitude."

"You can keep it." She flushed at his praise but paled when she caught me watching. "I like you well enough, Nicodemus, but not so much that I would step between you and your—"

His cold stare froze her on the spot, the terror she exuded when staring at me now leaking out in front of him.

I had taken a half step forward to diffuse the situation when what she said registered. *Nicodemus*. Not Cole. Not Heaton. Not any combination of the two. But Nicodemus. A name I had never heard applied to him. And yet she had known. *How* had she known?

"Forgive me," she whispered. "I misspoke."

"You got your assurances," Cole snarled. "Now go."

The woman crumpled in on herself but nodded and backed into the darkness until it absorbed her.

Cole rubbed a hand over his face, sighed in my direction, then went after her.

I let him go without a word.

"He never told you his name," Wu surmised, touching his knuckles to the side of my neck.

"No." I cleared my throat. "His secrets are his own."

"Trust will come in time," he assured me, and a knife to the heart would have hurt less.

For all that I trusted Cole, he didn't return the favor. I couldn't blame him. But forgiving him was hard.

Conquest shared history with him, and its depth and breadth had formed a chasm between us I was still bridging, plank by plank. But this woman leapt the divide with a single bound, a single word.

His name.

Nicodemus.

"Thish ish better—" Sariah slurred, "—than televishion."

The handcuffs had lost their shine by the time I clamped them around her wrists and hauled her to her feet. We gave Cole fifteen minutes to return, and when he didn't, we took his SUV back to the hotel.

Wu kept his own counsel, and I returned the favor. Some burdens weren't lessened by sharing them.

Up in our suite, Maggie curled against the arm of the couch with a book in her hands. Miller sat on the floor, his shoulder almost touching her ankle, a manual pulled up on his phone if the array of components fanning around him were any indication. The quiet week I spent at the bunkhouse, surrounded by books, felt like it happened years ago, to someone else.

Armageddon was hell on a TBR pile.

They glanced up in unison, but the first snarl shot from the far corner of the room, where Santiago hunched over a table scattered with circuits and wires.

"What the hell is she doing here?" He shot to his feet, brandishing a Phillips screwdriver like a sword. "Are you insane?"

"You bartered with her." Miller figured it out first. "Do you trust her to keep her word?"

"We do," Wu answered for me when it turned out I was still having trouble finding my voice.

"What does Cole think about this?" Portia, who set aside Maggie's book, stood and joined Santiago. They stood shoulder to shoulder, ready to bar Sariah from our rooms. "Does he know?"

"He picked us up," I rasped. "He knows."

"Luce?" Portia's voice wavered, teetering on the edge between personalities. "Are you okay?"

"I'm fine." Worst lie in history. No one believed anyone who claimed to be fine because they never were. "He gave me these." I lifted Sariah's linked arms and let them catch the glint off her wrists. "She won't be a problem. If she breaks her word to us—" and I had no doubt she would attempt to wriggle out of our deal now that she was free, "—these will keep her in line."

Or so I hoped until Cole explained how they worked in full detail.

"I know what that is." Miller flared his nostrils. "How—?"

"Lorelei," Santiago swore. "That's why she met Cole here."

"Where is he?" Thom strolled in from the mini kitchen, holding a raw fish in his hand. "He was waiting on you."

"Who knows?" I flapped a hand at him. "He's gone to find this Lorelei person."

"Is she lost?" He crossed to me and sat on the floor at my feet. "I saw her earlier."

"She got her feelings hurt." Emotions I didn't want to identify in my present mood. "She bolted after he presented his gift to me, and he went after her."

Miller turned his head to hide his expression from me, but Santiago I could trust to make the direct hit.

"Who is she?" I would know no peace until I understood what wasn't being said so loudly.

No one answered me. Not even Santiago, and the force of maintaining his quiet caused his jaw to bulge.

Thom held the fish aloft, offering it to me, and it took every ounce of patience in me to reach down, sift my fingers through his hair, and tell him, "It looks fresh. You should keep it."

"I caught it after I finished scouting the area where the body washed ashore." He bit into its belly, his teeth having sharpened to catlike points. "I stole one from the market, but it wasn't fresh caught today. The man lied on his sign."

"People do that." I cupped Sariah's elbow and led her into my room. "Come on."

"I'm not sleepy," she grumbled, her speech already solidifying. "Or are you going to lock me in there?"

"I'm going to let you shower, find you some clothes, and locate a map." She would fit into my spares until I could buy supplies for her. "You took an eight-hour nap. It's time for you to earn your keep." I didn't notice Wu slipping in behind me until I turned and smacked right into him. "I can handle her."

"I don't doubt it." His gaze touched on the bed, king-sized, like I might be sharing. But there were no dragons here. No Coles either. And he gave the impression of liking that just fine. "You're the one who captured her."

Eyebrow cocked, I let him get away with herding me. "Then why are you backing me up, in my bedroom?"

"You're emotional," he said calmly. "I only came in case you needed assistance."

"You did not just say that," I growled. "Just because I'm a woman—"

Wu closed his hand over my throat, his thumb caressing my carotid in a slow glide that turned my blood to honey. "You don't think clearly where Cole is concerned, and any distraction around a predator will get you killed."

Pulsing slowing, head clearing, I bobbled my head on my neck. "You've done this before."

The night we confronted Famine at the Trudeaus' home, he had calmed me with the same technique. Chokeholds weren't exactly soothing, but since I hadn't kneed his balls so far up his throat he sprouted a second pair of tonsils, my boneless response must be a charun thing. Biology at work. Yeah. That sounded good. Better than any other excuse that leapt to mind.

"To you?" Gold warmed his brown eyes. "Only once."

"It's a dirty trick." I exhaled slowly. "But I needed it. Thank you."

For another thirty seconds or so, he kept caressing me, and I kept letting him. The more he touched me, the less discordant he became, until I had to wonder if he hadn't somehow attuned himself to me. How, unless he hid his rosendium better than us, was he resonating with me at all?

Wu might look at me like he wanted to take a bite out of me on occasion, but I always wrote it off as posturing. That it might mean more . . .

The skip in my sluggish pulse furrowed his brow, and I broke free of him before he figured out why my heart had broken into a samba.

"Luce." Tablet in hand, Santiago shouldered past Wu into the room. "We got a problem."

The intrusion spared me from answering the question in Wu's eyes, and I blessed Santiago and his lack of personal boundaries.

"Is that—?" A security feed clued me into what I was seeing. "You're spying on Lambert?"

"He's awake." Santiago pressed the device into my hands. "We might ought to do something about that."

"Do something?" I studied the image, and the bottom dropped out of my stomach. "One, two, three . . . " I counted the hospital personnel in the room. "There are four people seizing on the floor." I spun it around for Wu to see. "You said he wasn't contagious."

"He shouldn't be." Wu cut his eyes toward the bathroom. "Keep an eye on Sariah. I'll go check it out."

And risk him dismissing this incident out of hand too? No thanks. "Santiago, can you babysit our guest?"

"Sure thing." His smile was all teeth. "I'm sure we can find some way to entertain ourselves until you return."

"Don't let her near Miller," I warned him. "I don't want either of them hurt."

Last time they butted heads, Sariah almost killed him. She'd had help. Lots of it. From her siblings. That didn't mean I wanted them left unsupervised. Miller was dangerous, that's what everyone kept telling me, but all I saw when I looked at him was a pool of blood on the kitchen floor in the farmhouse where I grew up, and a friend we had scrambled to save.

We left Santiago in the bedroom and gave Portia orders to select clothes that would fit Sariah. As dangerous as it was to let the two of them tag team our spy, I had no other choice.

A tentative hand on my elbow stopped me near the door, and I found Miller beside me. "Yes?"

"I'm not a liability." A flash of hurt made it clear he resented getting benched. "Santiago and I can handle Sariah. Maggie isn't ready for this."

"You're not a liability," I agreed quickly. "That's not why I'm asking you to stay out of that room and away from Sariah. I just don't want her near you unless I'm here to mediate."

"She can't kill me." He gentled his tone. "Not without signing her own death warrant."

So everyone kept telling me. "Remember when we agreed to try and understand each other's perspectives?"

"Yes."

"I thought I was going to lose you." I removed his hand from my elbow and squeezed his fingers. "I don't see you as some world-ending super demon. You're my friend, Miller, and you lost more blood than most horror houses use at Halloween because of her. Just humor me this one time. Can you do that?"

"For you." He pressed a fond kiss to my forehead. "But I will open her stomach and feast on her entrails if she harms Portia or Maggie."

Aware of the signals my body transmitted without permission, I smothered my fear, grasping the cold place with two hands and diving deep before the predator in Miller scented my panic. An unearthly calm spread through my limbs, and the tension in his shoulders eased. With emotion walled up behind bricks of ice, I saw things more clearly.

"I expect nothing less." Frost crackled in my mouth. "I respect your right to protect what is ours."

"It's time to go." Wu studied me, his eyes flecked with gold, his lips thin. Conquest always put him in a mood. For someone so eager to watch her rise in me, he sure preferred her tamped beneath my personality. "Your coterie can handle Sariah." Glancing past me, he singled out Thom. "Come with us. You have a soothing effect on her."

Thom discarded the remains of his fish sullenly then washed up to his elbows in the kitchen sink.

The urge to laugh plucked my vocal cords. "I can soothe myself just fine."

"Maintaining a partial shift for too long is dangerous. You need to settle your nerves."

Partial ... *shift*? Embracing the cold place ceded that much of me to her?

"Come on, Luce." Thom took my hand. "Let's go."

A flash of warmth spread up my arm, thawing my heart, and that calculating place in my head dismissed Wu. The cold place lasted for as long as it was required and not a second more.

Thom led the way, and Wu looked on, amused. Thom had a set of SUV keys in his pocket, but he passed them over to Wu. I claimed shotgun, and Thom climbed in behind me. After we cleared the parking lot, a rush of energy tickled my nape, and a boxy tomcat leapt onto my lap. His purr rattled my teeth when he leaned against my chest to scratch the underside of his jaw on my shirt buttons. That, or he was scent-marking me. Probably the latter. Clearly, I wasn't the only one with possessive issues.

"Does that help?" Wu flicked a glance at Thom. "The purring, I mean?"

"I like the sound." Already, I was more myself. "I like the feel too." I rested my hand on Thom's back, and he revved up his motor. "She must have too." He understood I meant Conquest. "All the coterie appears to have feline attributes."

The sound Wu made, a tight half-chuckle, had me glancing his way. "What's so funny?" I scratched behind Thom's notched ears. "Conquest, Scourge of the Terrenes, was one charun away from crazy cat lady status. Does that amuse you?"

"Yes," he admitted so quickly I knew that's not what had tickled him.

"Come on. Spill." The cold place had evaporated, leaving me in my own skin. "Why the laugh?"

"I'll show you one day." He dared me with a glance that left me with sweaty palms. He really shouldn't take his eyes off the road while driving. "Will that work?"

"I'm guessing I don't have a choice, so sure." Scooping up Thom, I cradled him against my chest while he kneaded my shoulder with wickedly sharp claws. "Thank you, Thomas."

"*Mmmrrrrpt.*"

"You identify most with your coterie in their natural forms," Wu mused. "That's unexpected."

"People are hard to parse." People lied, manipulated, stole, cheated. "Animals are simpler. Their motivations are easier to read. So are their moods." I used Thom as an example. "When they're happy, they purr. When they're not, they bite or scratch or both."

We reached the hospital before Wu could psychoanalyze me further. Thank God.

Thom hopped in the back while Wu parked. When we exited the vehicle, Thom did too. On two legs. He sniffed the air a few inches from my ear then licked the upper shell with his dry, raspy tongue that never seemed to shift back all the way.

"You'll be all right," he pronounced. "Your elevated testosterone levels have normalized."

"I, ah, okay." Resisting the urge to wipe my ear dry made my fingers twitch. "Good to know."

"Comb the lobby," Wu told him. "Keep your ears open for gossip. We must consider public opinion when deciding how best to suppress the spread of sensitive information."

The order curled Thom's lip, but he did as he was told and walked ahead of us into the hospital.

"I'm part of a cover-up," I muttered. "I can't believe this."

"Would you rather we warn humans about the end of days? Open their eyes to what lives among them?" He scoffed at the idea. "Imagine if this boy is contagious, if the origin is in Death, what then? Humans would sensationalize a zombie plague, and mass hysteria would reign. Consider how many more lives would be lost." He tamed his exasperation. "Humans die, thousands of them, sometimes hundreds of thousands of them, each time the cadre breaches. It's inevitable. We do our best to minimize the casualties, but there are environmental factors as well."

Thom was gone when we entered the lobby, so we hit the elevators. "What environmental factors?"

"Cadres unbalance the worlds they claim. Between them, they hold too much power. It disrupts the ebb and flow of the environment. That's why they aren't given the same chance at rehabilitation as other charun."

"You let me live this long," I pointed out.

"You were only *one*," he said, shuttering his expression, "and your condition muted your significance. You weren't expending energy, you weren't disrupting the natural order. Even with all the power at your disposal, you left no footprint. There was no harm in monitoring you."

"Now there are three of us." The elevator spit us out on the third floor. "What have I missed?"

"Small atmospheric disturbances. Low-grade tornadoes, minor earthquakes, a weak tsunami. Weather that might cause a meteorologist to remark on an active season, but nothing alarming."

I heard the *yet* clearly.

"No one told me." There was so much I didn't know, so much I didn't want to know but must learn.

The problem was that survival was taking up all my spare time. I was being given the CliffsNotes version of my past on a need to know basis instead of being handed the entire book to peruse, but I had come awake too late to catch up on my reading.

"Conditions will deteriorate quickly once Death arrives."

Note to self: Download weather app.

We turned the corner onto madness, and that spared him from answering more questions.

Wu at my side, I waded in. "What in the . . . ?"

Gurneys clogged the hall, convulsing bodies strapped to them. Nurses huddled in groups, some in triage mode while others wept and fluttered over fallen coworkers. Doctors waded in, and hands clutched at their white coats. Security officers milled among them, pushing the crowd back. More men in blue arrived and began herding anyone symptomatic into rooms down the hall.

One of them noticed us and whistled in our direction. "You'll have to come with me."

Wu started to protest, his hand reaching for the badge at his hip, but I gripped his wrist. "All right."

"What are you doing?" He pitched his voice low as we kept to the path the officer cleared for us.

"We need to find out what's wrong with these people. It will be hours before the staff is settled enough to answer questions, and we'll have to stand in line for a turn." I patted him reassuringly. "Why not go right to the source?"

"They might be contagious." He hesitated on the threshold of a room that would be difficult to fight our way out of if it came to that. "Assuming this illness spread from the corpse, we might be at risk."

"Well, that's one way to prove I was right." I waltzed right in. "I'll try not to gloat."

"I hope we live long enough for you to fully enjoy proving me wrong."

That made two of us.

We worked the crowd for two hours. There were three dozen people sequestered. Almost half of them wore scrubs. The first three or four had no information. They had been herded in here before grasping the situation. The next five or six had either been visiting family or seeking treatment when a commotion drew them out into the hall. The rest were starting to sweat and tremble.

"Are you ... cops?" Winded from the short walk across the room, a nurse wearing baby pink scrubs latched onto Wu's arm to keep her knees from buckling. "I saw . . . you interviewing . . . everyone."

"We're with the FBI." Wu adjusted the woman and reached for his badge. The flash gave me a pang of envy. I felt naked without one. Done impressing her, he put it away. "Can you tell us what you saw?"

"I was meeting a friend for lunch. I work in maternity. He works in ICU. I waited at the nurses' station on his floor, but he never showed. It's not like him to stand me up without calling, but sometimes we get busy. It's easy to lose track of time. I gave him fifteen minutes then I went looking. I found him collapsed in the hall outside Jay Lambert's room. He was foaming at the mouth and speaking in tongues."

"Speaking in tongues?"

"The way some religious people do? It's all gibberish to me."

Wu tensed beneath her hand, his face a calm mask that hid the cracks I heard in his resolve. "Can you remember anything he said?"

"There was so much of it, but he kept repeating 'ah-tru-ha-dal'."

The sheen sparking off Wu's brown eyes was in no way human, and the nurse wasn't so far gone not to notice.

Power radiated off him in waves that lifted the hairs down my arms. He was going nuclear, and there wasn't enough time to insulate everyone from the blast. I had to get him calm and fast. God only knew what charun lived beneath his skin. This was not how I wanted to make that discovery.

"Here, let me help you to a chair." I accepted her weight from him and guided her to the conference table. The crowd around the oval had thinned a bit as people grew bored and started pacing or standing in front of the doors like they might forge their combined will into a key that would open them. "There you go. Just sit tight. I'm sure it won't be much longer."

"I'm a nurse." The stare she leveled at me would have done Rixton proud. "I've worked in this hospital for fifteen years and been certified for twenty. Go pull someone's else's leg. Your arms will get tired if you keep yanking on mine."

CHAPTER TEN

Wu and I huddled in a corner as far from the others as space allowed. I wasn't convinced rubbing his arms like he was cold and I might warm him was the best idea I had ever had, but touch soothed the coterie, so why not him? Eventually, the fury vibrating through him abated enough he could open his eyes without gilding the room. He captured my hands in his and placed a kiss to the back of each, a formal gesture that nonetheless sent tingles radiating up my arms.

I wondered if it had to do with the fact he had cranked the dial on his power so high a moment ago, but I didn't ask. Tipping him back toward anger in the presence of so many innocents might spell disaster for us all.

The burning question of what "ah-tru-ha-dal" meant and why it flipped his switch was sidelined too.

I would get my answers, but first I had to get us out of here.

"The windows are all locked this high. We can't jimmy them without drawing attention, and I doubt we can break them without causing a riot. Odds are high they're plexiglass. We'd have to hammer on them to make a dent." I scanned the room, talking to myself as Wu calmed. "Looks like there's a bathroom." I tipped my head back. "Breaking those foam board tiles is easy, but the grid is weak. The drop ceiling won't hold us if we try to climb out that way."

"There's a window in the bathroom." Wu massaged his hands, as if they ached from clenching into fists. "It's high and narrow, but we could fit."

"Same problem," I reminded him. "We have no way to break it. Can we even reach it?"

Gold flecks sparkled in the depths of his brown eyes. "I said I would show you."

"You did," I agreed carefully, not at all certain I wanted his revelation. Let alone here and now.

"I'm going in." He shrugged out of his jacket and tossed it in the corner. "Wait five minutes and follow."

"People are going to think we're trying to join whatever the hospital bathroom equivalent is of the Mile-High club."

The imperious eyebrow he arched informed me I would be so lucky. "And?"

The dare unsettled me after his fit of temper. I wasn't touching it with a ten-foot pole.

"And nothing." I shook my head and set a timer on my phone just to be a smartass. "See you in five."

While he disappeared into the unisex bathroom, I took a moment to check in with Thom via text. I gave him an update on our situation and let him know extraction might be required. Santiago told me once that most of Thom's bodily fluids were considered medicinal. I had to believe that came with one heck of a top-tier immune system too. But we were dealing with an unknown contagion at this point, and Wu and I were both compromised.

After I unloaded everything we'd learned from canvassing the crowd, I let Thom make the final call. As much as I wanted out, I would rather suffer confinement in a hospital than harm him, or the others.

A *bing-bong* notification announced my time was up, and I started toward the restroom. I had my hand out, reaching for the doorknob, when a woman slid between me and the handle.

"Get in line," she snapped, glaring at my clothes. The belt, in particular, appeared to offend her. But maybe she was looking for the badge I didn't yet have. "That uniform doesn't mean you get preferential treatment."

Since my outfit could have passed as business casual, thanks to its quality, I assumed the woman had spoken to enough of her fellow detainees to know Wu and I were posing as FBI. The tone, paired with the sneer, made me wonder if she had to use the bathroom or if she just wanted to make sure I couldn't without going through her first.

"Sorry, but my partner doesn't feel well." That much should have been obvious by our huddle. "He texted me for assistance. I'm going in there."

"Let him choke on his own tongue." The woman honed her glare. "You suits are all the same."

A flare of ice singed my nerve endings, the cold place rising to cool my temper, but I beat it back until my head cleared.

"Yes, we are." I played up her insecurities. "So you know what will happen if you don't get out of my way."

Some of the color left her cheeks, but she kept her glare trained on me as I entered the bathroom and shut it behind me, taking care to lock it. I expelled a slow breath, regaining control of the trembling in my hands, and noticed a few things.

The bathroom was large, one of those all-purpose deals. Handicap accessible and family-sized with a fold-down changing table.

The window was indeed high. Long and narrow, impossible for a human to reach, let alone damage.

And the final thing, perhaps the most important thing, was the winged man who stood below it.

Stripped to his waist to give himself a better range of motion, Wu rustled his feathers. Preening. For me.

I'm not proud of the gasp that escaped me. Or the awe I felt climbing my face and rearranging my features. Or the desperate urge to reach out and caress the downy feathers on his—I counted them—three sets of wings. Six total.

"You look like an angel" was the dumbest thing I could have said about Wu, so of course that fell out of my mouth.

Aunt Nancy and Uncle Harold would have come unglued at the seams thinking of him in their house.

"Don't let the wings fool you." He held out his hand for mine, and comforting warmth lapped up my arm. "I'm no more angelic than I was five minutes ago."

"I get it now." The joke. The reason he had laughed. "I'm the crazy cat lady with a bird man for a partner."

Talk about a cosmic joke.

"I'm going to fly up there and shatter the window. We won't have much time after that. You've got to be ready." He squeezed my fingers so the bones ground together, snapping my attention from his wings to his face. "You're going to have to trust me."

I tugged on my arm, but he held firm. "That ... doesn't sound good."

"You'll have to get yourself onto the ledge and out the window."

"Out the window." Visions of splattering on the pavement danced in my head. "Climb *out* the window?"

"I'll catch you." His wings slid forward, gliding down my forearms, almost cocooning us. "Look at me." His eyes were solid gold, molten. "I won't let you fall."

"I will be very pissed if you do." I shut my eyes, kicking myself for putting us in this situation. "Mark my words—I will live long enough to kick your feathery ass if I die."

Okay, so that made more sense in my head. Considering I was about to kiss pavement, who cared?

"I believe you." He tucked his wings tight to his spine and kicked off his shoes. He leapt onto the wall and climbed, his fingers and toes cracking tile as his talons dug into the grout. "Move over there, and make yourself as small as possible."

Following his orders, I squatted in the far corner and curled into a ball, covering my head with my arms. I didn't see Wu punch out the window, I kept my eyes shut to protect them, but I heard the dull thuds as his fist hit. Over and over, the force terrible, and then *crack*.

Fresh air stirred tendrils of hair against my cheek, and I peeked up in time to see him slide through the opening that was maybe two feet tall by six feet wide. I grimaced as a sleek feather caught on a ragged tooth of glass, leaving a crimson smear on the bottommost portion.

I was guessing his stomach had taken the worst of the damage to preserve his wings, but that was worry for later. He was injured, and I didn't want to waste his time when I had no clue how long he could hover there in wait for me.

Plus, smashing the window had drawn attention to us. Raised voices called out from inside the room, and fists pounded the door while the knob rattled. Too bad Wu hadn't told me how he expected me to make my escape. The window was a good eight feet off the ground. The only way I could make it work in my head was going to hurt. A lot. Good thing I had charun healing on my side.

Still, I did what I could to mitigate the damage. Scooping Wu's shirt off the floor, I ripped it in half then wrapped my hands with the fabric. It wasn't much help, but I would take all I could get. That done, I kicked off my boots but kept my socks on to protect my feet. From there, I had to hope Wu's handholds and footholds worked for fingers as well as they did for talons.

The tiles bit into my fingertips through the makeshift gloves, but I clenched my teeth and climbed. I didn't have far to go. The window was placed just high enough you couldn't see more than a slice of sky when you glanced through it while handling your business. It was worse for my toes. The cracked tiles split beneath my weight, slicing me through my socks when I slipped on them. Once I got three feet off the ground, I was able to reach the window. "This is going to suck."

There was nothing for it but to grab the windowsill and haul myself onto the lip. Glass sliced open my fingers and ripped into my palms. The cold place hit me with such force, I almost lost my grip before the icy balm numbed the pain and allowed me to situate myself half in, half out of the opening. Hanging over the edge, I got a good look at how far I would have to fall to hit the ground.

Wind snapped loose hairs around my face, and I wished with all my might for the familiar iridescent glint of dragon scales, but Cole was nowhere in sight.

"Adam," I breathed, thinking it was odd I had never used his first name. "Don't make me regret this."

All I had to do was swing my leg over the ledge. That's all it took to unbalance me and send me tumbling through the air. I sank like a stone, unable to tear my gaze from the grave zooming toward me.

Strong arms hooked beneath mine, wrenching me back, popping my shoulders but not dislocating them. "I've got you."

"Okay," I squeaked, staring up at him. "I'm a fan of being gotten."

The panic over him flying away with me, legs dangling over nothing, got no chance to manifest. He didn't go up, as expected, but down. Backbeating his wings, he lowered us to the cracked asphalt of the parking lot. My feet touched down, and then my knees cracked against the pavement. I was happy to slump forward onto all fours and tempted to keep going until I kissed the ground.

Wings.

Why did everyone and their momma have to have wings?

Terror lent my voice an edge. "Did anyone see that?"

"No." He had the gall to sound affronted. "Of course not."

The *how* would only make my head hurt, so I didn't even ask. Beholding Wu in this form made my skull ache. Yet another one of those cracks was splintering my façade, the human shell I was having more trouble holding closed with each step I took deeper into the charun world.

"You're hurt." Wu crouched next to me, prying open my hands. "We need to get the glass out before your skin heals over it."

"I don't have any tweezers, and we need to get out of here more." I accepted his hand on my elbow as he helped me stand then grimaced at the pain in my feet. "We need to quarantine ourselves until the incubation period has passed."

"Your coterie is here in Vicksburg." He tilted his head. "Can we use the bunkhouse in Canton?"

Allowing him into their home—*our* home—rankled, but it didn't get more isolated than the swamp.

"I doubt they'll mind." I texted Thom to be sure. "Thom gave us the green light. He'll let the others know."

Some of the more mountainous members of my coterie might not be thrilled to learn I was holed up with Wu for forty-eight hours, but Cole would have to deal, the same as I had when he vanished on me earlier.

Petty? Who? Me?

"We'll make better time if we fly." Wu left the statement dangling the same as I had from his arms.

"Fine." I patted my queasy stomach. "You're lucky I'm sitting on empty."

Wu opened his arms and let me interpret how he meant for us to travel. Miles of bare chest snagged my gaze. Most of it smeared with drying blood and crusting scabs. I would be pressed against him and his ridiculous abs no matter how he held me, and I couldn't decide which of my options was the least intimate. Giving up, I asked for his preference. "Where do you want me to put what?"

Wicked heat licked the gold in his eyes, and I saw the naughty thought perch on the tip of his tongue before he swallowed it down. Without Cole around to antagonize, it seemed I wasn't worth the effort.

"The easiest thing— No," he amended, "the *safest* thing, would be if you wrapped your arms around my neck and your thighs around my hips."

Logically, okay, I could see that being easier for him. But I had never let a man other than Cole hold me for any length of time.

This is Wu, I argued with myself as I chewed on my bottom lip. *My partner.*

He was the one who gave the big speech about how there were no fraternization laws for charun. The spay and neuter program meant females no longer went into heat, and males no longer experienced the urge to procreate.

There was more to it, there had to be, if demi charun existed. But I didn't have much choice about going with him if I wanted to minimize the risk of infection for the coterie, and any humans we might contaminate if we lingered.

"Okay, we'll do this the *safest* way." I walked into his arms, hopped up when he bent his knees, then wrapped around him like a kudzu vine, careful to keep my hands linked at his nape and my ankles locked at his spine. His hands gripped the backs of my thighs, and his fingers dug into my muscles. His breaths puffed warm in my ear, and his heart raced where our chests touched. "Fair warning, I will go for the feathers if you touch my ass."

"How about this?" He slid his ironclad grip closer to my knees. "Comfortable?"

"Not the word I would use, no." I resisted the urge to hop off this ride before it got started. "I can handle it, though."

"Brace yourself," he said, breathless with anticipation.

He loved to fly, and why wouldn't he? He had been born with wings, made to carve his own path through the skies.

His vertical takeoff had me cinching my arms into a choke-hold, and I glanced down to make sure the pressure from my thighs locking hadn't popped him in half.

Sharp winds hacked at my cheeks, slashed water from my eyes, and I buried my face in his neck to lessen the sting. His scent made my nostrils tingle and my lungs tighten an instant before I softened against him.

Whatever he was, he had gotten one thing right. He was no angel.

Angels, I felt certain, didn't have this narcotic effect on people. Though, if they did, that might explain the depictions of them wearing halos. The artists might have been hallucinating.

The rhythmic pump of his wings, the sequence as each set gave way to the other with such precision, tempted me to peek up from his neck. Each feathered limb stretched longer than he was tall, reaching out to brush the stars to either side of us. How had he crammed them under his shirt? His jacket? How had they fit in the bathroom?

Dad once accused me of being *special*, a softer word for having magic, but this— This was true magic.

If I asked, Wu would probably science it away the same as Cole, but I wasn't one of those people who could only enjoy a magic show if I knew how all the tricks were performed. I was happy to sit and watch, to be amazed without questioning the mechanics.

"You can touch them if you'd like," he murmured against my cheek. "I won't drop out of the sky if you do."

I curled my fingers into my palm to keep from taking him up on his offer. "Isn't that ... intimate?"

"Very," he husked, his voice threaded with midnight. "As long as you avoid the wing joints, you're not taking liberties."

Unsure if I believed him, I knew I wouldn't pass up a second invitation. I brushed a fingertip down the wrist of his topmost wing, admiring the silken texture of his feathers, and chills dappled his skin. "Can you feel each set individually? Each wing? How do you coordinate them?"

"You're giving me too much credit." His laugh was lighter than the darkness around us. "I can feel each wing like you feel your arms or legs. I can move them independently, but they move in tandem without coaching from me. I was born for the skies, and my brain came with the manual already downloaded."

We didn't talk during the rest of the flight, and I kept my hands to myself as much as possible considering I was clinging to him like a barnacle on the hull of a ship.

"Hold on." His warm breath cut through the chilly night air. "We're landing."

Worried oxygen deprivation might cause him to pass out and us to plummet into the swamp, I loosened my arms, but I kept my ankles hooked and held on for dear life.

Wu's descent was as elegant as the rest of him now that he

wasn't plucking fallen women from the sky. I slumped with relief and rested my forehead on his shoulder when his knees bent to absorb my weight as he landed, as light as a feather.

The clomping footsteps didn't register at first. The howling wind had my ears ringing in the silence, and the *thump, thump, thump* wasn't all that different from the banging in my chest. No, what clued me in to the fact we had company was the tightening of Wu's fingers, how they dug into my thighs and kept me flush against him.

"Put her down," Cole rumbled, his voice barely human. "I don't want to spatter her with your blood when I rip out your throat."

"*Cole,*" I barked. "What the hell are you doing? We came here to get away from you."

A thunderous rumble vibrated the planks under our feet, and a vicious smile cut Wu's mouth. He was enjoying this.

The growl I shot back at Cole was pathetically human in comparison. "We might be infected. I wanted you and the coterie to stay in Vicksburg until we knew for certain."

Given my fit of jealousy over what's-her-face, I had been looking forward to the break. Okay. Fine. So I remembered her name was Lorelei. Whatever. But this hurt. Cole doubting me hurt. Wu enjoying his pain hurt. And fine, yes. Cole wandering off with her hurt even more.

"Let me go," I told Wu, kicking him in the tailbone. "You've had your fun. Now let me talk him out of eviscerating you."

As I slid out of Wu's arms, I got an eyeful of what we were up against. Cole was vibrating. It hadn't been his growl or approaching footsteps. His whole body hummed, seconds from exploding into his dragon form, and I doubted I could talk that version of Cole down from swallowing Wu in one gulp.

One good thing came from this steaming hot mess. No

inflight nausea. Hurray! Who knew staring down dragons with murder in their eyes worked better than sucking peppermints to soothe an upset stomach?

"How are you here?" I straightened my clothes and smoothed my windblown hair. "You must have broken speed records beating us to the bunkhouse."

"It wasn't that hard," he said flatly, and Wu bristled on my periphery.

"You're supposed to be in Vicksburg—" I tried again, "—where it's *safe*."

"Our culture forbids a female in your position to spend a night, however platonic, with an unmated male who is not a member of her coterie."

Our culture implied we shared some common ancestry, but what he must mean is it was an Otillian custom enforced by their conquered peoples.

"Under the circumstances, I think an allowance could be made." I anchored my hands on my hips. "You haven't touched us, breathed on us, or drank after us. No blood or other bodily fluids have been spilled. You should still hole up somewhere to wait out the incubation period to be safe, but you ought to be fine if you leave now."

"You're right," he allowed, appearing totally reasonable.

It made me immediately suspicious.

Just as I was about to smack him in the face with another warning, he gave the dragon his skin. The beast gazed down at us, crimson eyes hard, and wrapped his tail around his favorite ankle. Great. Now he'd gone and done it. He'd touched me. Holding Wu's gaze, he ducked his head and rubbed noses with me, breathing me in.

Oh no. No, no, no. I saw where this was heading.

I had no handy drink for him to gulp, and he would never

have bled me to prove a point, but he did lick me with his coarse tongue from collarbone to hairline.

Wu shuddered at the display, his hand going for the pocket of a shirt or jacket he no longer wore. I wondered if he would have offered me his handkerchief if he'd still had one. "There are more pleasurable ways to exchange saliva, dragon."

Scales rippled, a precursor to the change, but I captured the beast's face between my palms. "Our first kiss will not be the result of a dare."

The fury propelling the dragon stalled under my touch, and he ceded its form to his human one.

"Our first kiss," he echoed, clearly liking the way that sounded, "will also not have spectators."

Wait. Cole was agreeing there would be kissing? *Hot diggity dog.* "That sounds fair."

"You can take Thom's room," Cole informed Wu. "I'm sure you can find your way."

Given the years of surveillance, yeah. I'm sure he could too.

"You will remain in our room." Eyes on mine, he made it an order. "It's the most central and easily defensible."

"No arguments here." Home was where the AC hummed, after all. "What about you?"

"I'll be staying with you." He cut his eyes to Wu. "Unless you prefer I stand watch out here."

I like to think I'm a strong woman, but turning down Cole when he offered to share a bed with me was just plain dumb, and I also liked to think I wasn't stupid.

"Stay," I said, and stay he did.

CHAPTER ELEVEN

———◆———

Cole herded me into our room before Wu got a chance to say goodnight or ask for a clean towel to go with the shower he'd mentioned. As my heels scraped over the threshold, and I thought about him showering, I wondered how he would fit. After seeing him with wings as a natural extension of his body, I had trouble picturing him without them, but it was silly. He would just tuck them into whatever dimensional pocket or whateveryoucallit and that would be that. I could have let it go then except . . . "I have to go check on Wu."

"He's fine," Cole assured me. "You saw him two seconds ago."

Guilt sparked from his jealousy made me squirm. Having been a green-eyed monster earlier myself, maybe I should have relished paying him back, but I didn't. He deserved better than tit for tat over each little hurt accidentally inflicted while we figured each other out. Retaliation was purposeful, after all, and I wanted a relationship, not a scoreboard.

"We got sliced up making our escape." I held up my hands and clocked his grimace when it hit him one of us had to cut the glass from under my palms. My skin had grown over it during the flight. "He took the worst damage on his chest and stomach. He might be able to swing it solo, but we ought to offer anyway."

"There's a first aid kit under the bed." Cole made no move to help me locate it. "I'll shower while you examine him."

"Are you sure you don't want to come with?" I retrieved the medical supplies and dusted off the box, its seal intact. With Thom around, who needed mundane gauze, tape, and antibiotic ointment? "You could hold the flashlight for me."

"I can't be there when you touch him skin to skin." A fine tremor rippled over him, the dragon gnashing its teeth. "I will tend to you when you return."

Prolonged contact with Cole at the low, low price of him using a scalpel and tweezers to remove shards of pesky glass. "That's the best offer I've had all day."

On my way to Thom's room, I stopped by the kitchen and lifted an icy bottle of water. Maybe the cold would help numb him for what came next. With my hands full, I had to knock on the door with my foot. Wu opened on the third kick, sans feathers, and wasn't that a pity. I would have loved to inspect them closer. Except that kind of touching might convince the dragon across the way to eat hot wings for dinner.

"We've got maybe fifteen minutes to do this before Cole gets out of his shower." I held up my supplies then jerked my chin in the direction of the wrought iron patio set. Holing up in a bedroom with Wu was asking for trouble, but I fudged on my reason for the location switch. "This might get messy, so we'll do it outside."

Though, now that I thought about it, Thom thought Wu smelled delicious. He might not mind having avian-scented blood in his room. Maybe Cole had come to the same conclusion.

Or maybe he picked Thom's room because it opened onto the back of the house and was as far as he could put Wu and still claim him as a guest.

"Sit." I would have a bruise tomorrow from using my hip to bump out a chair for him. "Holler if it hurts."

"I don't *holler*." He did perch on the edge of the seat and lean back. "I'm surprised your leash stretches this long with a boulder like Cole tied to the other end."

Feminine as always, I snorted. "I call him Mount Heaton. In my head." I shoved his shoulder. "Let's keep that between us."

The idea of a secret lent his voice warmth. "Thank you for caring for me."

Words shouldn't carry such weight, but these did, and I wasn't convinced he meant me playing nurse.

Undercurrents swirled and eddied between us, but I was too smart to wade into the deeps. I already had my feet wet with Cole. Whatever Wu meant, I would rather keep ignoring the implications. I was good at that and getting better all the time. Before long, someone would owe me a trophy.

"You're welcome." I cracked open the kit and performed a quick inventory. "Besides, you can't blame it all on Cole. My fuse is shorter than Portia's attention span when Santiago opens his mouth these days."

"You're learning to control your instincts. They're new to you. Cole has had lifetimes to master his."

Despite Wu viewing Cole's behavior as adolescent, it cheered me. I liked drawing out his possessive instincts. Even now, when I owed him a scolding for endangering himself, I wouldn't push him away again. I'd used up all my self-control the first time I tried to send him packing.

"Hold still." I pulled out my phone and used it as a flashlight. "Stop clenching." I smoothed my hand down the valley between his pectorals then lower, over his abs, and he shivered under my questing fingers. "The worst pocket seems to be here. Your skin has grown over the glass. I'm going to have to cut it out. Is that okay?"

"You can't hurt me."

"Wu, I don't care who or what you are, some rules still apply. When someone cuts you open and digs around in the wound, it hurts."

"All right." His soft chuckle ceded the point. "I should have said— I can bear it."

"I'm still sorry it has to be done." I worried about the angle. It wasn't great, even with him leaning back and me wedged between his thighs. On second thought, maybe the last part was what gave me the twitches. "Can I convince you to stretch out on the pier?"

"You're the doctor," he teased, sounding too pleased by half considering what I was about to do. "Perhaps I might suggest you straddle my hips to give yourself the best access." He sank to his knees, then lowered himself onto the treated planks. Each of them scarred by claws and teeth. He crossed his feet at the ankles and rested his head on his linked hands. "I would suggest you straddle my face but—"

Crack.

The scent of blood hit me first, a testament to my heightening senses. Crimson smeared Wu's face, weeping from the gash opened on his cheek and across his upper lip. At my feet, Cole's tail writhed against the wood. I couldn't see the dragon, but it was plain he could see and hear us just fine.

Taking my life in my hands, I stepped on his tail. "You're supposed to be in the shower."

An unapologetic rumble came from around the side of the house, in the direction of the bathroom.

The anger spilled out of me the second he wrapped his tail around my ankle. Just once. That's all he could reach. I simply had no defense against him.

"I am such a sucker," I murmured. "That doesn't change the fact I need to treat Wu so he can shower. Hurry up, and don't use all the hot water."

The dragon growled uncomplimentary things under his breath but didn't let go.

"I'll make you a deal." I pinched the bridge of my nose, my gut tying itself in knots in preparation for what came next. "I'll let you take me flying if you do this one thing for me."

A pleased hum, almost a purr, vibrated through his grip on me, and then he withdrew.

I stood there, hands on my hips, until the shower kicked on. It got me wondering if the flying thing hadn't been the problem the whole time. Other men getting me airborne must be yet another no-no in his book.

Boys and their wing-measuring contests.

Standing over Wu, I nudged him with my foot. "You knew he was listening."

"Yes." His smile flashed pink teeth. "I did."

That right there was the reason why I couldn't take the heated looks he shot me too seriously. The man was a pot-stirrer, and I didn't want him sticking his spoon in me just to piss off Cole.

"Males make me tired." I sank to my knees and set to work, allowing a touch of soothing ice to rise enough to dull the edge of discomfort that resulted from knowing I was about to hack away at another person. I had promised the coterie to try and limit the old crutch, but it was reflexive. I wasn't convinced I could quit cold turkey even if I wanted to attempt life unanaesthetized. "What would you have done if I hadn't offered to do this?"

"The healing process would have pushed the glass out of my skin." He twitched his shoulders. "Eventually."

I uncapped the water and poured half over his chest to rinse away the crusted blood. "Bet that itches like crazy."

He hesitated a moment. "It does."

An itch was easier to admit to than pain. Gotcha.

"I'm going to focus on the big pieces. I see maybe seven that need to come out. Can you handle that?"

"You're the one who's procrastinating."

Blanketed in the cold, I fell into an easy rhythm. I drifted a bit, aware but unaware, and I appreciated the buffer between me and the blood slicking my fingertips. It reminded me too much of Uncle Harold and how I had made him bleed too.

"Your scent changed," Wu observed. "And now it's altering again. Are you with me, Luce?"

"Where else would I be?" The fading tendrils of crystalline focus thawed, and I blinked first at the precise cuts and then at the handful of shards stacked in a neat pile. "Looks like we're all done." I poured the remaining water over his chest and down his abs. "There are tiny lumps, but if you're sure you can eject those on your own, I need to go see a dragon about a rollercoaster ride."

Wu pushed up into a sitting position while I cleaned up the mess. After testing his skin with his fingertips, he smiled at me. "That feels much better."

"Glad to be of assistance." And I was. He had saved my bacon. Granted, he had convinced me to throw my bacon out a third-story window first, but still. "See you in the morning. There's got to be some remote work we can get done. We'll be at each other's throats if we don't find some way to keep ourselves occupied."

The thoughtful sound he made low in his throat almost convinced me he was about to say something inappropriate.

I waited for it, ready to hear the punchline, but he kept his thoughts to himself.

Ah well. Maybe I had been projecting. Dirty jokes were Rixton's wheelhouse, and he was irreplaceable. No one else had his sense of humor, so it's not like Wu was the only one who couldn't compare.

Wu's sense of humor was of the blink-and-you'll-miss-it variety. Very dry. Sahara Desertesque. But I was learning to appreciate both his wit and his deft hand at hiding it behind a blank expression. Subtle. That's what he was, when Rixton had always been more of a sledgehammer to the face.

"Santiago must have equipment we can borrow." Wu stood and helped me put away the kit under the kitchen sink then tossed the trash. "With his help, we might be able to surveille the hospital. The news will give us an idea of what humans think is happening, but we need to discover the truth."

"This is really our job?" I scratched at my palm, which was beginning to itch. "We cover up charun activity so humans don't become suspicious?"

"We investigate charun activity so that we grasp its undercurrents. We must be informed, and that goes double during an ascension." He scratched his jaw, annoyed when his nails encountered scruff. "Our reports determine the scope of what is required to insulate charun from exposure. Our work determines if there will be casualties and how many." He let that sink in. "You're in the place where you can do the most good."

"Hunting my sisters does the most good." I rinsed my hands one last time. "This is cleaning up the aftermath."

"How bloodthirsty of you." His eyes glinted in feral appreciation. "This is how the game is won. We must unmask all the players before we can determine their strategies and build our own."

"I know, I know."

Rixton taught me through example that being a good cop—a good detective—was ninety percent drudgework. These days, people left behind cyber trails rather than fingerprints. Following the breadcrumbs was a desk job. It was tedious and not at all what I signed up for, but there was no stopping progress, and we were making progress.

We were getting a bead on Death through tracking the corpses and those infected by them. Famine was behind bars. War was the only free agent, and Santiago had been hot on her heels even before Sariah joined us.

I patted my tender hands dry. "It's just frustrating."

"This is your first ascension, in a way," he mused. "I forget that."

"You want to forget." He wasn't getting off the hook that easy. "You want me to be Conquest."

"No." He turned to leave then stopped and glanced over his shoulder. "I want you to be more, better."

I watched him go then cracked open a bottle of water and went in search of Cole. I didn't have to go far.

"He's right," Cole said from where he leaned against the wall outside the kitchen. "Your scent changes when you go cold."

"Let's pretend you didn't mention my scent again. I'm honestly developing a complex." I offered him the bottle, and he took a long draw. "What makes you think I go *cold?*"

The coterie noticed when I slipped away, but I couldn't recall ever explaining the sensation to them.

"You shut down your emotions, your expression. You're a blank page and then someone else fills it."

"You mean Conquest." I waved off the water when he offered it back, unable to swallow past the lump in my throat. It's not like I hadn't figured that part out on my own. The calm wasn't like a hit from a drug, it wasn't physical. It was mental, sliding into a mindset with such vast experience that I drew upon that knowledge when I smashed into the boundaries that made me Luce. "You can scent her? On me?"

That must be what Wu meant when he claimed it was a partial shift.

"Only then, and only a little."

A shiver raced down my spine that reminded me of one of Aunt Nancy's old sayings. "Someone just walked over my grave."

"You're changing." He polished off the water. "It's to be expected."

"I don't want to change," I admitted, "but I understand I have no choice."

"You could stand with your sisters. You could refuse to take a stand at all. You could have locked yourself away after meeting us." He sounded proud. "You chose to stand and fight. You chose to sacrifice a part of yourself to protect what you believe in."

"I worry that the stronger these ... urges ... become, the harder it will be to ignore them, to stay me."

"Wu wasn't wrong when he said that all charun must learn to curb their appetites, especially when they're inhabiting a terrene that's not their own. The struggle eases, but the urges, as you call them—" he swept his gaze over me, "—they never go away."

"So basically 'Buck up, Buttercup?'" I exhaled on a laugh. "If charun toddlers can do it, then surely I can too. I'm a tad older than most of my classmates, but maybe I can blame a growth spurt for being the tallest kid in the room."

Cole belted out a laugh that had me grinning in response. He was probably laughing at me and not with me, but I couldn't resist him when tiny pockets of his soul exposed themselves. Or any other time, if I was being honest.

Maybe he was picturing baby dragons towering over me,

gumming me to death in preparation for the day they sprouted steak-knife teeth. Unless they were born with teeth like other reptiles. Not that I had ever asked if Cole identified as reptilian. I figured it rated up there with questioning a charun about their true form.

Revising my mental picture of that imaginary first day of school, I winced as things got a lot bloodier a lot quicker than when I pretended they shared mammalian traits.

As his amusement waned, Cole gazed out on the horizon. "Lorelei is Convallarian."

So was he.

A bitter taste flooded my mouth, and I couldn't tell if it was a more intense form of jealousy because she shared biology with him, a home, a culture, or if it was a ragged form of grief that in recognizing those things, I had to accept the hand I had in destroying them. "Did you know one another before?"

"No." His dipped his chin. "Her mother came through with the cadre during the last ascension. She barely escaped with her life. Lorelei was born here. She's never seen Convallaria."

"How did you find one another?" The NSB's program made it easier for charun from the same terrenes to hook up, but Cole had avoided their facilities. "Is she registered?"

"No, she's not."

The strained note in his voice had me searching his expression. When I understood, I wished that I didn't, that I could take it back, but the knowledge was mine to own now.

"She's unmated." The way his throat worked when he swallowed was all the confirmation I required. "She's off the NSB's radar, so that means she's able to reproduce." And he was male and also fertile. "She approached you. She wanted to mate with you."

"She wanted a child from me," he clarified. "She's married to a demi of another species. They're incompatible that way. They can't have children."

An icepick buried itself in my temple. That's how it felt. And through the hole leaked ... memories?

"Atru, Atru," *a breathless voice calls.* "Atru, Atru, Atru."

Hidden behind the planter, sheltered by its crown of fronds, I watch the small predator flare her nostrils as she homes in on her prey. Her head jerks toward me, crimson eyes as vivid as spilled blood, and she smiles.

She will make a glorious huntress one day.

"Atru," *she cries in triumph, toddling up to me. Her pudgy hands fist in my skirt.* "Atru."

"Luce," Cole roared in my face. "*Luce.*"

"Give her air," Wu ordered. "She can't breathe."

"She's convulsing," Cole thundered. "That's why she can't breathe."

"What did you say to her?" Wu's voice was a blade. "What did you do?"

He had no satisfactory answer for that, and his quiet pain ripped me back into the present.

"I saw her," I sobbed. "I saw her."

Gathering me in his arms, Cole pressed his lips to my ear and exhaled liquid syllables that splintered my heart into shards that wedged deep, that cut true.

"Forgive me," Wu breathed low. "You must sleep now, Luce."

Warmth spilled through me where his fingers brushed my forehead, and I ceased to exist.

CHAPTER TWELVE

———◦◦◦———

"Learn to shut a door, dragon," I grumbled, rolling onto my side. "It's hot in here."

"The door is shut," Cole murmured. "Should I lower the thermostat?"

I popped awake to find him stretched out beside me. Naked. No, not naked. He wore a pair of loose, jersey shorts that left little to the imagination.

Gah.

His eyes aren't down there, Luce.

"Hey." I withdrew to hide my morning breath from him, and then I remembered—charun. He could smell me across the house, let alone across the pillow we seemed to be sharing. To be on the safe side, I curled my fingers into my palms to keep them from roaming his body. "Now I see why I was all hot and bothered."

Sweat plastered my pajama shirt to my skin, and my shorts were twisted from tossing and turning.

Concern raked furrows across his brow. "How do you feel?"

"Hungry." I laughed until I caught his expression. "Why? What's wrong?"

Muscles fluttered along his jaw as his molars grated together. The words he'd almost spoken didn't have a chance. They were ground to dust.

"Talk to me." I wriggled closer. "What's got you riled up so early?"

"You had a seizure." Cole placed his hand on my cheek. "You were unconscious for almost a full minute."

"I don't remember ..." I gripped his wrist and noticed the lack of pain. He must have removed the glass from my palms while I slept. "Does that mean I've caught what Jay Lambert has?" I jerked back, struggling to put space between us like it mattered when he had slept with me. "You shouldn't be so close if I'm contagious."

"You're not sick." He hooked his arms around my waist and hauled me against his chest. "Our conversation triggered you, and you ... went away."

"I don't remember." I curled my hands between us to keep from reaching for him. "What set me off?"

"I'm not sure I should remind you." His sigh rustled my hair. "You might have the same reaction."

"Okay." I tipped back my head and searched his face. The grief I found there pinched my heart. "You saw what happened. You can make the call. I trust you."

"Then let me shield you from this for a while longer," he said, voice raw. "Let me keep you while I can."

There was no point in telling him he could have me for as long as he wanted me. Neither of us had any idea how long that might be. And I had no doubt he was aware I was his for the asking. He had always known.

Conquest must be pressing against the cracks, widening them, for me to have blacked out, but I felt no different.

Actually, after searching myself for new fissures, I had to admit I felt more whole today than I had in months.

Whatever happened last night, it must not have been all bad if I woke with a firmer grasp on myself.

"Are you both decent?" Wu called through the door. "I would like to check on Luce."

"We're decent." I buried my face against Cole and couldn't resist the urge to press a kiss over his heart. "Come on in."

Cole didn't growl as Wu entered the bedroom. That struck me as odd. Really odd. Downright unprecedented. This was his den, and I was his . . . I was his. Full stop. And yet he let Wu enter without so much as curling his lip.

Lifting my head, about to demand an answer, I intercepted the grim look they exchanged. It was only slightly less scary than the truce they must have forged while I was inspecting the backs of my eyelids.

"Okay." Glancing between them, I pushed into a seated position. "You guys are freaking me out."

"We've decided not to revisit the events of last night," Cole told him, sitting up beside me. "I think it's for the best."

Playing devil's advocate or genuinely curious, I couldn't tell, but Wu studied me. "You're sure you don't want to know?"

"Yes?" Chilled despite my sweat-dampened shirt, I rubbed my arms to warm them. "I don't remember what happened, but it's nothing good if you guys are this spooked."

"I possess sensitive information as well." A politician couldn't have been vaguer with campaign promises. Wu was slick. "Would you like me to withhold that too?"

Walking on eggshells wasn't great for morale, but I had to remain functional. I had Dad to look after, a case to solve, and a sibling rivalry to survive. "Will it impact my ability to do my job?"

"No," he said, after some thought. "We can proceed."

"All right." I dropped my hands then linked my fingers in my lap. "As long as that remains true, keep it to yourself. The second it compromises me, tell me. Make whatever arrangements you deem necessary, but I expect you to hit me with the truth stick. Even if it knocks me out again."

Lips mashed into a bloodless line, Wu nodded once. "As you wish."

Unnerved by their good behavior, I swung my legs over the edge of the bed. "I'm going to forage for breakfast." I slipped on a pair of house shoes good for preventing splinters as I crossed the pier. "After that, we need to touch base with Santiago and find out what's happening inside that hospital."

"I updated the coterie on your condition a few hours ago." Cole leaned over and slapped his palm on the nightstand. "He said to give you this."

"A tablet." Feeling around the topmost edge, I found the power button and woke it. "Is it just me, or does he have a million of these now? Amazon must have been bundling them."

The screen flickered to life, and up popped a video chat app. Three seconds later, Santiago's pinched face filled the screen. Distracted, he didn't speak but typed on a keyboard angled across his knees.

"I don't get it. He's not saying anything." I looked to Cole for answers. "Is this a recording? Can we fast forward?"

"Give me a minute, damn it." Santiago glared at me. "Brilliance takes time." More keys clacked, more time slipped past. "Open the White Horse app on the home screen."

"Okay." The logo I would have known anywhere, but it didn't hurt that I had seen him use the app when he hacked the black phone Wu gave me. I tapped it then sucked in a breath. "Where are the rest of them?"

Several tabs had opened at once, but the topmost one showed the room Wu and I had broken out of last night. Almost three dozen people had been corralled in there while the hospital figured out what to do with potential carriers. I counted less than a third remaining, and the brutal black and white feed cast their pallor in a ghoulish light.

"As best I can tell, a baker's dozen are residents in ICU. The rest . . ."

"They're dead?" I shifted the windows until I had a split screen view that made Santiago easier to see. "From symptomatic to dead within twenty-four hours?"

"Seventy-two," he corrected me.

"What?" I whipped my head toward Cole. "I was out for forty-eight hours?"

"Yes." He glared at Santiago, who stared back unrepentant. "We were going to update you after breakfast."

"You're still you, aren't you?" The question, coming from Santiago, was as good as a fit of hysterics from a normal person. I must have really worried him. All of them. "I can't smell you through the screen, but you don't look like you've got a hard-on for world domination all of a sudden."

"I'm still me." I smothered my grin before he spotted it. "The forty-eight-hour nap explains why I woke up feeling so refreshed."

The glare Cole turned on Wu would have withered a lesser charun to a husk on the spot.

Wu returned the look with teeth, an open-ended invitation Cole had only to accept.

Santiago, unable to see them, grunted. "The good news is, this means quarantine is over."

"You three represent multiple species of charun," Thom

said, his voice muffled in the background. "Since none of you showed any signs of infection, it's safe for us to assume we have an immunity to the virus."

"Is it a virus?" I heard myself ask.

"The way it's transmitted leads me to believe it is, yes." Thom's face appeared over Santiago's shoulder. "I'm on my way to the morgue. A few of the bodies have been released for autopsy. I'm going to see what I can learn."

Already dreading the answer, I still had to know. "How is Jay Lambert?"

"Alive." Santiago peered at another screen as though double-checking himself. "He's recovering."

"Patient zero," I sighed. "Does this mean he's developed immunity from the virus?"

"We'll find out soon enough." Thom leaned closer. "He's being kept in isolation, but we need to pay him a visit. Any hope of creating a vaccine depends on us getting a viable blood sample."

"We'll go." I let the guys in the room determine which *we* I meant and returned my attention to Santiago. "Have you pinned down what happened to the other floaters?"

"Charun found them," he chimed in. "They were taken to secure facilities."

"How did you manage that?" I aimed the question at Wu. "Do you have something to share with the rest of the class?"

"An aquatic species of charun located the first body. Diorte. They're scavengers. They were drawn to what at first appeared to be an easy meal, but the meat smelled wrong. One of their elders called Kapoor, and he had the body collected." He shrugged. "The elders offered their assistance to make the waters safe for their offspring. They're the ones who located the second and third corpses, but they found Jean Ashford too late. The teenagers were already in the water, and the Diorte shied away from human contact. They updated us as the situation progressed, but the damage was already done."

"Two things." I held up a finger. "Offspring? How is it their elders knew to contact Kapoor, which means they're beholden to the NSB, and yet they have children?"

"Otillians are the most resistant to the NSB's methods." Tube-ties for females and snip-snips for males. That's what he meant. "Our scientists pioneered IUDs as a secondary means of compliance."

For which I was grateful. I wasn't a fan of invasive procedures. Or hospitals. Or doctors.

"There are other species with similar, regenerative capabilities. Their bodies repair what is perceived as damage over time and they become fertile again." He returned to the matter at hand. "The Diorte cull their own periodically since they reproduce at will. They're long-lived, and they see the chance to procreate as a fair trade."

Exchanging their lives for their children's. What parent wouldn't make that sacrifice?

"Their size is a factor too," Cole said quietly. "There are only so many adults that can shelter in the same body of water. The pods would outgrow the rivers and lakes where they live, making them impossible to hide, if restrictions on their numbers and sizes weren't enforced."

All this made me question how old these elders could be unless they were celibate. Or unless someone else made the sacrifice, if one was required, so their offspring had an anchor to their past.

Adding a second finger to the first, I wiggled them. "Does this mean demi charun are also immune?" Wu didn't answer. "Has anyone checked on Kapoor?" His grimace told me all I needed to know. "Nice, Wu. Real nice. You're saying my boss might have kicked the bucket during my first week on the job, and no one noticed. This isn't building my confidence in the taskforce."

"He would have reached out if he required assistance." Wu sounded certain, but his hand reached for his phone. "He's aware of what we're doing. He would have seen the news coverage and made the connection. He wouldn't have risked himself or his team if he had any reason to assume he had been exposed to a contagion."

"Except you just said charun reclaimed the body. Without a human there to conveniently get infected and die, how would he know to be wary? If he's the only demi on his team, and the others don't get sick, he might think it's the flu."

"Charun can't catch the flu," Wu informed me.

I leveled my best cop stare on him. "You know what I mean."

Cole interrupted before either of us blinked. "Are you sure it's safe for you two to return to the hospital?"

"Santiago?" The security feed was our biggest concern. We didn't need people making connections between our previous visit—and subsequent disappearance—and this one. "Can you make us disappear?"

"Already done," he sighed, disgusted with my lack of faith.

"That leaves us with the witnesses we interrogated, and they're all dead, in ICU, or confined." I checked with Cole. "We shouldn't run into anyone who might recognize us if we go straight to Lambert's room then leave."

"Okay." He stood and selected a fresh uniform from his closet. "I'll drive."

"I'm her partner." Wu kept his tone this side of civil. "I can protect her."

A headache blossomed behind my right eye. "No one is questioning your ability to protect me."

"I am," Santiago volunteered.

"Not helping," I sing-songed.

A frown gathered on his brow. "Who said anything about being helpful?"

Massaging my temple did zero good. "I bet the other coteries don't talk smack to the cadre."

"The other coteries are sheep," Santiago bit out sharply. "*We* were sheep."

"I have never been a sheep," Thom said, affronted. "Sheep are prey, and not worth hunting. Their meat is fair, but their fur gets stuck in my teeth for days."

Putting aside the fact this tomcat could take down sheep, I had to diffuse the situation. "I shouldn't have joked about that." I set the tablet on the mattress. "Sometimes I forget the others don't have what we do. The sarcasm doesn't come across how it's meant."

"We're family," Thom supplied, his glare daring Santiago to disagree.

"We're something all right," he grumbled, which was better than an outright denial.

From the moment I met them, I had no doubt they functioned as a cohesive unit. I was the odd man out, and I was working to get in their good graces. So, yes, I saw them as a family cobbled together in order to survive. They protected each other, provided for each other, and stuck together no matter what fresh hell Conquest dragged them through. That kind of bond couldn't be broken. The best I could hope for was that it might be expanded by one more link.

War bound her coterie with blood, but I had yet to meet Famine's chosen. Death was also a mystery. I had suspicions about what we would encounter when she breached, but I didn't want to think too hard about them. I had my hands full with animated corpses and potential zombie viruses without adding a heaping helping of tomorrow's fear onto today's plate.

"I'm proud of the lives you've built for yourselves," I told

them. "I'm proud of the work you do, the people you've become."
Security might be a mercenary business, but it hadn't escaped my
notice that when given the chance to start their own business,
they had monetized helping others. Sometimes for far less gain
than the expense to them. "I don't want you to hold back. I want
you to be honest with me. I want us to work, and that means you
all help keep me in line."

"You should get dressed." Wu reached over and turned off the
tablet. "They're old enough to know you meant no harm. Your
apology was more than sufficient."

"These bonds are what keeps the coterie steady." Cole covered
my hand with his where it rested on the blacked-out screen.
"Luce is finding her way, and so are we. Her instincts are good,
particularly where Miller is concerned. If she feels she owes them
an apology after a misstep, show her the courtesy of allowing
them to accept."

"She's coddling them." Wu transferred his scowl onto me.
"They aren't human. They aren't fragile. They're predators, killers.
They don't need you to hold their hands or kiss their boo-boos."

"They're my friends."

"You heard them." Cole searched my face. "We're family."

Uncertain if he meant the words for me or Wu, I clung to
them all the same. Dad was all I had left in this world now that I
had alienated the Rixtons. Maggie was coterie, and I considered
her family. Portia and the guys were a melting pot, and I was
happy to dissolve into their ranks if they would have me.

Wu exited the room then returned with a box he passed to
me. "You'll be needing these."

"New boots." I rubbed a thumb across the label. "I'll try not
to lose this pair the first time I wear them."

Crooking his lips, he backed out onto the pier. "I'll leave you
to dress."

Uniform tucked under his arm, Cole shut the door behind him. "I'll dress in the corner." He turned his back to me. "Let me know when I can turn around."

The room was large, it had to be to accommodate a man built like Cole, but he didn't give me a chance to get far before his shorts hit the floor.

A strangled noise clawed up my throat, and it didn't cut off until he glanced over his shoulder at me. And smiled.

"You—" Heat swept up my neck and stung in my cheeks. "*You.*"

If ogling his bare ass was wrong, then noticing the muscular indents in the curve of each cheek was worse, but that didn't stop me from staring.

"Take a picture." Making no move to cover himself, he chuckled. "It'll last longer."

"I'll do that." Given permission, I fumbled around the bed until I palmed my phone and used burst mode to make sure I got at least one picture that wasn't blurred. "Thanks."

The red painting his cheeks when I called his bluff was precious, but as much as I wanted to cross to him and press a kiss to the underside of his jaw, I wasn't dumb enough to get that close to so much naked Cole. Until he initiated, I was keeping my hands to myself.

With the exhibition over, Cole started dressing in an economical fashion that still had me salivating as I watched from the corner of my eye. And if I noticed him watching me right back while I stripped off my PJs and donned my suit, I behaved. Mostly. Okay, so maybe I never wore thongs to work, but it's not like I'd ever had a reason to scintillate in polyester, either. And if he bit off a pained groan when I *accidentally* dropped my bra and had to bend down to pick it up, well, I'm sure blue was a lovely color on him. It would complement his eyes.

CHAPTER THIRTEEN

———◆———

As promised, Cole drove us to the hospital. I rode beside him and found the landscape too fascinating to meet his eyes. Thinking about the picture on my phone, I half expected either it or my panties to melt. I had the worst flush in the history of flushes, and Wu noticed. Of course he did.

"Are you feeling all right?" he drawled from the backseat. "Your face is splotchy."

"I'm good." I flipped down my visor. "It's probably all that direct sunlight burning my cheeks."

"Mmm" was all he said, and I was grateful.

Desperate for a distraction, I texted Kapoor to check his pulse. He pinged me back seconds later, assured me he wasn't dead, and asked when to expect my latest report to hit his desk. No wonder Wu had hesitated to contact him. Paperwork sucked. Consider me schooled. In the future, I would assume no news meant good news too.

Playing the role of chauffeur to the hilt, Cole guided the

SUV beneath the portico. Wu hopped out, but I hung back long enough for Cole's fingers to brush my cheek, tracing the path blazing across my face.

"I'm keeping the photo," I informed him primly. "It's mine, and you can't have it back."

"It's yours," he agreed, sounding far too agreeable.

His feline grin made me wonder what I had started with those pictures.

I jumped when Wu rapped his knuckles on the glass then blushed even harder at being caught having inappropriate thoughts while on the job.

"On my way," I assured him, forcing myself not to look at Cole one last time.

"Clearly." Wu pulled out his phone, checked its display. "That's why I had to come and fetch you."

The text lit a fire under him, and he started walking before my feet hit the pavement.

"So . . . " I had to jog to match his long legs. "What's the plan?"

"I have ID." He pulled his jacket to one side to flash his FBI badge. "We go to Lambert's room, we interview him, we establish our right to be there should it be required, and then we hit the lab on our way out."

"Simple and straightforward." I popped my knuckles. "I like it."

The lobby was bustling, and each elevator arrived packed to capacity then left that way. News anchors held court in opposite corners of the lobby, updating the public on the mysterious outbreak.

Having them ignore me was surreal. It made me wonder if I shouldn't have moved or switched uniforms a long time ago, but no. I had loved living in Canton, both in my own apartment and sharing the farmhouse with Dad. Factor in Uncle Harold and Aunt Nancy, the Rixtons, and Maggie, and it had been paradise.

Thanks to War, it was paradise lost, and I was happy to have put the city limits behind me.

Though, once Dad recovered, he might decide to return home. That would be hard, on both of us, but so was moving on.

Wu and I shuffled out of the elevator when it reached our floor, after stopping on each one in between, and he cut a path straight to Lambert's room. This time slipping in wasn't an option. The hospital had positioned two security guards in the hall to monitor his door. They spotted us, took in our suits and Wu's purposeful stride, then exchanged a look.

"We need to speak with Mr. Lambert," Wu informed them, smooth as glass.

"We'll need to see some ID," said the one on the right.

"Of course." Wu exposed the badge on his hip. "I'm Special Agent Adam Wu with the FBI."

And the funny thing was, in a roundabout way, it was the truth. The taskforce was a division of the NSB, and the NSB was a branch of the FBI. That had to be the reason Wu could present his credentials so boldly. The alternative, that he was such an accomplished liar, shook me. Though it's not like he hadn't had centuries—or something like it—to perfect the art.

"This is my partner." He jerked his chin toward me. "Special Agent Luce Boudreau."

"What's your interest?" the one on the left asked. "Or is that classified?"

Wu leaned in closer and pitched his voice low. "The body Mr. Lambert discovered belongs to a suspected drug mule. We're investigating cartel ties and want to clear Mr. Lambert of any wrongdoing."

"Foaming at the mouth," Righty said. "Like from an OD."

"Yeah." Lefty grimaced. "Some of that shit is just whatever

chemicals some dumbass found under their kitchen sink and mixed together."

Righty nodded then frowned. "That doesn't explain why it affected the personnel, though."

"We suspect the compound has hallucinogenic properties," Wu confided. "It's possible a friend or coworker attempted to mask Mr. Lambert's withdrawal symptoms by sneaking him more product. If it was an inhalant, an aerosol perhaps, that would explain its widespread effects."

"And if it was cooked up in someone's bathtub," Lefty said, "that would explain why it killed so many people."

"We have a meeting in a half hour," I reminded Wu in a solemn voice. "We better make this fast."

The guards, convinced we were the good guys, held the door for us. Their muted conversation continued after it swung closed. From all appearances, they could have talked louder without bothering the room's occupant.

Jay Lambert was out cold. We just had to hope it was natural sleep and not medically induced.

"That story is going to be all over the hospital by the time those guys clock out." I huddled at the door by Wu. "You really shouldn't have implicated the poor kid. He's already young, tattooed and pierced. Folks will peg him for a hooligan as it is."

Wu looked amused. "Would you feel better if I released an official statement clearing him of all wrongdoing?"

"Can you do that?" I reached in his jacket and tapped the badge. It was metal. Solid. "Is that *real*?"

"I didn't get it out of a gumball machine, if that's what you're asking."

"If someone calls in our credentials," I wondered, "will they validate us?"

He chuckled at my seriousness. "Is this one of those *if a tree falls in the forest* questions?"

"Uh, no." I jabbed him in the ribs with my pointer. "This is one of those *covering my ass* questions since I didn't exactly get an orientation."

"You're thinking of your father." Wu saw right through me. "He's free to dial them up. Rixton is too. Anyone who calls looking for you at the FBI will be routed to your phone."

"What if they come to a physical location?" Dad thought I would be working out of nearby Jackson. I could envision him wanting a tour of the office. "What happens then?"

"We create a paper trail for a transfer you forgot to mention then establish a protocol if anyone comes searching for you in the future." Wu cocked an eyebrow. " I thought we had an urgent meeting to attend?"

Rolling my eyes, I crossed the room to check on the patient. The kid was gaunter than the last time I stood over him, the bruises under his eyes more pronounced. He might have survived whatever virus hit his system, but it had cost him. "Mr. Lambert?"

"Five more minutes," he mumbled before rolling onto his side. "Tired."

"I'm Special Agent Luce Boudreau with the FBI." *Say that five times fast.* "My partner and I would like to ask you a few questions if that's okay."

"S'okay."

I started him off light and easy. "How did you and your friends come to be down by the river?"

"Picnic. Tryin' to impress a girl."

That tracked with the police report. "That's why you dove in the water?"

"I thought that woman was drowning," he protested. "It was the right thing to do."

"Yes, it was." Time to dig deeper. "When did you first realize there was something wrong?"

"I touched her in the water. Her skin was clammy, but I thought . . ." He rolled onto his back and used the control to raise the head of his bed. He must still be too weak to sit up without aid. "I think I could tell before I reached her. There was this smell . . . but she was moving. When I got closer, I thought—but she wasn't swimming. Trying to swim. She was twitching in the water. I didn't get it until I dragged her onto the shore."

Pay dirt. "What didn't you get?"

"This sounds crazy, I know it does, but I think . . . I think she was already dead before I found her."

Talk about dirt, this kid was digging his own grave with Wu in the room. I sensed, rather than saw, him shift on my periphery and angled myself between him and the kid. "How long after you found her did you get sick?"

"Yes!" His eyes brightened. "I kept telling my doctors, but they wouldn't believe me. I never get sick. Ask my mother. I never had seizures. Nothing like that." He touched the tattoo of an eagle in flight on his arm, and I noticed the sleeve he was working on was flight-themed. Ironic given death might come for him on swift wings if this went sideways. "I don't do drugs. I don't drink. My old man did both, and I do neither. Ink is my only addiction, and it doesn't hurt anyone."

"I believe you."

"You do?" His eyes sparked again. "For real?"

The hope in his voice made my chest ache. "For real, I do."

"Good." He exhaled and gripped the rails on either side of his bed. "They won't tell me what happened to those people who got sick from being in my room."

The kid was fishing, but maybe letting him catch something would build trust. "A few of them are in ICU, just down the hall.

More of them are in quarantine until the doctors figure out if they've been infected." Though he deserved to know, I hated being the one to tell him. "The rest died."

"That's what the news guy said, but I hoped he was wrong." He smoothed his thumb over a square lump on the rail nearest me. The image had long since been rubbed away, but it must have been a button at some point. "They took the remote, but they forgot about this. I watch TV sometimes during shift change when it's quiet."

Odds were good the nurses were letting him get away with it, but I couldn't blame them. He must be bored out of his mind, and he was too weak to do much else. Though maybe they ought to be policing exactly what he was watching. "How do you feel now?"

"Better. Still weak. Still . . . tingly." A hint of warmth splashed his cheeks. "Will you think I sound like a baby if I admit I just want to go home? They won't let Mom in here, and I could use a hug right about now."

Another woman might have acted as a surrogate or offered at least. Maybe he was hinting he wanted exactly that, but humans were still hard for me to touch, and I didn't want his hands on me.

"Do you have a card?" I patted my pockets for show. "I seem to have left mine at home."

"Of course." Wu removed a sleek black case from his pocket, flicked it open and withdrew a crisp rectangle with the contact info printed in bold ink. I skimmed the details in passing and almost dropped the card. "I always carry spares."

The card Wu handed me was the feminine version of his. I almost didn't want to give it up, but I couldn't gawk at the FBI seal or all my fancy titles without giving away the fact this was my first time holding my new identity. "Call me if you remember anything you might think is important." With reluctance, I passed the card to Lambert. "Reach out if you overhear anything that worries you, or if they attempt to move you from this location."

"I can do that." He rubbed his thumb over the seal, and I experienced a moment of concern that the metallic sheen might flake if he got his nail involved. "Can you get a message to my mom for me?"

"Keep it brief." Wu passed over the pad and pen from the nightstand. "We don't want to interfere with hospital protocol more than necessary." He was looking at me when he said, "Protocols are in place for a reason."

There was a message there, not buried too deep, either. A subtle warning, if you will. That I shouldn't get attached to Lambert. The taskforce's new janitor, whoever had replaced Kapoor, would be through at some point to clean up the mess. Right now, Lambert was in danger of being swept under the rug.

"Okay, finished." Lambert ripped off the topmost page, folded it and passed it to me. "There you go."

He didn't spare Wu a second glance, hadn't so much as spoken to him. As often as I wondered how my new partner passed for human, I was starting to think they saw him just fine. The nice suit and fancy shoes distracted, sure. It gave him a polished air I suspected he cultivated either because classy was his default, or his dry sense of humor was at work again.

After seeing my uniform, I had poked fun at him, calling us the men in black. I was starting to wonder if the joke was on me, and Wu had been playing it on humans for a long, long time.

"We'll see to it that your mother gets this." I tucked it in the pocket of my jacket and gave it a pat. "Put that card where you won't lose it."

He saluted me with the paper between his fingers. "Yes, ma'am."

We left without Wu managing to get a word in edgewise, and I didn't breathe easy until we stood in the hall. The guards all but clicked their heels together and saluted Wu, which amused him. I could tell by the slight crinkles gathering at the corners of his eyes. Only someone who knew him would catch the subtle amusement, and it was only mildly terrifying to count myself in that small number.

"The lab has been temporarily relocated to the top floor," Wu said, sticking close. "The facility is undergoing an extensive renovation, and they're operating with a skeleton crew."

"That plays in our favor." About time we caught a break. "The location won't be secure."

"Since their in-house facilities are diminished, they're sending most blood samples out for testing." He checked the time on his phone. "It's too early for the courier. We should have time to get in, get Lambert's vial, and get back out."

"How are we going to store it?" The suits were nice, don't get me wrong, but they didn't come with refrigerated pockets. "What's the shelf life of blood at room temperature? Thirty minutes?"

The hotel had a mini fridge and complimentary ice. Either would do for transport until Wu got the sample to the White Horse lab. And I had no doubt that's where he intended to go. He wouldn't be able to resist rubbing Cole's nose in the fact he held a contract with them, a longstanding one, that no one had connected to him until he asked me to drop samples there for testing.

I couldn't even be mad about it, really. I was a resource. I expected to be used. I also expected to return the favor. However, I was less enthusiastic about the taskforce using me as a conduit to access my coterie.

"We must keep it chilled." Wu brought a black fabric pouch out of his pocket, about the length and width of a cigar. "The vials have anticoagulants to prevent clotting, but the blood will still hemolyze. This will be our only chance to collect a sample without rousing suspicion. One tube might be lost or mislabeled. Two, on a high-profile case, will earn the nurse transporting them guards until the transfer is made."

With the risk of infection so high, he was right to emphasize how important it was we get this right on the first try.

The elevator ride up to the lab thinned the herd until only the two of us were left. We stepped out into a construction zone. Plastic sheeting sealed off hallways to the left, but the right side appeared to be finished. A temporary sign that read "Laboratory" complete with a red arrow showed us the way.

The hospital had set their workstation as far from the chaos of construction as possible. The floors were new and gleaming, the walls covered in fresh paint. The smells burned my eyes. Even Wu squinted from the fumes.

"Only hospital personnel are allowed on this floor." A security officer wearing the same uniform as the two posted outside Lambert's room stepped forward, hand on the Taser at his hip. "I'll have to ask you to leave."

"We're here on official business." Wu flashed his badge. "We won't be long."

"I'm sorry, sir." After sizing up Wu, the man wet his lips. "No one cleared this with me. I have my orders. I can't allow you in that room without verification." He unclipped his radio. "This won't take but a minute."

"Of course." Wu gave every appearance of compliance, until he didn't.

Plucking the radio from the guard's hand with preternatural speed, he crushed it in his fist. *That's going to be hard to explain later.* The man gaped as Wu swept his legs from under him. He landed in a heap with a short cry, eyes huge in his narrow face as Wu loomed over him.

"That's enough," I said softly. "He's just doing his job."

The creature who lived in Wu's primal core peered out at me, sizing me up as if I had exposed a weakness it was helpless to resist exploiting. I stared him down, dipping my fingers into the cold place so he understood I wasn't prey. His shoulders rolled, resettling wings he lacked in this form, and he struck the man too fast for me to stop him.

"Hey," I snapped, baring my teeth.

"He's unconscious." Wu's voice was silk as it caressed my ears, and I shivered. "I didn't kill him."

"What a polite monster you are, Mr. Wu."

Oops. Judging by the scowl cutting his mouth, I guess I'd said that last part out loud.

CHAPTER FOURTEEN

━━━◦◉◦━━━

Kapoor leaned back in his chair, propped his feet up on his desktop, and let his sandpaper eyes close.

Luce Boudreau might not be offering up the next vacancy in her coterie to him, but he had earned a spot in her regard. Otherwise, she wouldn't have sent that damn text and derailed his train of thought. One chugging steadily toward a cliff's edge at breakneck speed.

The worst part was not the brief message but the thought that had gone into sending it.

Wu, whom he had known most of his life, hadn't spared a thought for his health after his brush with the reanimated corpses. Yet here was Luce, checking on him like he mattered when the truth was he had been married to the job for so long no one would notice if he croaked on the john in his hotel room.

However pretty the wrapping, Conquest was the prize at the bottom of that box.

Kapoor had to remember that. Some damn body did anyway. Adam sure as hell wasn't thinking straight.

His phone buzzed with an incoming text, and he checked to see if Luce was offering to bring him chicken noodle soup. No such luck. This message came from General Isadora Valero, and any news about The Hole was guaranteed to give him a headache. He dialed her up anyway.

"Ezra paid the facility a visit today," she said in lieu of a greeting.

Yep. Pain, as promised. "Inspection, interrogation, or inquiry?"

"Interrogation. He requested his guards and ours remain in the hall while he spoke with Famine."

The news, while not great, wasn't as bad as it could have been. Ezra was bound to confront Famine once he learned she was caged. Harder for her to outrun his sermon that way. "Any idea what he was after?"

"No." A few seconds later, she cleared her throat. "He asked if the protocols were still in place."

A chill of foreboding slithered down his spine. "He didn't elaborate?"

"No."

Frustration lent his voice an edge. "You didn't ask?"

"I'm alive, aren't I?"

Point to Valero. Challenging Ezra had a negative effect on your life expectancy. "Keep an eye out. Let me know if he circles back."

"I risk discovery for *chala*." Her voice softened at the mention of Wu, who she viewed as a son even if he wasn't wired to reciprocate. "He does good work for our people. I don't want to see his efforts undermined."

"That's treason," Kapoor teased, but it was true.

"I am an old woman," she said, laughter edging her tone. "We should be allowed our minor rebellions."

He agreed because that was the polite thing to do. It didn't change the knowledge they both accepted what was on the line each time one of these conversations occurred: their lives. "I couldn't agree with you more."

Valero signed off, Kapoor texted Wu an update, and then he allowed his gritty eyes to rasp shut again.

For a man with near-eternity on his side, he never seemed to have enough hours to spend quality time with his bed. But, he supposed, he could always rest when he was dead.

CHAPTER FIFTEEN

—————◈—————

Without knowing how often the guards checked in with one another, we had no clue how wide our window of opportunity extended. For all we knew, the guard had checked in with a benign-sounding code when he first spotted us, and reinforcements would pound up the stairs once his radio silence was noted.

I had no illusions that Wu wasn't capable of physical violence. It required zero imagination to picture him snapping necks with one hand while disemboweling with the other. But his reactions felt off to me, more intense than usual.

Maybe this was the real Adam Wu, and I was meeting him for the first time. Now that we were partners, it's not like I could do much about his methods except mitigate the damage for humans. But the way he butted heads with Cole reminded me of Thom's warning that Wu saw me as his. Factor in Cole starting to see me in the same light, and I had to wonder if all the bunk Wu had spouted about there being no need for fraternization laws within the taskforce was a crock.

The heat thing made me head-explodey. Mentally, I stuck with ovulating. That was a nice, human word. Normal. Plus, it sounded far less likely to end with me thrown over a male's shoulder and brought to his cave for impregnating.

The coterie was quick to point out when Cole got me hot and bothered. Wu was attuned to my scent as well, but his possessiveness had me questioning if I wasn't the problem. And how we fixed that without fixing *me*.

That charun-friendly IUD was starting to look better and better if its hormones did the trick. It's not like I planned on following in War's footsteps. Birthing cannon fodder—I mean, offspring—was not part of my strategy to win this.

What I had done to Sariah to get at War could and would be done to any children I had and me. Payback was a bitch, and no kid ought to be used as leverage. That was perfect-world thinking, though, and my new reality was a far cry from that. Strategic advantage or not, Sariah might have earned clemency if not for all the blood on her hands.

I recalled the first time Wu set eyes on Nettie, the predatory gleam in his gaze, the inhuman spark that had me shoving her into her father's arms and putting myself between them. Babies were pink and plump. Tender. Barely a mouthful. Their skin soft, their bones fragile—

Nettie might not officially be my goddaughter, but Rixton had been my partner on the force for years, and I loved them both like family.

A wave of dizziness rocked me back on my heels, and my gorge rose. Wu gripped me under the arms to keep me from collapsing in a heap, but his support couldn't stop my gut from roiling.

"Your scent changed," he said, echoing my earlier thoughts. "What's wrong?"

"I'm good." I forced my knees straight. "I had a thought that didn't agree with me. That's all."

Warmth spread through his hands where he touched me. "What kind of thought?"

"I . . ." I screwed up my face. "I was thinking about Nettie." There was more, there had to be. I missed her and her parents, they were three pieces cut from the cloth of my soul, but I had made my peace with their safety. I wouldn't hit the deck mid-op remembering what this war had already cost me. "Wu." It took a lot for me to admit it, but I had to get it out there. "I can't hold onto them, but . . . I get these flashes. Memories that aren't mine, thoughts I would never have, urges that are more instinct than anything."

"The wider you open your bond to Cole and the rest of your coterie, the more often this will happen." He hesitated. "Your senses are heightening, and your instincts are coming back online too. Denning with your own kind is thinning the walls between you and Conquest."

I didn't miss how he singled out Cole, but I was too tired to argue. "That doesn't sound like a great idea."

"You need to access your abilities." He gazed down at me. "Your coterie needs you strong, and so do I."

"You also need me to be *me*." Supernatural powers did no one any good if I switched teams and took my coterie with me. "I'm steady now." I straightened my clothes. "Thanks for not letting me eat floor."

A hint of weariness—or was that wariness?—pinched his expression. "What are partners for?"

I huffed out a laugh then took a good look at our surroundings. "No one came running when we busted in here."

"We're alone." Wu flared his nostrils. "The tech's scent is fresh. We must have just missed her."

I checked the time on my phone. "She must be on lunch. That's handy."

Wu scoffed at the idea of serendipity. "There was a reason why I chose midday for infiltration."

"How do we do this?" The room was large but still cramped for its purpose. Two bulky machines dominated the center of the room, and three laptops sat open and on stands that pressed against them. Four industrial refrigerators lined one wall. That was our first stop. "They should be labeled, that's the easy part, but how are we getting a viable sample out of here?"

"With this case." Wu flashed the black pouch at me again. "Diabetics use them to cool their insulin during trips. I soaked it in cold water prior to our departure to activate the gel crystals. It's good for forty-five hours in temperatures up to one hundred degrees. It's the best option we've got on short notice."

Easy to conceal too. That always helped. "All we have to do is make it back to the SUV."

"What do you mean?" Comprehension dawned a moment later. "Cole."

"I once saw him ice over the staff lounge at Madison Memorial. This should be nothing."

"That was a brute show of strength," he countered. "A lack of self-control that required Kapoor's direct intervention. This requires a delicate touch."

"Let me worry about that part." I had an idea that didn't hinge on finesse. "You take that one, and I'll take this one."

We each tackled our assigned fridges, and it didn't take long for me strike gold: Lambert, Jay.

"Got it." I lifted the vial, slid it into the pouch Wu held open for me, then started wiping down surfaces I had touched. "Are fingerprints something I should worry about?"

His grin spread slowly. "What do you think?"

"That I no longer exist?" I meant it as a joke, but Wu wasn't laughing. That was just . . .

Damn.

While I wrapped my head around becoming a figment of my father's imagination, Wu tucked away the sample then exited into the hall. He paused to check the guard's pulse, but I deducted points for humanitarianism when he made certain I was looking first.

"He's fine," Wu assured me. "I'll call for assistance as soon as we're out of the building."

Uncertain I believed him, I sharpened my scowl on his back as he led our escape. "You do it, or I do it for you."

We hit the elevators, shuffling closer as more people piled in with us then wriggling out once we reached the ground floor. Okay, so I was the one doing the shimmy. People parted for Wu, but they huddled together again just as fast. Safety in numbers and all that. Even when humans didn't shriek and point at charun, they tended to know they were there on a subconscious level.

All in all, I was impressed with how smoothly we pulled off our mission. Right up to the point where we located the White Horse SUV, and I spotted the person waiting in the passenger seat.

"Sariah," I growled as my heart skipped a beat. "How did she get here?"

Wu filled his lungs then shook his head. "I can't pick up her trail."

We reached the SUV together, and I approached on the driver's side. Cole didn't fool with lowering the window. Instead, he popped open the door in an invitation to check for myself that he was whole and unharmed, which I did to the best of my abilities without hauling him out and patting him down.

Downplaying my initial burst of concern, I glanced between them. "I'm listening."

"Miller called," Cole said before she could open her mouth. "Sariah claims to have time-sensitive information on a cluster of nests within a few hours of town. He asked me to pick her up so you two could discuss the viability of her intel."

"I was scaring the blonde." Sariah cheered at the mention of terrorizing Mags. "He knocked me out twice, but what can I say? I inherited my mother's hard head. I kept bouncing back."

"Miller will kill you if you harm her." Better the threat come from him than me. The target would still be painted on her back, but it might be a few inches smaller. "Try it sometime if you don't believe me." If the coterie was showing her Maggie instead of Portia, Sariah would be in for a nasty surprise when she made a move against them. "Granted, he'd take the rest of us with him, but maybe he's made his peace with that."

Sariah cocked her head to one side when she realized I was serious. "He wouldn't."

"The last thing he wants is to hurt her." I believed that, and she could read my honesty if her discomfort was any indication. "Defending her honor while also killing her in the process would probably not earn him any brownie points, so he'll avoid it. Unless you piss him off so much his switch flips."

Cole watched me during our chat, his expression neutral, but curiosity burned in his eyes. I could see him mentally reviewing every interaction between Miller and Maggie he'd witnessed, and the grim set of his mouth made it clear he wasn't happy about this latest development.

"You can fill us in on the ride to the hotel." Wu spoke over my shoulder, his breath almost in my ear.

Once again, Cole kept his lips buttoned, and it was all I could do not to reach out and pry them open.

The caveman routine was a bit much, and the chest-beating was overdone, but I still experienced a thrill every time he bristled when another male paid attention to me.

Dragon logic was so much easier to parse. He would have eaten Wu by now. Message sent and received.

Checking on a hunch, I located one of the coolers that seemed to come standard in every White Horse SUV trunk. I brought it to Cole, who breathed ice along its insides, and we stashed the sample there until we could have it flown out for testing.

The idea of riding with Sariah behind me made the hairs prickle along my nape, so I let her keep her spot then slid in behind her. Wu sat behind Cole, and I didn't miss the tiny smirk he wore. One I assumed the driver noticed if his white-knuckled grip on the steering wheel was any indication.

"Look, Tweety." I pegged Wu with my best cop face. "We all have to work together, and that means we all have to play nice together too."

"Tweety?" Wu cast me an affronted look.

Sariah craned her neck. "Tweety?"

"Hello?" Outing him, even without a proper name for his species, wasn't happening. "Didn't your mother ever tell you it's rude to eavesdrop?"

"No." She frowned. "As a child, I was able to hide in places too small for adults. One of my duties, until I outgrew them, was to spy on the cadre whenever they convened."

I bit the inside of my cheek to keep from telling her how messed up that was when she had no frame of reference for what a normal childhood ought to be like. Mine wasn't exactly average, either, but Dad made it as smooth as possible, and I had Maggie as an example too.

"Tell us about this nest," Wu said to get us back on track. "What makes the location time-sensitive?"

"Each unit rotates from nest to nest. There's a system in place that allows empty locations to be restocked and cleaned in addition to letting the heat to die down if the coterie has drawn attention to itself." She twisted around in her seat. "We're two days from a rotation. It would garner too much attention for the entire coterie to relocate at once, so a unit per week makes the transition."

"You're talking about a massive network." I swallowed hard. "How many members are in War's coterie?"

Sariah offered a negligent shrug. "I have no idea."

"Is that your final answer?" Wu asked, his voice a silken invitation.

"Mother won't risk herself with a pregnancy to increase our numbers, not when she's tipped her hand, but she's got enough children they can start building our forces without impacting her ability to realize her vision."

I couldn't hide the judgment in my voice. "Incest?"

"The offspring are disposable." Sariah frowned at me. "What does it matter if they're deformed? Or their intelligence is diminished? Mother wants as many bodies between her and you as she can get, and she's not picky where they come from as long as they report for duty."

"Is that why you've killed so many?" Not the question I meant to ask, but it popped out anyway.

"I have a certain reputation, it's true." She toyed with the cuff on her wrist. "I earned it."

"But?" I prompted.

Baffled, she glanced up at me. "What makes you so sure there is a *but*?"

"No one is born a killer. No one crawls from the womb irredeemable. Parents guide us, and circumstances shape us. The world gets its licks in too." I spread my hands. "I'm a prime example of nature versus nurture. I am this person because my father loved me, taught me, and invested in me. I'm this version of me because I want to be someone who makes him proud."

"Are you serious?" Sariah cocked her head at me and then included Wu in the gesture. "Is she for real?"

Wu pinched me, and I yelped. Cole snapped out his arm toward the greatest threat on reflex and fisted Sariah's throat without decelerating.

"She feels real enough to me," Wu said, ever-so-helpfully.

"Let her go." I pried at Cole's fingers, and he let me peel them away. "She didn't try to hurt me."

"Turn around and sit down," he barked at her all the same. "Conversation can wait until we get back to the hotel."

"Sure thing," she croaked, shooting me a grateful look.

All hope for evaluating her intel went up in smoke, but I would bet money that wasn't the reason for our extra passenger. Cole had defused a delicate situation by moving the lighter away from the tinder, nothing more.

"You won't break through to that one." Wu offered the advice in a matter-of-fact drawl. "Forget saving her."

"I'm not—" The protest died in my throat when it occurred to me it might be true. Hard to tell if it was guilt on my part or deeply buried fondness from Conquest guiding me. And by fondness, I mean she wasn't the only one who recognized a solid-gold resource when she saw one. One bound into our service made it even better. It meant even if we couldn't earn her loyalty, we still reaped the benefits. "How do you know? Look at my coterie."

"Your coterie was loyal to Conquest. Most were with her of their own volition." The back of Cole's head drew his eye. "Or they gave consent to be taken." He tapped his fingers on the seat beside us. "You've given them a taste of freedom, and the fact you didn't walk up and immediately snatch it back has earned you their goodwill. Adaptation isn't the same thing as transformation."

"You're saying coteries are like packs of rabid dogs. The pack master can kick and beat and starve them, and the one time he shows up with a bone, all is forgiven. Even if it's only one bone, and they have to fight amongst themselves to claim it."

"You see the face they want you to see." Wu's fingers stilled. "The coterie you know is a fiction they've created, one that complements your goals and ideals, and you'd be a fool to trust your eyes."

Thom explained to me how the first thing charun did on a new world was learn the food chain to integrate at its peak. They observed a society, selected its top predator, and then mimicked it. On this world, that meant humans. Charun were resilient. My own species, apparently, were the ultimate chameleons, selecting mates and then altering our biology to mimic them on a cellular level. But hearing his theory that the coterie had crafted personas to reflect mine set my teeth on edge.

I shook my head. "You're wrong."

Wu once accused me of believing my own propaganda, and maybe he was right, but this was a prime example of him doing the same.

Conquest was a title, not a person. That's what he told me. Well, coterie was a label, and it was up to us how we defined it.

What mattered to me was they had been given fifteen years of freedom, and they had spent it building a quiet life for themselves. They had done no harm. At least not to humans. Charun politics were a river I was unqualified to paddle in, so I floated no opinions on the topic.

The coterie had evolved from whoever they had been, however she had molded them, to who they were now, a shape they defined themselves.

I was a blank slate gifted with a fresh start, so why shouldn't they get the same second chance?

Secrets aside, I believed in my coterie, and I trusted them. They were being as honest with me as they could without compromising me or endangering themselves. And I was returning the favor. Ezra was the only skeleton hiding in my closet, and I couldn't be certain they hadn't watched me stuff him in there.

I had a theory that our bond flowed like a river between us, that wading in was what had eroded the touch-aversion that plagued me until I met them. And while I might have been oblivious to the current for the last decade and change, they had been swept along in my wake.

The coterie was, I speculated, fundamentally altered at its source. I was the fount, and I had been reborn. How much had my regenesis christened those waters? Had it anointed them with fresh purpose as well?

Sink or swim.

They had more than survived the swirls and eddies of change. They had thrived amid the chaos.

"I hope your faith isn't misplaced." Wu frowned at that. "None of us are who we appear to be."

I patted his twitching fingers. "Most of all me."

CHAPTER SIXTEEN

———◆———

Our arrival was met with groans from Santiago and glares from Miller. Portia was doing her best Maggie impersonation, and she winked to let me in on the secret in case I hadn't seen through her charade. Whatever her game, I was glad Portia was the one playing it. I wanted Maggie far away from Sariah.

Personally? I would put five dollars on Portia and Santiago hoping to provoke Sariah into an attack using fake Maggie as the sacrificial lamb. Predatory instincts were difficult to suppress at the best of times, and these were far from those.

Wu prowled behind Sariah as she strolled toward the desk Santiago had arranged as her workstation, close enough his breath must have hit the base of her neck. No wonder she sat down so fast.

Cole entered at my side, and we sank onto the couch to see who cracked first.

"I vote yes," Santiago announced.

"No one's asked a question," I pointed out.

"You're the *let's put it to a vote* type these days," he countered. "Trust me, it's coming."

"Sariah," Wu intoned from his position beside her. "The floor is yours."

"Mother has outposts in Greenville and Jackson in Mississippi, as well as in Alexandria and Monroe in Louisiana." She stood and lifted the tablet Santiago had loaned her, proving they really did pour out of his ears, then indicated the virtual pins she had stuck in the map. "The Jackson nest is the largest. It's about forty-five minutes from Vicksburg. But the nest in Monroe has the best fighters. It's closer to an hour and a half away."

She held everyone's focus now, and she preened under the attention.

"I've already explained how the system works, so I'll skip that part." She paced between her chair and the wall, four quick strides that told me she thought best on her feet. "We've got two days to take out as many nests as possible. There are no direct lines of communication. Mother distrusts technology. Her grasp is only as firm as the hosts her soldiers have taken, and their understanding is too thin for her liking. She has no time to become proficient herself, so she's sticking with what she knows best. She's running scouts between locations. I have their timetable memorized. If we disrupt their lines of communication, we can, potentially, take out two of the four nests before she realizes what we've done."

"This could be an ambush," Miller said, tossing in his two cents.

"I've kept her offline," Santiago protested. "She's had no way to reach out and touch anyone."

"She's fresh from The Hole," Wu agreed. "She was clean when she arrived."

"She won't betray us." Cole dipped his gaze to her wrists. "Her intel is good, or it was prior to her incarceration."

"Then the question becomes—" Thom exited his bedroom and crossed to my side, "—which two do we hit?"

"A forty-eight-hour window isn't realistic," Portia agreed. "We can only take out what we can hit in a single night. Otherwise, word will travel, and an ambush will really be waiting."

After a brief debate, I became aware of all eyes falling on me. I was their leader, what was left of her, and it was my duty to make these calls. Or it would be one day. Call me a coward, but I wasn't willing to shoulder the decision alone.

"What will give us the tactical advantage?" I posed the question to all of them. "Taking out more of her fighters or her better fighters or splitting the difference?" I looked to Cole, who had led them for so long, to get a read on which way he was leaning. He gave away nothing. Great. It was down to me then. "I vote we strike the two weakest outposts. We'll lose the element of surprise, which will cost us our chance at the bigger targets. But the fact is, we don't know how far to trust Sariah's intel. After Famine's capture and Sariah's disappearance, War might have initiated emergency protocols."

"You're throwing away your chance." Sariah huffed. "Hit her hard and fast, take out the two prime targets."

Seven of us, counting Wu, wasn't going to make a dent in the numbers she implied. "I won't risk the coterie."

"We could split teams," Wu offered. "Strike the weakest links simultaneously then regroup." He eyed Sariah. "If we take out the scouts, we can isolate the remaining nests. We could take three out of the four in one night."

"Given the opportunity," Santiago grudgingly agreed, "we should take full advantage."

There was always a chance the individual battles would take

longer, that we wouldn't have time to regroup or the means to plan another attack. A girl could hope, right? "I can live with that."

"All in favor," Cole said, lips curling with amusement. "Say *aye*."

A chorus of ayes filled the room, Sariah's the loudest.

"Aye—" I elbowed him in the ribs and immediately regretted my life choices, "—can't believe you said that."

"We're a democratic coterie these days." Amusement glinted in his eyes. "All I did was save you the trouble."

"All opposed," he called, still grinning. "Say *nay*."

"Nay."

We whipped our heads around in sync. Miller stood with his legs braced shoulder distance apart, and his arms fisted at his sides.

"Miller?" Cole and I rose in tandem. "What's the problem?"

He tagged Portia with a gaze harsher than any he would ever turn on Maggie. I still imagined her cringing inside, even though I had no clue if she was cognizant of what happened while she was waiting her turn.

"Let's discuss this somewhere private." Anything we said in close quarters would be overheard. Crossing to my friend, I hooked my arm through his. "Come on. Stop dragging your heels." I trailed my fingertips down Cole's arm. "We'll be downstairs. Give us a few minutes."

We left the suite and took the elevator down to the lobby. There was a plush sitting area, and we put it to use.

"Portia is climbing the walls." I twisted so we faced each other on the couch. "She needs an outlet."

"Maggie is untrained." He shook his head. "Her fear will cause Portia to doubt, and they'll both get killed."

"Portia has been training, which means Maggie has too. Even

if she's not an active participant. Muscle memory will have kicked in, and all Portia's knowledge is right there if she takes over." I crossed my legs and started kicking to burn off energy. "I don't love this idea either." I held his worried gaze. "You know I would do anything to keep Mags safe. I already have."

"I know," he said softly. "Let me have their back?"

"Santiago is usually Portia's partner, isn't he?" It was a hunch, but it made sense.

"Yes." He tipped his head back and stared up at the ceiling like he might glimpse Mags through all those layers of wood and plaster. "They've always worked best together."

"Then it makes sense to let the pairing stand." I squeezed his hand. "He knows her weaknesses, so he'll be there to shore them up, and he'll be the first to notice if she falters."

"I hate logic."

"Me too." I sat there a moment longer. "I'll give him a direct order to get her out if she defaults to Maggie. I'll let Cole have the honors if you think he'll listen better if the news came from him."

"Santiago isn't sexist."

"No, he's Luceist."

Miller chuckled, a ticking time bomb defused. "We've got an odd number. Who gets Sariah?"

"I hadn't planned on allowing her in the field." Funny how he was shifting all the big decisions onto me. "It seems dangerous. One look at her, and it's as good as beaming an SOS to War. Any survivor will tell War who led the charge and who was with her. She'll suspect Sariah, but she won't have all the pieces unless we hand them to her." Figuring the rest of the coterie would be getting twitchy, I uncrossed my legs and stood. "I guess that leaves you the odd man out."

He spread his hands. "Guess so."

"Looks like you'll have to play third wheel for someone."

He glanced up at me. "Guess so."

"I told you—" I took his hand and hauled him onto his feet with me, "—I'll do anything to keep her safe. You can't get in the way of Santiago and Portia, but you can act as backup, and you can do me the huge favor of keeping an eye out for Mags."

"Portia isn't used to sharing," he agreed. "She's the dominant personality. For now. She ought to be able to hold on, especially if Maggie gives her permission."

"But emotions run high in battle, and attentions slip." I nodded that I understood. "We need to make sure Portia doesn't lose her grip."

With that settled, we rejoined the others, who were deep into planning our various infiltrations. Guess they weren't all that concerned Miller might go kaboom after all. As much as I wanted to take credit for that, he was the stalwart one.

Miller joined Santiago and Portia in their huddle while I joined Cole, Thom, and Wu in theirs.

Asking Santiago for a favor was almost as smart as sticking your head in a lion's mouth, but I took a quick minute to text him my request all the same. He angled his head toward me, lips pursed in thought, then gave me a terse nod.

"Everything settled?" Cole shifted so that his arm brushed mine, drawing my attention back to him. "Miller seems calmer."

"We've come to an understanding." I cast my gaze around the group. "Are we all going in together?"

"Yes." Thom stared at Wu, unblinking. "This evens the teams. Three and three."

Three plus three didn't equal seven. Even I could do that much math.

"Great," I grumbled. "I'm the liability."

"You're the bait," Wu corrected me. "Her coterie has their

orders. War might want to take another swipe at you, but she won't shed a tear if someone guts you before she gets her chance."

I rubbed my stomach. "You guys are big on disembowelment, huh?"

"Yes," Thom answered, distracted. "It's fast and simple, a solid strategy."

A bullet between the eyes was fast and simple. Evisceration was up close and personal. It allowed them to get their claws wet, and I couldn't say boo about it. Brutality was in their nature, and the same was true for our enemies. I couldn't leash my coterie when War allowed hers to roam unfettered. "Do we have our marching orders?"

Wu caught my eye. "Are you ready for this?"

"I have to be." I rolled my shoulders, but his judgment weighed on me. "We passed the point of no return a few miles back."

Wu dipped his chin then vanished into the hall with the cooler in one hand and the note to Jay Lambert's mother in the other. How he ended up with either of those things mystified me. Light-fingered indeed.

"I don't like this," Cole murmured.

"Which part?" I leaned closer. "That we're using Sariah's intel? That we're raiding War's nests? That Maggie is going out on her first mission? That Portia is sharing consciousness with a civilian?"

"I meant the part where you have to fight."

"I could say the same for you." I rested my cheek against his upper arm. "You've all got this feral core, I get that, or I'm trying to, but I don't want this for any of you. You might enjoy a good brawl, but it terrifies me that I might lose one of you."

"We've been doing this a long time." He kissed the top of my head. "It might not seem like it, but this plan is low-risk."

"I'll have to take your word on that." I cut my eyes toward

Sariah, busy arguing with Santiago about who knows what. He would fight you on any point, no matter how trivial, if he didn't like you. Since he didn't much like anyone, cue histrionics. "What are we doing with her?"

He had his answer primed and ready. "You're going to order her to remain here."

"You're that confident the bangles will compel her into good behavior?"

"She can't disobey a direct order while wearing them. She can find loopholes and manipulate those, but she must follow your instructions to the letter."

A shiver rolled through me at having that much power over another person. I could tell the coterie what to do, yeah, but they could argue. They could fight back. She couldn't do either of those things if I forbade them. No wonder Lorelei wanted them destroyed ASAP.

"Good to know." I almost wished I had the option of ignorance here too. "There's something ..." A headache throbbed behind my right eye. "I get a migraine if I look at them too long. That can't be good." I blinked clear of the pain. "They didn't bother me at first. Maybe it's from too much exposure? Can they affect me?"

I might have a charun core, but I still thought like a human, and I still wore a human shell.

Cole's answer came slower this time. "Do you have a long-sleeve shirt she could wear to cover them?"

"I'm sure I have a spare in my bag." I rocked back on my heels, waiting to see if he had anything else to add. "I'll dig that up then get her settled. I'll pop some ibuprofen while I'm at it. Maybe that will help."

"Santiago is setting her up with what he's calling an unhacka-ble tablet that will link her to his party and ours. We can check in with her and coordinate with each other through the White Horse app."

"That's one heck of a handy app." And they called me chameleonic.

"Santiago reprograms it for every occasion." A smile tugged at his lips. "You better look fast. This incarnation won't last the night before he shreds it and starts weaving the strips into something new."

Shaking my head, I went to raid my clothes and left the coterie to finalize our plans. In my room, I found a pleasant surprise that punched me in the feels. A pair of black tactical pants and matching long-sleeve shirt was folded on the duvet, waiting on me. I ran my thumb over the white war horse stamping its front hoof embroidered above the pocket. Heavy tread boots waited at the foot of the bed with black socks sticking out of their tops like tongues flapping. The nylon belt clashed with my leather shoulder holster, but I couldn't care less. I suited up and left the room grinning like a fool.

We drew Greenville, leaving the other team Alexandria. Monroe and Jackson could wait. We had an hour and a half drive ahead of us, while the others had closer to three. That meant we would strike first, but it also meant our entire plan hinged on us taking out the scouts at our location. No pressure.

Night fell as Wu drove, and Thom rode beside him in silence. He was leaning over the console, too close to be polite, but Wu was determined to ignore him.

Thom might give sheep a run for their money in his tomcat form, but Wu made for a damn big bird.

Rixton would love that. Calling Wu Big Bird. Talk about your missed opportunities. Ah well. Tweety I had called him, and Tweety he would remain.

Thinking about Rixton pinched my heart, so I locked down all thoughts of him and Sherry and sweet Nettie before I got sniffly. The last thing I wanted the guys to remember about my first op was how I kicked it off by bawling the whole way there.

Our first target was an abandoned fast food restaurant on the edge of town. Just looking at the broken sign made me hungry. I couldn't remember when I ate last, and that couldn't be a good thing. Maybe the headaches were my stomach's attempts at getting my attention.

Wu parked three blocks away, and we huddled on the sidewalk at the rear of the SUV like it was a barrel fire in the middle of winter. Cole popped the trunk, pried up the carpet, and exposed a storage compartment that would make any spare tire envious. The weapons cache he revealed made me take an involuntary step back. It was like the middle ages vomited its surplus. Small swords, axes, medium swords, maces, big swords, and a dozen smaller weapons I couldn't imagine a use for—let alone name.

One for you, one for you, one for you . . .

"I'll pass." I waved off the shorter sword with a broad tip he offered me. "I don't know how to use one."

"You'll need a blade. Trust me." He unfastened my belt and fed it through the loops on my pants then added a scabbard before buckling me up again. "The falchion is a decent size and weight for you." Happy with the fit, he sheathed the blade and adjusted its position at my hip. "How does that feel?"

"Clunky," I admitted, fingers brushing the pommel. "And unnecessary."

"Just wait." His grin bordered on feral. "You'll change your mind."

The sword he chose for himself was tall enough to pass for my twin. The familiar way he handled it told me they were old friends reunited. That was a comfort. Me? I wasn't trusting my sword not to bite back.

Wu, to my surprise, came equipped with his own twin swords that looked so at home in his hands I had no trouble flashing back to all those portraits of avenging angels. Clearly, there was some truth in the myths.

"I'll take zone one," Thom said. "Smaller targets are harder to spot."

"Be safe." I ruffled his hair. "Don't take any chances."

Thom leaned over and rubbed his cheek against mine, a light rumble in his chest. "I will, and I won't."

Laughing softly, I watched him go. "Cole and I will take zone two."

Cole's eyes glinted in the dark. "Double the manpower in case Thom flushes out a scout."

"That leaves me with zone three." Wu sighed, clearly unhappy drawing the short straw—the one least likely to see action. "Report back in one hour."

That left us a thirty-minute window to plan our attack before Santiago's team arrived at their destination.

Wu turned on his heel to leave, but I caught him by the upper arm. "Be careful."

"I didn't know you cared." His smile was wicked and meant to incite Cole, but Cole ignored him. Huh. Maybe their truce was more binding than I first thought. "I haven't died yet. I doubt this will kill me."

"Asshat," I muttered to his retreating back.

He chuckled in response then vanished into the gathering shadows.

The streetlamps flickered and dimmed, one of Santiago's time-delayed tricks. The absence of light might confuse the Drosera for a minute, but they would come investigate as their hideout edged toward absolute darkness. Luring War's coterie out into the open, using their curiosity against them, was the point.

This was a stealth mission. No chatter allowed. Even though I longed for a distraction to keep my mind off what came next, I couldn't risk the inattention. Conversation might not get us killed, but it would get us noticed, and that amounted to the same thing. The best I could manage was caressing my Glock in its shoulder holster with my fingertips in anticipation of the draw.

I drifted in Cole's wake, learning the way he moved, a shadow larger than the rest. I don't think I would ever get tired of the view, but I had to keep a clear head. If my coterie could pick up on scent cues, then so could the Drosera. As satisfying as it might be to gawk, I couldn't let myself get hot and bothered if it meant leading the enemy straight to us.

Once he got over being pissed about me blowing the entire operation, Santiago would never let me live it down.

I could hear his *I told you so*'s from here.

We circled the block but encountered no charun. This end of town was quiet so late, most of the stores closed, and traffic was light. It hit me then that if the fight bled out onto the street, humans would get hurt. Maybe not in the initial strike, but any who witnessed the battle would be silenced.

Jay Lambert's fate was already a burden on my conscience. Add too many more, and I might crack.

Movement snared my attention, a motion too quick to be human, a smudge too large to be an animal.

Ahead of me, Cole walked on without a hitch in his stride, and I mimicked his placid demeanor.

A second patch of darkness shifted with inhuman quickness on my periphery.

We were being hunted.

Heart kicking my ribs, I expected fear to drench my mouth or sweat to coat my skin. But with Cole at my side, I wet my lips, anticipation zinging down my nerve endings.

Cole glanced over his shoulder at me, his nostrils flaring, a red sheen coating his eyes.

That ... did nothing to help with the whole anticipatory thing.

Squeezing my thighs together as I walked, I forced my brain to focus.

The smirk that kicked up his lips had me seeing red too. He was riling me up on purpose.

Newsflash. I was not going to be the Pied Piper who lured out all the charun with her pheromones.

The scuff of boot on asphalt rang out behind me, and I didn't wait to take my cue from Cole. I pivoted on my heel, raised my arms, and sighted my gun. I squeezed off two quick bursts before my brain caught up to my reflexes.

The cold place lapped at my senses, blanketing me in a thick calm. The part of me second-guessing my decision to kill another being suffocated.

Kill or be killed.

This wasn't Canton. I wasn't on the force. These weren't people breaking human law. They were charun. *Other.* And they would raze this world if I let them.

CHAPTER SEVENTEEN

———◆———

The man went down. The *skin suit*, I reminded myself. He wasn't human anymore. But still ... I couldn't look away. The cold place nipped at me, taking bigger and bigger bites of my self-control, but I refused to surrender. What if ... ?

A gasp echoed down the empty street, the man's dying breath. *Oh, God. Oh, God. Oh, God.*

I rocked forward, ready to sprint to his side, but Cole clamped a hand on my shoulder.

"Trust your instincts," he growled. "There are no humans out tonight."

A groan reached my ears that built in volume to a roar as the man split down an invisible seam, and the super gator pulling his strings burst onto the pavement. Light glinted off its beady eyes, turning them red, and he snapped his massive jaws at me.

"Watch my back," Cole ordered as he drew his sword. "Don't let them box me in."

Cole charged the Drosera and leapt over its head. He landed on its back, fisted his sword with both hands, and stabbed downward through its spine.

The creature screamed and thrashed as Cole gripped the hilt of his sword like the pommel on a saddle. A second blade, this one shorter and curved, appeared in his dominant hand, and he started hacking at the base of its skull.

Bullets wouldn't kill them. I scowled at my gun, my *pacifier*, hating no one had bothered to tell me that, and traded it for the falchion sheathed at my opposite hip. I tested the weight of the blade and hoped like hell I didn't hack off my own fingers or toes wielding the blasted thing.

The second shadow coalesced behind Cole as he finished off the first beast. With his back to the skin suit, he didn't see the attack coming.

This time, there was no bargaining with the cold place. There was no dipping my toes in its waters. It rose up, sank its hooks in me, and plunged me into its depths.

As much as I'd wanted to run to his defense, I prowled, closing the distance. The skin suit held a handgun I doubted would kill Cole since my weapon had been about as annoying as a mosquito bite to the Drosera I dinged, but that didn't mean it wouldn't hurt, that it couldn't damage him in other ways.

As quick as that worry surfaced, it drowned beneath a pulse of soothing numbness. Wresting control of my body off autopilot proved impossible. All I could do was ride the wave as I crept up behind the skin suit, cradled his jaw in my left hand, wrenched his head back, then slashed a gaping smile across his throat with the blade in my right.

Blood poured hot and wet through my fingers, and the urge to lick them clean had my mouth watering.

I swallowed once, twice, three times then spat excess saliva on the ground when that didn't help.

"Release him," Cole rasped, his voice husky, riding the edge of adrenaline. "He's dead."

Finger by finger, I willed my hand open and let the body drop.

"You're still here." He gazed at me, into me, through me. "You're still Luce."

Luce.

Yes.

The cold place snapped like a rubber band, and I melted into his arms.

"Are you sure?" A tremor rocked my voice. "How can you tell?"

"I would know you anywhere," he murmured into my hair. "You are the other half of my soul."

Tipping my head back, I searched his face. "Not her?"

"Never."

"Okay." I breathed through the panic fisting my heart and stepped away from him. "I'm not done with this conversation, but I also don't want us to get sniped out here in the open."

"We need to finish clearing our zone," he agreed. "We can pick this up in our room back at the hotel."

I might have gulped, and he might have nipped my bottom lip hard enough to hurt.

"Bad dragon." I rubbed away the sting. "I'm waiting on a first kiss, not a first chomp."

He smiled, all teeth, and we set out to finish our circuit.

On the way, we intercepted Wu, who had gotten bored and decided to come help us.

His gaze lingered on my swollen lip. "Were you two making out or fighting Drosera?"

"You can't tell?" I arched an eyebrow. "I see you sniffing me. You're not that subtle."

"You're getting better at locking down your emotions." His bland expression made it impossible to tell if he thought that was a good thing or a bad thing. "You don't leak as much."

"Good." Finally, one benefit to inviting Conquest to the party. "Did you have any trouble?"

"I convinced a few humans to be somewhere else for the next few hours, but I saw no sentries or scouts."

"We need to backtrack to our rendezvous point." I scanned the streets, at their darkest and most silent since our arrival. "I hope Santiago wasn't going for a total blackout. I don't have night vision."

Back at the SUV, we checked in with Santiago's unit then made certain Sariah hadn't gotten into any trouble. I was signing off when Wu shoved an eyeglass case in my hands. "New toy?"

He measured the night around us. "A necessary one."

After tucking away my phone, I cracked open the case. "Night vision?" The wide yellow lenses set in a black frame resembled sunglasses more than anything. "They're not those nighttime driving glasses, are they?"

"Spoken like a true infomercial connoisseur." Wu removed them and slid them on my face. "They cost more than $19.99 if that's what has you worried."

Through the lenses, the night flared to light around me. I turned a slow circle, stalling out when I spotted Cole, who had believed himself to be hidden. But I noted the tightened fists, the sawing motion of his jaw, and the murder promised in his eyes when they landed on Wu. Maybe their truce wore on him more than I first thought.

Wonder if they would give me a copy of the terms and conditions if I asked? Nah. Probably not.

Silly dragon. Did he really think he had competition? Wu was nice and all, but he was no Cole. And it's not like he had declared any intentions for me beyond partnering up to wipe my sisters off the face of the planet.

A text on his phone distracted Cole, saving our gazes from clashing and me from getting caught.

"Okay, I'm impressed." I adjusted the frames until I was comfortable. "Mine to keep?"

"Greedy little thing," Wu said, amused. "Yes, they're yours."

"That was Thom." Cole flashed me his phone. "He can't come to us. We're going to have to go to him."

Panic quickened my breaths. "He's okay?"

"Snug as a bug," Cole assured me. "He's in a sweet spot to watch our backs and doesn't want to give up prime real estate."

"Good." An exhale gusted through my lips. "Hold on— I thought he went cat?" I glanced at his phone. "No thumbs for texting. How does that work?"

"Ask Santiago." Cole put away his cell. "This is the field test."

Packing away my questions for later, I slid a fresh clip in my pocket—bullets might not kill a charun, but they slowed them down—then palmed the falchion. "Ready."

Wu set the pace, gliding through the darkness, as silent as a cat on soft paws.

Basically, he fit right in.

Cole stuck to my side, his flash of temper extinguished, his body quivering in anticipation of the fight.

"I'll be pissed if you get yourself hurt," I murmured. "Super pissed."

"I know." Feral intensity burned in his gaze when he turned it on me. "The same goes for you."

"I know," I parroted back to him, taking comfort in our small ritual.

I flexed my fingers, rotating my wrist, getting used to the weight of the blade. It should have felt stranger, less familiar, but it didn't. Eyeing Cole's sword, I experienced a moment of kinship. Something told me if I lifted it, I would find its strength a comfort too.

Zone three remained quiet and contained. Zone two was bloodstained but empty. Zone one buzzed with frantic activity.

Smoke poured from the rear of the building, and flames licked up its sides. Men and women hustled to contain the blaze, but it burned too bright. Unnaturally hot. I was sweating from here.

"*Mmmrrrrpt.*"

A slight weight touched down on my shoulder, and a furry cheek brushed mine. "Nice job, Thom-cat."

"Are the scouts neutralized?" Wu stared into the blaze. "Did you have to burn them out?"

"*Mmmrrrrpt.*"

"Fast and effective," Cole praised him. "We don't have long. The authorities will be notified soon if they haven't been already."

The winged kitty glided to the ground, shook out its wings, then rose on two legs as Thomas.

"There were eggs," he said. "Rooms of them. They've dug deep and carved out a true nest. It's easier to boil them en masse than scramble them individually."

Eggs. We had to cut down War's numbers, but it still made my heart ache. "Any children?"

"No." Thom turned compassionate eyes on me. "There are no young, only the unborn."

"All right." I packed away those bothersome emotions for later examination. "Let's do this."

Cole was watching me, assessing my reaction to the grim news, but he dropped his gaze before I caught him at it.

"Bring up the rear," Wu ordered me. "Thom, you're with Luce."

Cole offered a tight nod of agreement indicating they ought

to be the ones who led the charge. I didn't argue. I was weaker, and I glitched between stone-cold killer and bleeding-heart. I couldn't be trusted to have their backs, no matter how much I wanted to guard them.

Distracted by the fire, the Drosera didn't notice us converging on them until Cole roared his battle cry. That sent them into a fresh tizzy, and they tossed aside buckets and grabbed anything that might work as a weapon. I counted two dozen of them, give or take. It was hard keeping them straight with the black cloud swirling around them.

Wu raced forward, twin swords raised, and sliced through his opponents without uttering so much as an undignified grunt. Each strike was as elegant as a courtly bow, his attacks a vicious waltz with more partners than any dance card should hold. He actually paused once to grimace as blood splattered his shirt. Thankfully, he got his head back in the game before it was separated from his shoulders.

There was no hesitation in Cole. There was no stopping him, either. He raged at them like a pissed-off bull with a matador in his sights. He swung his sword like it was an extension of his arm. Powerful. Merciless. He cut down his opponents then snarled a challenge for more.

What it said about me that I actually panted watching him work up a sweat, I didn't want to know.

It was easier accepting them as *other* than recognizing the same urges and desires in myself.

"Our turn." Thom flexed his hands down at his sides. Claws the length of my thumbs emerged from the tips of his fingers. "We must cut down the cowards who flee."

Suddenly, I had a much clearer picture of how those sheep had met their ends.

Thom was one scary son of a biscuit.

Three Drosera decided they had had enough and bolted down streets headed in opposite directions. I charged after one, but Thom trailed me instead of hunting down the others. And I wasn't fooling myself. He could dispatch ten to every kill I managed with those razorblade fingertips and his centuries of experience.

"Go," I growled at him. "They're getting away."

"Your safety is my priority." He wasn't even winded. "We'll catch the others." He tapped the side of his nose, and I half expected him to lop off the tip. "I can track them. They won't get far."

"All right." I trusted his assessment. I didn't have much choice. Truth be told, I didn't want to be out here alone. I was scared what I might do without someone to anchor me in this skin. "Let's do this then."

The first charun decided he couldn't outrun us and hid behind a dumpster. Blood poured from his side, and his eyes barely tracked as Thom took his head. At this point, it was a mercy killing.

"The others have a head start." I kept my expression and voice neutral when he searched my face for signs of ... revulsion maybe? He was my friend, and I showed him none. "Get tracking, tracker."

When Thom smiled, his mouth was full of needles, and he rolled his r into a purr. "With pleasure."

Chin up, he drew in air to fill his lungs then exhaled with manic glee written across his face. Faster than I could ask what he'd scented, he turned on a dime and bolted in the direction his nose told him to go.

To keep up, I had to pull on the reserve that made me a bit faster, a tad stronger, than most humans.

We breezed past zones two and three. This outer area hadn't

been cleared, and the odds of running across innocent bystanders skyrocketed.

"This way," he breathed, legs pumping until I worried he might lift right off the pavement.

I stuck as close to him as my shorter legs and lesser endurance allowed, and soon I saw what he had sensed all along. The two stragglers had banded together. Now the odds were even.

Thom flexed his claws. "They'll only kill more humans if we allow them to escape."

There was no way to tell how many skin suits they had cycled through in their lifetime. Thom was right. The longer they lived, the more humans would die, and the war hadn't even kicked off yet.

As far as motivational speeches went, it was a short but effective one.

The Drosera noticed us at the same time, and they made their stand in the middle of the freaking street. It's not like there was any traffic, but there would be eventually. We had to wrap this up quick.

"Take the one on the left." Thom's nostrils flared. "He's already wounded."

"Got it."

We advanced while they held their ground. That made me nervous, like they knew something we hadn't figured out yet.

Right before we got level with them, I grasped the situation and yanked Thom back a step. Had the unmarked sedan not been pointed in the opposite direction, the cops would have spotted us. Me with my blood-crusted falchion, and Thom with his claws still dripping.

Shit on a shingle. This just got more complicated.

"There's an undercover unit parked on the corner," I told Thom. "See that glint? It's a light bar mounted flush with the back windshield. Looks like two officers. Both plainclothes."

"We have to lure them away," Thom snarled softly, his disgust at their cowardice apparent.

The big rule was not to involve humans, to fly under their radar, but these two were willing to drag bystanders into the fray to save their tails.

"Damn it." I wiped the back of my hand across my sweaty forehead. "They know I'm a cop." I bit the inside of my cheek until I tasted blood. It didn't matter. Amending that to *I was a cop* would hurt even worse. "They don't think I'll put the officers at risk."

Thom spared me a glance. "Will you?"

I didn't like the way he was looking at me. "Will you?"

"No," he said slowly, as if sounding out the right answer.

Shocker, I wasn't the only one who pulled on a blank face to conceal their true emotions. The coterie was trying, and so was I. I had to believe that was enough, that we could find some middle ground where their morals and mine didn't clash so loudly.

"We can't wait them out, and we can't let them go." Our chances of striking a third target evaporated if we stood here much longer. I still wasn't hot on that plan, but majority ruled. "Can you incapacitate them?"

A flash of needle teeth. "Yes."

"I'm going to engage." I tested my grip and found my palm bone-dry when it should have been as sweaty as the rest of me. "When the officers exit the vehicle, take them down. Easy."

"I won't hurt them," he promised, sounding more certain.

"Wish me luck." I didn't give him a chance to follow through before charging toward the startled charun. One blanched while the other pointed to the sedan in case I had somehow missed the police presence. I grinned at them, and it was a nasty twist of my lips that snarled up my face. "They can't save you."

The cold place burst over my head, chilling my thoughts and freezing my reservations.

Whatever change they perceived on my face or in my body language sent them scurrying.

Behind me, I heard car doors open and footsteps hit pavement.

"Stop," a woman barked. "Drop your weapon and put your hands in the air."

Trusting Thom to have my back, I kept up the pursuit.

The Drosera sprinted for the nearest lighted area, a grocery store by the looks of it. The lot wasn't empty of vehicles. Far from it. There were people in there who would eventually need to come out and get in their cars to go home. These two knew I valued human life. They were making me work for the kills. The only way to protect the shoppers was to take out the charun before they hit that spill of light and claimed their safety.

Diving deeper, I pumped my legs harder. I drew on that calm center until it enveloped me, until its focus encased me in an impenetrable bubble where things like exhaustion and ethics ceased to exist. Even the worry I had nursed for the humans faded to a half-formed thought, easily swept aside by the tide of hungrier urges.

The faster charun stepped in a pothole and lost his footing. Those precious seconds cost him. I was on him a heartbeat later. I clamped my left hand on his shoulder then thrust my blade through his kidneys. He cried out, thrashing. The wound, while painful, wasn't life-threatening. It was a petty strike, a toll exacted from him for making me waste my time. He should have stood his ground, died in the fight with his kin. But no, he had abandoned them to save his own skin.

I shoved him forward, and he landed on his hands and knees. From there, it was easy to take the three steps that lined me up with his shoulders, to raise my blade, and sever his neck with one surgically precise blow.

His head tumbled to the asphalt and rolled to a stop with his face gazing skyward. I watched the light go out of his eyes, and I was satisfied. No, I was horrified. But I couldn't shatter the icy bars of the cage holding me. There was nothing to do but piggyback on that spark of Conquest's consciousness while ancient instincts ruled my body.

The second charun hadn't waited around to see what fate befell his coterie member. He was a dot growing smaller on my horizon as he fled toward the perceived safety of the light.

He didn't make it.

Thom slammed into his side, and they went down together. A feral snarl tore past his lips as he punched the Drosera in the chest. His hand came back bloody, and he clutched a fistful of pulpy meat in his palm.

His heart.

Thom had ripped out his heart.

Bile splashed up the back of my throat, the heat of it thawing me until I registered the dried blood making my hands itch. I clamped my lips closed as Thom rose. He tossed the shredded organ onto the dead Drosera's chest like a ball of yarn he had grown tired of playing with then strolled toward me.

"We need to sweep the area. I've got their scent now. I'll be able to locate any of their nest mates." He reached in his back pocket and removed a thin packet that crinkled. He pulled out one baby wipe for me and took another for himself. He watched me until I started cleaning my hands then began the meticulous process of scrubbing blood from his knuckles. "Better?"

"Much." I deserved a gold star when my voice didn't crack. "Thank you."

"This body isn't as flexible as my natural one," he said

mournfully. "The texture of the human tongue leaves something to be desired as well."

"I'm, uh, sorry about that." All I could think of was how cats stretched one leg high over their heads while they cleaned their junk and about how there were rumors about a rock star having two ribs removed so he could fellate himself. I wasn't sure if Thom had a sense of humor or if it was too dry for me to discern it, so I wasn't taking any chances. "So . . . You can track any deserters?"

"Yes." He took my trash and shoved it into a pocket alongside his wipe. "We should get started. The cops won't be out long. I didn't bite them very hard."

I rested my hand on his arm. "Thanks for not hurting them."

"Hurting them would hurt you." He went solemn on me. "I would never do that."

A humid wind stirred around us in a sudden rush that left me searching the sky for storm clouds.

Thom brushed his shoulder against mine. "Cole."

Sure enough, a gust of hot breath blasted in my face, the scent coppery but pleasant.

"Come to check on us?" I groped air until my fingers tangled in his silky mane. "We've got everything under control."

The dragon made an inquiring noise, almost a trill.

"He's on clean up detail," Thom informed me.

"You're collecting bodies for disposal?" I clenched my hands, a sick feeling in my gut when it occurred to me to wonder how the coterie made bodies disappear fast in an urban setting. "Or are you the disposal?"

A huff of breath, the bright punch of new pennies, fanned my cheeks.

"FYI." I kept my tone light, my expression smooth. "You're flossing when we get back to the hotel."

The great beast nudged my shoulder, and I took the hint gladly. He had cleanup to do, and he didn't want me here when he chowed down.

We almost made it out of range when I heard the first crunch of bone. The sour taste coated every surface in my mouth, but I swallowed until I felt certain I wouldn't toss my cookies. I avoided thinking about how my dragon BFF was a man eater. Corpse muncher? Charun nibbler? Did that make him a cannibal?

Look, brain, I can't afford to backslide into shock. This is my new reality. Adapt already.

The pep talk must have done the trick. I managed to help Thom clear the zones, adding three more kills to my tally, before we backtracked to zone one to rendezvous with the team.

Wu stood in the rubble of what should have been an inferno, but whatever accelerant they used had reduced the old fast food joint to blacked bones jutting from the cracked foundation. He glanced over when he heard us coming. He examined my hands and then my face. A grimness pinched his mouth, and it looked more at home on his face than any smile I had ever seen him wear. There was something sad about that.

Leave it to him to cut to the chase. "Are you steady?"

"Rock steady." I grinned, but he didn't get the reference. Rixton would have laughed. Maybe even sang a few bars of the R&B classic. Probably made a dirty joke that would get him slapped if Sherry heard him talk about her that way. He viewed his wife as a sex goddess, and she was cool with that, but it was the sharing—the *oversharing*—with his coworkers that mortified her. "Never mind."

"Luce handled herself well." Thom came to my defense. "Next time, she needs a bigger blade."

Hefting the falchion, I twisted the handle so light played off the stained blade. "I would have to upgrade to a broadsword to get bigger than this."

Thom nodded in agreement. "Cole has yours."

"I have a sword?" The fingers in my right hand tightened. For a moment, the sensation of carved wood vanished, and braided leather molded by time and sweat and blood warmed my palm. "Maybe he should keep it safe for me. I drew on the—" I almost said *the cold place* but didn't want to explain myself. "I remembered how it feels to fight with a sword, maybe with that sword, so let's avoid giving Conquest another touchstone."

Memories were trickling in faster than ever. I couldn't afford to touch an old sword and black out again. I had no clue what triggered my last episode, and I aimed to keep it that way, but two days? What kind of landmines were buried in my head that exploded on that scale?

Maybe everyone had been right all along. Maybe it was only a matter of applying enough pressure in the right spot. After all, something was making me go *boom*.

CHAPTER EIGHTEEN

———◇———

Santiago greeted me onscreen wearing a maniacal grin. Gore smeared his face, and his hair was plastered to one side of his scalp with dried blood. Portia crammed in behind him and let Mags surface long enough to wave at me before tucking her back in where it was safe.

Call me optimistic, but I figured that meant their mission was also successful.

I wasn't sure yet if that was a good thing or a bad thing beyond the obvious that I was grateful we had all made it out the other side unscathed. "Where's Miller?"

Santiago cranked up his deranged smile into berserker territory. "Digesting."

"I see." The division of assets made a lot more sense once he put it like that. "Cole is too."

"Cole is probably wishing he had a toothpick right about now. Miller doesn't have that problem."

Meaning . . . he swallowed his victims whole versus chewing first?

Not gonna ask. Don't wanna know. I'm happy living here in Ignoranceville, population: Luce.

He peered around me but got an eyeful of headrest since I was holed up in the SUV. "Where are the others?"

"Cole is on aerial surveillance, Thom went cat in the driver's seat to clean up, Wu is on the phone with Kapoor." I spun the tablet around to give him an eyeful of Thom licking his unmentionables. "And I got the pleasure of checking in with unit two, which would be you."

"Uh, no." He laughed with an edge of challenge. "We're unit *one*."

Exhausted, filthy, and smelly I might be, but I couldn't resist needling him.

"'Fraid not." I tsked at him. "Cole and I are both here. That makes us number one."

"I said we're *unit* one." Santiago's face got a lot closer to the screen. "If we're talking *number* one—"

"Are you two children really fighting over this?" Portia palmed his forehead and shoved him back. "Now?" She caught sight of my face and sighed. "Him, I get. I made peace with the fact he's a man-child long ago. But I expected better from you, Luce."

"I'll try to behave." I don't think the smirk sold her on my contrition. "Now that we've got that out of the way, report."

"The nest was exactly where Sariah indicated. It was located in a warehouse district, which made it easier on us. One human was injured in the skirmish—a security guard on watch—but we left him at the hospital. We counted a dozen Drosera and maybe another dozen charun of various species. All local."

Mixing ranks couldn't be a good sign. "She's recruiting?"

"You remember Veronica? The receptionist at the lab? The one you hid from to avoid having your feet kissed?" Santiago smirked at my unease. "There are fanatics like her on every terrene. Each member of the cadre is idolized. Some charun worship the four as goddesses. There are entire sects devoted to furthering your goals, and that means planting agents throughout the terrenes. All the cadre has to do is ask, and their vessels will sacrifice themselves on the altar of your ambition."

"Good to know." Pieces were shifting in the back of my mind, connections snicking into place, but I couldn't afford to get distracted. "Anything else to report?"

"We won, obviously." He snorted like it could have gone any other way. "Miller handled the runners, and we tossed the rest in the warehouse and set it on fire."

"Two fires, two cities, and two poor arson investigators who are getting wakeup calls right about now."

"Aren't you glad you're no longer one of the schmucks who gets lassoed into lending a hand?"

"I loved my job," I said softly. "I would trade them for the honor any day of the week."

The cat beside me paused his grooming, his sky-high leg drooping.

"But that would mean losing you guys." I scratched under the cat's chin. "I had that life, and it was a good one, but . . ." I shook my head, " . . . it was never mine. Not really." I included Santiago in my smile. "This is what I was meant to do, to be, and I can't regret learning how it feels to belong."

"Even if it means ending your nights sticky in places you can't mention in polite company?"

"What polite company?" Portia cackled. "You? Me? Mags, maybe. Okay, fine. Miller has manners."

"I have manners," Santiago snarled. "Want me to introduce you to them?"

"You didn't, did you?" She gawked at his lap then started baby-talking his crotch. "Did he name you guys *Manners*?"

"*What?*" Blistering purple scalded his cheeks. "No, I did not name any parts of my anatomy *Manners*."

"Guys." They ignored me. I tried again, louder. "*Guys.*"

"What?" they chorused, almost nose to nose.

"You're overlooking a critical detail here."

"Is that some kind of come-on?" Santiago frowned. "If so, no. You can't overlook my *details*."

"*Guys. Parts. Details.*" I spelled it out for them. "As in they're all plural."

They exchanged a puzzled look that sent heat rushing up my nape.

"And?" Santiago demanded at the same time Portia said, "So?"

"Never mind." I closed my eyes. "I don't want to know."

"Well that answers that question," Portia murmured.

Santiago glared at her. "What question?"

"Cole and her. Her and Cole."

He rolled his hand. "What about them?"

Portia formed a circle with one hand while sticking the pointer finger of her other through the hole.

"Why didn't you just say they hadn't screwed yet?" Santiago thumped her on the forehead. "Besides, if they were having sex, we'd know it. We'd smell her all over him. You know how Otillians have to mark every damn thing as theirs."

"I'm stepping out now." I left the tablet on in case Thom decided to shift and engage them, but I was done. The fresh air did me a world of good as I hunted down Wu, who was tapping his phone against his chin. "Hey."

"They're pulling your leg," he said, distracted. "Charun males have one penis."

A sigh gusted out of me, leaving me limp with relief. Cole was not a small man, and—since he had been carved from a blueprint for humanity and not born into his body—I imagined he

was proportionate. Everywhere. And let me just add that imagining said proportions was not doing great things for my focus.

"Well," Wu started, rolling an elegant shoulder, "unless they're
in their natural form . . . "

About to swallow my pride and just ask outright, I noticed
the merry twinkle in his eyes.

I smacked my palm against my forehead. "Not you too?"

"Charun are always in a good mood after a melee." His eyes
lightened to gold. "I'm no exception."

"So I see." I hooked a thumb over my shoulder. "I'm not going
back there and dealing with that."

"We must organize our next move." His entire being vibrated
on a frequency I imagined resonating in my bones. His happiness—satiation?—was infectious. "We've proven Sariah's
intel is good. We should squeeze every drop from what she's
given us."

Squeeze every drop? I squinted at him, waiting to see who
cracked first. "That was not a dick joke."

Wu raked his teeth across his bottom lip, but it did nothing
to counter his shoulders as they jostled from laughter.

"You're all impossible." I threw up my hands. "I'm going to
read until you guys tire yourselves out."

"You feel it too." He caught my wrist as I turned to leave,
whirling me in a complex spin that belonged on a dance floor
and left me facing him. "Your blood is humming." He cocked
his head, lashes fluttering against his cheeks. "I hear its song in
the beat of your heart."

"Invest in earplugs." I planted my palms on his chest and
shoved back, or I meant to, but my hands got stuck. Not literally.
Not in a charun superpower kind of way. More like I couldn't
convince myself to let go. The reaction was purely physical, but
not sexual, not wholly. "What is this effect you have on me?"

"Perhaps you're attracted to me," he murmured. "Is the idea so repugnant?"

"No." I smoothed a hand up to his shoulder then down his arm, marveling at how the caress calmed me more than a hot bubble bath and a good book combined. "But I'm pretty familiar with attraction, and while you're gorgeous—and you know it, so put up your fishing pole—this is not that. This is . . . I don't know what it is. That's why I'm asking."

"We resonate." He caught my hand as it was about to fall. "I feel it too. I have since the moment I first saw you. It's the reason why I believe we can do great things together."

"Cole and I also resonate." There was no other word for how attuned we were to each other. "How does that work? He and I are . . . " I searched for a comparison that wouldn't get Wu's back up. "We're tuned to a different frequency."

"Resonance is potential." He brought my hand to his mouth and kissed my knuckles, blood and all. "All it means is we're compatible. That compatibility doesn't mean we're fated mates or destined to be lovers. It's a component in most friendships, in all the best partnerships. There might be mutual attraction, but it's difficult to parse an emotional attachment from the physical reaction. It's why you should never enter into a relationship that resonates unless you're certain that person is the hum you want in your bones forever."

The hum in my bones.

I narrowed my eyes at him. "You're not psychic, are you?"

"No?"

His bafflement was not a great sign. It meant resonance was real, and even the word thrummed with a rightness within me. It had the ring of a thing once forgotten but now remembered. I had been thinking of the coterie along those lines, so maybe he was right. It didn't have to mean Wu and I were fated to be more than partners. Maybe all it required was a certain level of like-mindedness. That would explain why Cole sparked with me when he hadn't with Conquest.

"Do you want to . . ." I rolled my wrist, " . . . resonate with me?"

His tongue darted out to wet his lips. "Are you asking if I'm interested in more than being just your partner?"

I searched his face, curious for his reaction. "Yes."

"You love Cole."

Love was . . . a big word. *Huge.* But there wasn't an ounce of me willing to deny it fit.

I was in love with Cole Heaton.

More than shock, I felt . . . an overwhelming sense of inevitability. There was no path forward I could imagine walking without him by my side.

Until I met him, I had never been a big believer in fate. Now I believed our mating dance had already been choreographed. All we had to do was screw up the courage to hear the music and learn the steps.

"Yes," I rasped, the confession ripped from my soul.

"You deserve whatever happiness you can find for as long as you can hold onto it." Gold washed over his eyes, the metallic sheen reflective in the low light. "If Cole brings you joy, then you shall have him."

The ring of permission being granted puzzled me. Wu was in no position to palm me off on Cole. Must be the battle high warping his poor little bird brain.

"I'm going to read." I backed away from him. "Let me know when you've got a plan ironed out."

Three steps into my retreat, I bumped into a wall that might as well have been brick for all the give there was in dragon hide.

An inquisitive noise rose in Cole's throat as he snuffled me, taking his time at each point where Wu's touch had lingered.

An angry gurgle bubbled up through my shoulder blades where they pressed against his side.

"Upset stomach?" I reached up and scratched behind his tab ears. "I would offer you an antacid, but it would take a gallon of Pepto to make a dent after your binge."

The dragon sighed agreement then rubbed his cheek against mine, replacing Thom's scent markers with his own.

God save me from males of the species.

Really, I ought to be grateful for their under-chin scent glands. A cheek rub beat getting sprayed each time one wanted to mark their perceived territory. Maybe that was the *real* reason why the NSB spayed them.

"Sariah is online," Thom called. "She's demanding to speak to you, Luce."

"Of course she is." I patted the dragon then pushed off and headed for the SUV. "I'll take it." Thom passed over the tablet, and my niece stared out at me. "What's up?"

"Our plans go up in smoke if you don't get your asses in gear," she said, all business. "Santiago has called in the all-clear. We're good to move forward with the attack on the third nest. Have you decided which target to strike?"

"The larger nest," Wu said from beside me, saving me from having to choose. "We're in no shape to go up against their best. We would win, but it would cost us." All traces of his earlier flirtatiousness had vanished now that his blood was cooling. The dragon's appearance probably had something to do with it too. "We have better fighters, stronger fighters. We can take out more of them than they can of us."

"That works for me." I checked my phone. "It will take us two hours to get from Greenville to Jacksonville."

The screen split, Sariah's image compressing as Santiago popped up beside her. "It will take us three."

"You'll be racing the dawn," she warned us. "You'll have to fight quick and dirty."

"I've got it covered," Miller said in the background.

Not one single person questioned him. Odds were good I was the only one dumb enough to wonder what he meant by that, but a stomach could only hold so many bodies, right?

Miller had eaten people. No, skin suits. Most of them were buff guys or fit women. Fighters. I wasn't clear on how digestion worked since there was a super gator stuffed in the hosts too, like some seriously fucked up turducken. But even if I downplayed the height and weight of the other coterie's members, I was left with a disturbing gauge for Miller's size.

Cole was large as a dragon, and his head was massive, but it was only as long as an average human body was tall. Hence the crunching. The rest of him— I hadn't exactly whipped out a measuring tape. Reptilian tails could stretch two or three times the length of the body it was attached to, and that was certainly the case with him, but his whiplike tail alone had to be in the neighborhood of twenty feet.

And Miller was bigger. Much bigger.

"We're heading out." Santiago shot me a mock salute. "Don't get started without us."

His image disappeared from the screen, leaving me staring at Sariah, who gazed right back.

"You don't look thrilled," she observed. "I thought this would make you happy."

"Death never makes me happy." I closed the app before she drew me into another philosophical debate. I might feel I belonged with my coterie more than humans, but I was still an outsider with one foot in both worlds and no plans to change that anytime soon. "Load up." I switched off the tablet and passed it to Thom. "We've still got a long night ahead of us."

"Cole will join us there." Thom kept his voice soft. "He needs to burn off some calories."

"We need him to work up an appetite." The better to devour our enemies. "Gotcha."

Thom drove, and I rode beside him. Wu piled in behind me, his presence a tickle on my nape. Leaning my head against the window, I let sleep tug my eyelids closed.

I dreamed of verdant plants and walled-in gardens, childish laughter and the pitter-patter of tiny feet.

Jackson was a familiar stomping ground for me, and for the coterie. Finding our way around was simple enough without using the GPS. This time the Drosera had holed up in a condemned shopping mall, and that alone offered a chilling estimate of how many charun could hide within the warren of hollow stores and vacant halls.

We established our base in the parking lot attached to a grocery store about five blocks from our target.

"Having second thoughts?" Wu asked, his breath fanning my ear when he leaned forward in his seat.

"And thirds." I swatted him away then got out of the SUV to stretch my legs. "And fourths. You?"

"This is a good sign," he said, joining me. "A compound that size shores up our intel. So far, Sariah has been leveling with us."

"The bangles seem to be doing their job." A faint throb of what promised to be a migraine furrowed my brow, and I flinched when Wu smoothed it with his thumb. "Personal space." I swatted him again. "Have you heard of it?"

"Luce enjoys her *me* space," Thom said sagely. "Now he knows."

"Thank you, Thomas." I ruffled his hair. "You're a clever kitty, you know that?"

Wu looked on, amused. "Is that the equivalent of telling a dog he's a good boy?"

"Watch it, Tweety." I pointed a finger at him. "Or I'll let him use you as a scratching post."

Feral delight gleamed in Thom's eyes. "Yes."

"Down, boy." Wu stepped back when Thom sniffed at him and wet his lips. "Remember—" his fingers elongated, tapering into black talons, "—I have claws too."

A sound that was a close relative to a purr rattled Thom's chest. "I like when food fights back."

"You're not going to win this argument." I chuckled at Wu. "Thom is a predatory feline. Like it or not, you're a bird-man."

"You liked my wings well enough," he reminded me. "You looked disappointed when I put them away."

"I was," I admitted. "The coterie could use a new cat toy, but it's not the same without the feathers."

His flat stare kept the laughter rolling through my chest, and it felt good to have a moment of normalcy.

"We need to split into teams and secure the area." Wu tilted his head skyward. "Can you sense Cole?"

"No." I joined him in stargazing. "Usually it's the wind that gives him away."

"We have less than an hour until Santiago and the others join us." Wu caught Thom's eye. "Stick close to her and take zone five. I'll handle zone four. Cole can have three when he arrives, and we'll keep closing the net until the others get here."

"Don't take any risks." I bumped Wu's shoulder. "Find us if you need backup, and do not engage."

"As the lady wishes." Wu touched his fingers to his heart then set out in the opposite direction.

"He thinks you're his." Thom frowned at him. "He doesn't understand you can't be owned."

I waved him ahead, and we started our sweep. "Wu understands more than he lets on."

"Cole will kill him if he tries to claim you."

I tripped over air. "It won't come to that."

"No," he decided. "It won't." Claws sprang from his fingertips. "I'll kill him first."

"Tell you what." I drew my grungy falchion and refamiliarized myself with its heft. "If Wu ever tries to club me over the head and drag me into his cave, you have my permission to kill him."

"And eat him?"

"And eat him."

"Do you want me to save any of the feathers for the toy you mentioned?"

His earnestness slayed me, and I pretended to give it real consideration. "That would be nice. Thank you."

"You're welcome."

The outer ring was clear of charun, and we crossed paths with Wu a short time later as we spiraled closer to the nest. Cole remained MIA, but he might have stopped to purge. The weight of flying with a full stomach might have slowed him too. There was no reason to panic. Yet. Right?

He was the largest airborne charun I had met. Wu might be able to outmaneuver him, but he couldn't take him down without help. Lots of help. A whole flock's worth of help.

On the boundary of zone one, we met Wu for the final pass. Wu glanced behind us. "Still no Cole?"

I quashed the nervous quiver in my abdomen. "Not yet."

"I'll handle recon on the nest," Thom offered. "We'll meet back at the car."

The others ought to be arriving soon, and we needed to intercept them but still . . . "Are you sure?"

"I will be careful." He slid his cheek against mine. "Cole will return soon."

As alien as Thom's thought process struck me at times, I marveled at how well he read me.

Either he and I weren't so different, or his innate healing gift extended to emotional wounds too.

"We'll backtrack and intercept the others." I put on a brave face. "We'll be ready to hit the ground running when you report in."

In the blink of an eye, he transformed from man to cat. The scruffy tom flexed his wings and settled them against his spine before he strutted off, nub tail swishing.

I watched until I lost sight of him then started the walk back with Wu. We intercepted three charun, one solo in zone two and a pair in zone three, and Wu dispatched them without giving me a chance to mount a half-hearted protest that I ought to pull my own weight. For that, I was grateful.

The others were gathered around our SUV when we arrived, which had me wondering if Santiago was tracking the tablet or the vehicle, and I walked into Maggie's arms.

"You good?" I asked over her shoulder. "You can bow out at any time."

"I'm having trouble breathing," she gasped. "Otherwise, I'm . . . okay." She buried her face in my neck. "I'm going to need time to process this. Later. But I can hold it together a while longer. Portia is keeping the worst from me." Her voice lowered. "You should have seen Miller. He was . . ."

Terrifying . . . Horrifying . . . A monster . . . ?

"Magnificent," she breathed. "Like one of those heroes from your kissy books."

"My kissy books?" I leaned back and scowled. "You're the one who started sneaking me old school Harlequin novels when I was like twelve so I could avoid talking to Dad about the birds and the bees."

"Okay, so I got you hooked, but you're the one who started reading paranormal romance. It was never my thing."

Just like the small-town romances she favored with normal boys falling for normal girls hadn't been mine. Hard to relate when *normal* wasn't your default.

"I have some books you can borrow." I pulled back and grinned at her. "If you're ready to switch teams."

Mags rolled her eyes. "Now you're my demon romance dealer?"

"I didn't say anything about demons." Innocently, I fluttered my lashes. "Any demons in particular I should search my shelves for?" Flares ignited in her cheeks, and suddenly I was looking at Portia. "Thanks for taking such good care of her." I squeezed her hand. "And of yourself."

"And Santiago, and Miller." She flicked her wrist. "Boys are so helpless. They're all 'this Drosera is eating my spleen' or 'have you seen my pinky'. Losing a finger sucks, I'll give you that. But come on. No one even knows what a spleen does. Miller could have lived without one until it grew back."

Panicked, I searched beyond her to where Santiago cradled his hand against his chest. After patting Portia on the shoulder, I crossed to where he leaned against our SUV and held out my hand. He snarled at me, hunching over his injury. Someone had the presence of mind to bind it, but I wanted to see the wound for myself. Instinct was pushing me to be certain my people were intact.

"Stop being a baby." I grabbed his wrist and took care while unwrapping his injured hand. I stopped, blinked, then blasted Portia with an incredulous glare. "You put his pinky on backwards."

"Are you sure?" She widened her eyes and cupped her mouth with her palm. "I'm ever-so-sorry."

"Son of a bitch." Santiago curled his lip over his teeth. "You did that on purpose."

"I'm not a doctor." She shrugged. "How am I supposed to know what goes where?"

"You've got a hand full of fingers," he snapped. "That's how you know."

"Okay, kids." I rubbed my finger gently over the fused seam. "What do we do now?"

"It will have to be cut off and regrown." He shook his bloody hand at her. "That will take forever."

"A week tops." She cocked a hip and crossed her arms over her chest. "You heard Luce. Stop being a baby."

"You do realize we're kind of in the middle of something here." I pegged her with a glare I would never turn on Maggie in a million years. "Why would you do this?"

Chin jutting out, Portia said, "He told us our butt looks big in our fatigues."

Oh yes. Adrenaline had our hormones blasting off like fireworks. I've got to admit, it made me feel better knowing I wasn't the only one skirting the edge of conflagration. A five-dollar word I learned from my kissy books, so there. "Santiago, why were you looking at their butt in the first place?"

"They told me to kiss it," he said innocently. "I was debating where I ought to plant one when I noticed the options were endless."

An inhuman snarl clawed up Portia's throat, and her fingers hooked into talons.

"Let it go." I stepped between them. "He's not worth ruining your manicure."

Portia stuck out her tongue at Santiago, who responded by lifting his hand and biting off his pinky. He spat it in his palm then hurled it at her. The digit bounced off her forehead, leaving a smear, and she caught it in the vicinity of her cleavage.

"That's as close to copping a feel as you'll ever get." She tucked it away in her pocket. "Nice try, though."

"Quiet." The single command zipped all our lips as Miller coalesced from the darkness, his stride loose and his face serene. All he needed was a lit cigarette to complete the picture of post-coital bliss. A full belly was rare for him, from what I understood. Satiation wasn't a bad look on him. He strolled right up to Portia and peered down at her. "Show me."

The color drained from her face. "Miller . . . "

He leaned in closer, and Santiago palmed a dagger as he hissed, "Show. Me."

Maggie swam up to the surface, her ascent slower than usual. A sign of her reluctance or Portia's?

I mirrored Santiago's stance, falchion in hand, and watched Miller for signs this was about to go bad.

"Hi, Miller." Mags licked the pad of her thumb then wiped a piece of God-only-knows-what off his left eyebrow with a trembling hand. The reminder of what she used to be, of all the tiny faces she had once cleaned with equal care in her classroom caved my chest beneath the pressure of my guilt. Those smudges had been dirt, not blood, but his lost boy expression brought out the nurturer in her all the same. "I can't be here."

"You make it better," he said simply. "Your light lessens the darkness."

"You're not alone." Maggie extended her hand to him, and this time it didn't quiver as she squeezed his shoulder. "The only way the darkness wins is if you let it convince you otherwise."

"Go," he rasped. "I shouldn't have brought you here."

Portia blinked into awareness, lowering her arm, and Miller shuttered his expression.

I wrapped an arm around his waist and held him tight. I'm not sure I had ever side-hugged anyone, except maybe Maggie, but he looked like he needed one, and the instinctive unease I usually felt when maintaining contact failed to surface.

That's how Cole found me a quarter of an hour later.

Without breaking his stride, he prowled over to me. Prying me from Miller, he wrapped me in his arms. He buried his face at my neck and just breathed. Allowing him to settle, I scratched his prickly scalp and wondered at the texture. It must be time for a haircut. He usually kept it as stubble across his head, but I felt maybe a quarter inch of growth. It made me wonder how he looked with hair and if I would get to see it long one day.

"We're running out of time." Wu plucked his upper lip while he stared at a tablet screen. "Recovery took longer than expected." He passed the device back to Santiago. "We can call it now, go back to the hotel, and dream of War's pissed off expression when she realizes what we've cost her."

"Or—" I caught the drift of his motivational speech and filled in the blanks, "—we can take down one last target and cripple her." I stared at the others over Cole's shoulder and hated that this was only the beginning. "But skilled fighters can only do so much against sheer numbers."

"Nice." Santiago slow-clapped for me. "Now I feel all pumped up about our odds."

"I should have left the speechifying to Wu." I rested my chin on Cole's shoulder. "Sorry, guys. What I meant to say was 'Rah, rah! Go team!'"

"Shake your pom-poms for me," Santiago suggested. "Maybe that will motivate me."

Portia slapped the back of his head. "Pig."

"Oink, oink," he deadpanned.

"How have you put up with them for so long?" I whispered in Cole's ear. "I would have strangled them by now."

"I duct tape their mouths, hands, and feet once every six months, so I can enjoy the quiet."

"Smart." I laughed against his skin. "How are you holding up?"

"I can manage." He straightened to his full height. "We need to finish this then get Miller and me back to the bunkhouse before we crash." His expression tightened. "We'll be out of commission for a few days."

Snakes, depending on their size and the meal they consumed, could spend days or weeks digesting their prey and then go months without eating. I was guessing charun biology must speed up the process, or else there was no way Cole or Miller would be able to down a second helping. But I wasn't going to ask.

The same man whose breath on my throat gave me chills had devoured entire people.

At least he chewed them first. Did that make it better or worse than what Miller must do?

And did I really want to know? The portion of my brain still convinced I was human was screaming. It had been for a long time. Hours or days. Hard to tell at this point. I figured eventually it would get tired and shut up, but that hadn't happened yet. Each fresh horror I witnessed gave it a fresh lungful of air, and *here we go again*.

Tomorrow I would have to sit Maggie down and judge her level of okayness for myself.

Maybe we both ought to take Kapoor up on his offer of counseling. I was coping, but it was costing me. I wasn't as sure about Mags. With Portia acting as a buffer, she might be fine. But with Miller so invested in her, I couldn't afford not to take precautions.

Bad enough for one-quarter of the upcoming apocalypse to love her and want her safe. Toss in an infatuated being with world-ending capabilities, and Maggie just might be the single most important person on the planet.

"We stick to our teams." Wu seized control of the op when it became obvious the rest of us weren't interested in calling more shots. "Portia, Santiago, Miller." He snapped his fingers at them. "Cole, Luce, and me."

"Wait." A cold knot formed in my gut. "What about Thom?"

"He's not back yet." Wu met my eyes when he said it, like that might soften the blow. "We've waited as long as we dare."

"What about his com?" I spun on Santiago. "He was texting Cole earlier. Can we check in?"

"His signal went dark about twenty minutes ago." He raked his hands through his hair. "The tech is jury-rigged out of scrap. Just an idea I had on the fly. I'm surprised it lasted this long."

"We don't know if the tech failed or ..." I shut my eyes, breathed. "We have to get him back."

"Fuck," Santiago spat, summing up my thoughts exactly. "This just became a rescue mission."

CHAPTER NINETEEN

———◦◉◦———

With Thom missing, Wu claimed his right as my partner. Santiago and Portia kept their duo intact. As much as it pained Miller to let Maggie out of his sight, he paired with Cole.

The fatigue, the sarcasm, the flirtations. All of it had been wiped away as if it had never existed.

We opted for a three-pronged attack. Our heavy-hitters would waltz through the front door and provide the distraction. While the Drosera rushed to mend the breach, the other teams would enter from the sides and start clearing stores. And searching for Thom.

"Focus," Wu murmured too low for his voice to carry. "You're no good to any of us dead."

We crouched in a small courtyard overgrown with vines and waited for the party to get started.

"I'm good." And I was. No cold place required. They had taken Thom, and I was getting him back. End of story.

The look he turned on me was grim, and I wondered at the regret pinching the corners of his eyes.

He wanted me to access my inner charun. He wanted me to step up to the plate. Well, this was me. I had a bat in my hands—okay, a falchion—and I was ready to take a swing. This time, I wouldn't miss.

Inhuman screams erupted on the other side of the wall in front of us.

"Keep your head clear. Your head, not hers." He tapped my temple with his index finger. "Don't let her off the chain."

Wu shot to his feet and angled his body perpendicular with a low window. A metal pipe filled his hands, one he must have scavenged, and he swung. Glass shattered, a loud crack of noise, and he used the pipe to knock out the jagged teeth. He hopped through without drawing blood, and I followed his example. By the time he glanced back, I was at his side. We entered the building together, and the smell almost knocked me on my ass.

Urine and feces smeared the tiled halls, and the drag marks from scaly bellies reminded me of how gators slid down muddy inclines to splash in the swamp. The bulk of the nest must be keeping it au naturel on the home front. The ones wearing skin suits had to maintain those or lose them, but the pungent stench I learned well during my time on the streets convinced me they weren't playing human while safe behind these walls. Every corner was a toilet, and they were overflowing.

The room we entered might have been a clothing store in another life. Wads of dirty fabric mounded together to form nests on the floor, but we were alone. Wu had managed to give us the advantage of not dumping us out into the main hall. That must be what he and Santiago had bent their heads together over—floorplans.

Careful of his footing on the slick tiles, Wu led the way to the security door, which had been ripped from its hinges. He peered around the corner in both directions, flared his nostrils, and gave me a nod. I flowed out behind him, keeping the falchion down at my side and one hand on my gun. Bullets might not stop charun, but the familiar weight of the weapon grounded me in my skin.

Once out in the hall, I cast a quick glance over my shoulder. The mall dead-ended behind us. We didn't have to watch our backs.

Yep. Wu had definitely done his homework.

The first clot of Drosera, all wearing skin suits, guarded a door leading into a massive space that must have once belonged to one of the anchor stores. Wu sliced through the first charun before the others tore their rapt attention from the commotion down the hall to defend themselves. Clearly, they had been counting on the dead end to protect them too. A good reminder for me that there were no guarantees while inside the nest.

I swung the falchion and hacked through the neck of the second charun, and its head spun across the floor. Wu had moved on to his next target when a fourth rammed its shoulder into mine and sent me spinning into the wall.

Impact knocked the breath out of me, but I recovered and drove my blade through its heart. The organ's placement should have mirrored a human's while they were fused, but that wasn't enough to stop it. It hauled itself further onto the blade and closer to me, until the man it used to be could have kissed me.

"Butterflies can't ... fly ... without wings."

"Keep spouting crazy." I brought my knee up, smashing his groin, and the charun howled. At least that bit of anatomy remained the same. "Get out all the last words you want, I'll listen."

Surrendering my grip on the blade, I brought my gun up and blasted four rounds through his forehead.

The charun slumped forward, his weight crushing me against the wall, grinding the falchion's hilt into my gut.

"That was sloppy." Wu gripped the charun by the back of the neck, held him aloft while he retrieved the blade, then tossed him aside like he was nothing. "If you're close enough to chat, then you're close enough to die."

"Thanks for that gem." I accepted the falchion when he passed it to me. "It's not like I pulled up a chair and invited him to join my quilting circle. I was trying to kill him. He just wouldn't die."

"You need a bigger sword."

"Men always think bigger is better."

"Women do too."

I choked on a laugh before I remembered where we were, what we were doing.

The adrenaline dump flipped all kinds of interesting switches in charun. Gallows humor was nothing new to a cop, but this newly awakened side of me kept whispering there was a third option. Fight or flight was for humans. Fight or flight or fuck was for us. And we all seemed to skate the edge when our blood got pumping.

We dispatched four more stores full of charun. Three of which held more skin suits. The fourth, that was the nasty one. Half of those lounged like gators on a riverbank. We had to team up, and we still almost lost the fight. Wu did lose a chunk of his thigh, and I got a nasty gash to my upper arm that was slow to clot.

After that, we took a breather in the hall. Wu refused to go down, but he was weak, and I was determined. I forced him to sit. As disgusting as it was, I had to get him off his leg. I knelt beside him, unfastened his belt and yanked it from around his waist. It made a decent tourniquet, but it wasn't a miracle cure.

Once I had him patched up, he ripped off his shirt and tore it into ribbons he used to bind my wound. The pressure numbed me until I couldn't feel the pain. That was nice. But it also meant I couldn't use the arm. My dominant one. Of course.

"We're done. You can't walk. I can't swing a blade. We're dripping like wet paint, and soon the Drosera will scent us and home in on our location. Our part in this mission is over, and there's no hope of extraction." Down here, the smell was so much worse. That had to be why my eyes were burning, hot tears rolling down my cheeks. Wu's thigh would get infected if he didn't seek immediate medical treatment, and our medic was . . . Damn it. I was supposed to be leading the charge to find Thom, not sidelined in this cesspit waiting on a status report once the dust cleared. "There's no one to answer an SOS even if I could send one."

"Go," Wu panted. "Find one of the other teams and join them."

"I'm not leaving you." I let a growl enter my voice. "Partners don't leave each other behind."

"Thom needs you," he reasoned. "I don't."

"Mmm-hmm." I let him watch my slow perusal of his battered form. "How do you figure?"

"We've cleared the hall up to this point." He swept his arm out to encompass our swath of destruction. "I can fly out."

"Your wingspan is too large." I wasn't buying that for a minute. "You can't just soar down the hall and out that window. You'll get caught, and those pretty feathers will get ripped from your back."

The offhand comment set a distant alarm bell clanging in the back of my head, but I was too focused on Wu to tune in to its warning.

"I'm not going through the window." He pointed ahead to where a weak shaft of moonlight glistened on the tiles. "I'm going through the skylight." He lifted his hand and brandished the same length of pipe he'd used to clear the window. I recognized the neon paint splashed down one side. He must have traded out one of his elegant blades for a blunt-force weapon.

"Get me there, and I can handle the rest. I'll do recon outside and take out any runners."

"I still don't like this plan, but I can't think of a better one." That bell hadn't quieted yet, and its implications got harder to ignore. "What that Drosera said before he died … He was taunting me. About Thom." I got to my feet and helped him to his. He slung an arm across my shoulders, and I wrapped one around his waist. "We need to find him."

"They'll use him as bait."

"Tell me something I don't know."

"There's a town in the Atacama Desert in Chile called Calama that has never recorded rainfall."

Shaking my head, I set out toward the skylight beneath the defunct food court and hauled him along with me. "I forgot you're a trivia wiz."

He grinned, but it was strained. "It's amazing what factoids you accumulate over a lifetime."

"A lifetime like yours maybe." I cut him a look. "I get a headache when I try to imagine how old you are, all you must have seen and done."

"You're not much younger than I am," he pointed out. "Punching through the terrenes takes its toll. The differences in planetary rotations ages you more than living on one your whole life."

Talking kept his mind off the raw meat frontage on his thigh, so I kept going. "You're going to make my head explode."

"You've beheld more wonders than I ever will. It's all locked away in that clever mind of yours."

"Flattery? Really?" Heady relief swirled through me, though I hid it from him. "Your leg's hanging on by a thread, and you're stroking my ego?" I dug my thumb into his ribs. "Do *not* make any comments about what else you might like to stroke."

Gold washed over his eyes. "I would never."

"Liar, liar, wings on fire."

A dozen steps, and we would reach our goal. Ten, nine, eight . . .

A low reptilian growl reverberated through the space, and I whipped my head toward the sound. What might qualify as the world's largest American Alligator lifted its blocky head from the sludgy water in a shattered fountain I had dismissed as debris. Our eyes locked, and its nictitating lids blinked once.

"Wu." I stepped away from him, angling my body between him and the gator. "Get out of here."

"No." He panted with the effort of standing alone, but I needed both hands free. "I won't leave you."

"Then we'll both die." I mashed my lips into a flat line. No point arguing my own logic with him.

The Drosera climbed out, its weight cracking the fragile tiles underfoot. Jaws snapping, it roared a challenge then charged. The furious beast moved impossibly fast for such a large creature. I was trapped unless I abandoned Wu, and that wasn't happening. I raised my falchion, the blade the length of one of its arms, and braced for impact.

It never came.

An enormous snake—its wedge-shaped head longer than the gator's entire body—whipped in from one of the connecting hallways. Vibrant crimson and burnt orange scales provided camouflage for a foreign world. The snake pierced the gator's body with fangs longer than my legs, and the Drosera screamed while the beast kept pumping it full of venom in green, fragrant drops that slid down the creature's side to melt the tiles beneath.

"Miller," I breathed, and the snake cut its citrine eyes toward me.

"Don't move." Wu gripped my upper arm. "He might not remember you when he's like this."

"He knows me." I pried free of him with gentle hands so as not to hurt him worse. Then I made a gesture to indicate he needed to make with the wings. "Otherwise, me seeing him like this wouldn't humiliate him so much. If he wasn't in there, if he didn't remember, it wouldn't matter, but it does." On high alert, I waited for the cataclysmic explosions, lava flows and solar flares to start, but nothing happened. "I thought the world would end and spare me the headache if he shifted."

"This is a partial shift. He's in his natural form, but his size ... " Wu couldn't peel his eyes off Miller. "It ought to be impossible to fold himself into such a compact skin without it bursting."

"So should bird-men, and yet there you stand." I snapped my fingers. "Wings, Wu. Wings."

"He'll snatch me out of the air," he said matter-of-factly. "I'm prey to him."

Of all the mythical combinations, why did Wu have to be considered a delicacy among my coterie?

"I'll distract him, but you're going to have to work fast." I couldn't help sounding oddly proud, like I had anything to do with Miller's prowess. "He moves like lightning."

"Buy me five minutes." He hefted the pipe in his hand. "That's enough to break the glass and get out."

"I'll do my best." Inhaling deep, I exhaled slow. "Here I go."

The enormous snake angled its head toward me as I approached. Eyes the size of my head put on a good show of not being able to look at me, which was confirmation enough. Miller was in there, and he was ashamed.

"You saved our lives." I walked right up to him, projecting confidence. "I don't know what I would have done if you hadn't stepped in when you did." Upon closer inspection, I noticed each delicate scale was about the size of my hand. "Thank you."

Miller's head drooped on his muscular neck.

A memory surfaced of the night we located Angel Claremont, the kidnap victim who started it all. The naked longing in Miller's gaze when Thom revealed himself to me had made me ache then, and I hurt for him now. He wasn't majestic like Cole or adorable like Thom, nor was he beautiful like Wu. But he wasn't the grotesque he imagined himself to be, and it was time he accepted that.

Behind me, air stirred as Wu thrust his wings. Miller's tongue struck the air, tasting, debating.

"I'm going to pet you now." I reached out, careful not to let my hand be a conduit for my nerves. "And you're going to suck it up and deal." I smoothed a palm down his side, uncertain what to expect and delighted by his velvety texture. "How are you this soft? It's ridiculous."

A rhythmic pulse started under my palm, and I caught Miller studying me.

"You can purr?" Nice to know Conquest stayed on brand with her coterie. "We're going to talk about this later, mister."

No. Damn it. He was watching Wu over my shoulder, and his eyes were dilating in a not-very-comforting manner.

Shit, shit, shit.

I played a low card. "Even Maggie said you were magnificent."

That got his attention, but it didn't stick to me for long.

Time to lay the full deck on the table. "You can't eat Wu."

A ribbon of tongue lashed between Miller's lips.

"Seriously, he's my partner, and the best resource we've got."

Muscles flexed under my palm, and he started this side-to-side wiggle like a cat readying to pounce.

"Miller, no."

All that tension uncoiled in a strike that would do any death adder proud.

"*Wu!*" I screamed a warning, whirling away from Miller so he didn't crush me when he landed. Glass shattered overhead and rained down on me. All I could do was cover my head and face until the shower ended. The ground vibrated under my feet when Miller smacked the tiles, and I fell on my butt. "Goddamn it, Miller."

The snake looked smug.

I searched his mouth for feathers but found none.

"Luce." Wu's voice echoed through the food court. "Go."

That's when I put it all together. Wu must have struggled to break out, and Miller had fixed the problem.

"Okay, fine." I held out my hands. "You got me." With Wu safely out of the picture, we had no more time to spare. "Where are the others?" Miller angled his head in the direction of his tail, which was nowhere in sight. "Are you done clearing your quadrant? We've secured the mall from our entry point forward."

A shiver rippled beneath Miller's skin, and he made a rasping sound that came out pained. It seemed Cole wasn't the only one with an upset stomach.

"It's almost over," I promised him. "Let's go get Thom."

Retracing the length of Miller's body was surreal. His massive head filled the hall behind me as he doubled back on himself, but to the left was yards and yards of snake belly, and it grew more distended the farther we traveled. I didn't want to count the lumps that might have been heads or knees or elbows pressing against his skin, but I couldn't stop myself from noticing each blemish marring his sleek lines.

"Luce?" Portia marched over to me, scimitar in hand. "Where's Wu?"

"He's wounded." I scratched beneath Miller's lower jaw. "Miller saved our asses, and Wu retreated through the skylight in the food court. He can't walk, so he's going to hunt down stragglers from the air." I searched the other shop entryways for signs of the others. "Where are Santiago and Cole?"

"Cole is hunting for Thom." She glanced over her shoulder. "There's Santiago now."

Drenched in blood and grinning about it, he swaggered out to join us. He took one look at my hand where it rested on Miller and snorted. "Guess the snake's out of the bag." He thumped Miller on the tip of his nose. "Idiot. I told you she wouldn't care. You're the vainest damn charun I've ever met. Maybe this will finally let you get over yourself."

Stepping between them—like a giant snake needed my protection—I cocked an eyebrow at him. "I haven't seen your true form yet."

Santiago smiled, and it was ugly. "I'm shy."

Portia bit her lip so hard against a retort I worried it might bleed.

"Status," I snapped at him before he noticed, and they started bickering.

"The mall is shaped like an uppercase E. You and Wu cleared the lower leg and the hall leading up to this point. We've done the same for the middle. That means the upper leg is all they've got left."

"That's where they're keeping Thom." It must also be where Cole had gone. "Move out."

Santiago took point, and Portia fell in behind him. They moved like two halves of the same whole, their partnership a well-oiled machine.

I kept pace behind them, and Miller brought up the rear. That much of the building had already been cleared, but even if there were survivors, they couldn't very well get between Miller's coils to reach us. His body, doubled over as it was, clogged the hall until nothing could get past him.

The remaining Drosera had cleared out, falling back to defend the last unclaimed wing.

"Stop," a man barked. "Or I will pluck each of his feathers then use them to make you a hat."

We froze on the spot, Santiago and Portia shifting aside to give me a clear line of sight to where the speaker held Thom's small body aloft by a ragged wing. The other was broken, jutting out in front of him at a wrong angle, glistening bone punching through his fur. Blood slicked his fur and dripped onto the floor in a viscous puddle, and pain glazed his eyes until they failed to track our arrival.

"Release him," Santiago snarled, "and we'll make it quick."

"Retreat," the man countered, "and we'll let him live." He lifted Thom to eye level then sniffed him. "He doesn't have long. An hour. Maybe less. I'd make a quick decision if I were you."

Shouldering to the frontline, I growled, "What do you want?"

"You." His eyes gleamed. "What else?"

"Kill her," the woman beside him snarled. "Dead or alive, the reward is the same."

"Hush," he told her. "This one is special. The reward will be greater if she's still breathing."

"Release Thom," I said, cutting short their squabbling, "and you can have me."

"No offense meant, my lady, but no." He inclined his head. "I'm well aware of your prowess, even in this diminished form. Have one of yours walk you over to claim his body, and I'll have one of mine meet you halfway to escort you to my side."

Behind me, Miller shifted his weight, the rasp of his scales on tile rustling like corpse laughter.

"Luce," Mags begged on a ragged whisper. "Please, don't do this."

"That was low, Portia." I didn't look back, I couldn't if I wanted to finish this. "Santiago, you're with me."

"I hope you know what you're doing." He scowled down at me. "Cole will murder me if you die."

"Then you better not let that happen." I set out for the middle ground, Santiago at my side. "Take Thom and fall back."

"I'm not leaving you unprotected." He kept his face neutral. "Forget it."

"I won't be."

Cole was out there. Somewhere. I could sense him. Closing in on the Drosera from behind.

The ambassador for the Drosera passed Thom off to the woman beside him. Lip curled, she dangled Thom by the scruff of his neck. Once she reached us, she thrust out her arm toward Santiago. Unable to risk sheathing his sword in the presence of so many enemies, he reached for Thom the same way. The woman smiled, a cruel slash of her mouth, and yanked her arm back.

It happened so fast, I didn't get it at first. Not until Santiago wobbled like his knees might buckle.

Thom hung limp from his hand, but his broken wing was . . . gone. Ripped clean from his body.

The Drosera standing before Santiago used the wing to fan her flushed cheeks, and laughter rang out behind her. The man who had bargained with us winced, backing away from the cheering crowd. He must have been older. His actions proved him smarter. Too bad that still didn't make him intelligent enough not to pick a total moron to handle the exchange for him.

Ice spread through my body like a cancer, freezing me on the spot, and when I spoke, a white plume shaped the words. "You will regret ever being hatched."

CHAPTER TWENTY

Darkness swam before my eyes. Walls. I was in a small room. I shoved upward, and my palms sank into the plushness of a mattress. Panic swelled my heart, and I bolted off the bed. The frantic thump of my heart beat out a single name. *"Thom."*

"Here," he rasped. "I'm here."

Fumbling in the dark, I found my way to the bed and climbed back in with him. "Hey."

His eyelids fluttered, unable to rise, but his mouth curved. "You're in my *me* space."

Tears sprang to my eyes. "Thom—"

"Shhh." A wide palm wrapped my ankle, as familiar to me as my own hand. "Let him rest."

Eyes adjusting to the gloom, I could make out Thom's outline in the center of the bed. I had slept next to him on one side while Portia snuggled up to his other. Santiago lounged on the floor beside her, his head tilted back to rest on the mattress, and Cole had chosen to sit at the foot of the bed, guarding the door.

I noted another shadowy figure and identified Miller slouched in the far corner, using the walls to wedge himself upright.

"Come on." Cole rose, hauled me up, and led me into the living room. "Let me get you some food. Then we can talk."

While he puttered around in the kitchen, assembling a stack of sandwiches, I sank onto the couch. The bedroom had been so dark, I assumed it was night, but that couldn't be right. And out here, it was obvious a new day had dawned.

"What's the last thing you remember?" Cole sat next to me and balanced a plate on my lap. He carried soft drinks in the other, and he set those on the coffee table. "Take your time."

"Thom was missing." I bit into the first sandwich after he put it in my hand, and my stomach roared. I devoured it like I hadn't eaten in days instead of hours. "Wu escaped through the skylight." That part still gave me sweaty palms. I took my next bite slower. "I saw Miller. He wasn't thrilled, but he got over it."

"He associates his true form with his past." Cole popped the tab on a can and passed it over. "He finds them both hideous." He watched me polish off the first can then handed me a second. "Is that all?"

"No." I scrunched up my face trying to remember. "There's more."

"Don't strain." He noticed my first sandwich had perished and lined up another sacrifice. "I'll tell you."

"I get the feeling this isn't going to be happy news."

"Thom had been captured, he was injured. You traded yourself to the Drosera in exchange for him." He squared his shoulders, bracing himself. "They tore off his wing in front of you, and . . . you shifted."

The thunder in my chest rolled. "I did what?"

"You shifted," he said again, quietly, "and you slaughtered them all."

The hunger vanished, and I pushed away the plate. He captured it before it hit the rug and set it aside. "I . . . ate them?"

"Yes."

Feeling ten kinds of stupid, I pulled up my shirt and examined at my flat stomach. "How is that possible?" The full scope of what I had done smashed into me, and I shot to my feet. "I don't remember. Any of it. I ought to recall turning into a . . ." I had never asked about my true form. I hadn't wanted to know. It seemed so distant, so impossible, I dismissed it out of hand. But if I was at risk of exploding into that shape, rampaging without memory of doing so, I ought to at least have an idea of what I was up against. "Was I her or was I me?"

The answer was a long time in coming. "You were some combination of the two."

"Then why don't I remember?" I rubbed my face with my hands. "If she didn't kick me to the curb, how could I forget?"

"Human minds are fragile," Wu said softly, gently, like he was afraid of spooking me. I hadn't heard him enter the room. "They break so easily, and what you did would have shattered yours. I have a theory if you'd like to hear it."

I almost pushed the matter of what I had shifted into, but I was turning pro at ignoring things that caused my brain to stutter and smoke to pour from my ears. "Sure."

Cole gripped my hips and lifted me onto his lap. I curled against him, safe in his arms, and waited for Wu to get to the point.

"Your brain has a partition," he hypothesized. "The same thing that altered you when you entered this terrene built a failsafe into your mind. When Luce is in control, you're aware of everything that happens. She is your dominant personality now. She's the persona you revert to when the danger has passed."

I wet my cracked lips. "You're making me sound schizophrenic."

"You are, in a way." He rubbed a hand over his mouth. "The stress of your awakening is causing fractures, but it's not rupturing your core the way I feared. It's splitting you in two, giving you two personalities. One is Luce Boudreau. The other ought to be Conquest. The other *is* Conquest, but less." He gazed at me with what I hesitated to label as awe on his face. "You've leashed her. She can only do so much for so long, and then you snatch her back."

That sounded . . . not entirely terrible. "Does that mean I have no control over my other form? Is it hers?"

"Now that your body recalls how to shift, you might convince Cole to help you slide into that shape and test it." Wu dropped his arm. "I believe it's a mental shift, not a physical one, when Conquest surfaces."

That made sense given my access to the cold place had never been impeded by my human body.

"Okay." I blasted out an exhale. "I can deal with that."

Warm lips pressed against my temple, and Cole breathed in my ear. "You were magnificent."

"You would think so," Wu said dryly.

Needing a moment or ten to absorb what they were and weren't saying, I asked, "How is Thom?"

"I reattached his wing." The amusement slid off Wu's face to clatter on the floor. "I have a minor healing gift, as you've probably realized, and I could do that much."

So, his magic touch had a medical explanation. It should have relieved me of the guilt I felt when his touch sparked against my skin, but all I could think was *Thom, Thom, Thom*.

Tears welling, I swallowed hard. "There's a but in there somewhere."

"I can't promise he will ever fly again." He rubbed the skin over his breastbone, his mouth a tight line. For a winged charun, this must be akin to delivering news of a death to family members. "Additional treatments over the next forty-eight hours will fuse his bones and muscle faster than they could regrow on their own, but it will take months to build up his strength again. From there ... It's in his gods' hands."

"I never should have let him go alone." I wiped my cheeks dry. "He should have had backup."

"Thom is an experienced operative," Cole soothed. "He knew the risks, and he chose to take them."

"He lost a wing, Cole." I pictured his scarred face, his kinked whiskers. "What will he do if he can't fly?"

"He will adapt." He tucked errant hairs behind my ear. "He's a gifted healer in his own right, and his people are winged. This might not be a common injury for them, but it would have happened during dominance or mating fights. He'll know what he's up against, and he'll have ideas on how to treat it. Just give him time to mourn."

"Okay." I sank back against him. "As long as you don't think he'll do anything drastic."

"Thom is pragmatic." Cole tightened his arms around me. "He knows his own value. Even if he must wait until he returns home for treatment, he would endure. The knowledge he's collected is too valuable to lose."

Well, that answered one question. The coterie was aware Thom wasn't a permanent fixture, a fact that stabbed me through the heart imagining the day he left us. Having almost lost him, I saw clearly how it would be to go on without him, and I couldn't imagine parting with my friend even under happy circumstances.

"He agreed to act as our healer under the condition he was allowed to return home at a time of his choosing," Cole told me. "He never belonged to Conquest the way he belongs to you. He's your friend." Cole stroked a thumb over the banding above my elbow. Even through the shirt, it made my soul hum. "Thom was ready to leave after seeing Earth, that had been his goal, but then you . . . changed." He smiled. "The mystery proved too much for him to resist. He decided to stay on, and he hasn't left yet."

Unable to bear thinking on the topic any longer, I let it go. "How are the others?"

"Portia and Santiago are fine." Meaning so was Maggie. Physically, at least. "Miller is still resting. He needs a few more days to fully recover, but he can be mobile in twenty-four hours." He hesitated, debating a confession. "Maggie sat with him for a long time. She's never held control for that many hours. Portia was impressed with her endurance."

Hope and worry for my best friend clashed in the pit of my stomach. "How did the dogpile happen?"

"The coterie is yours," Wu answered for Cole. "They're drawn to you, and you refused to leave Thom."

"What about Sariah?" I hadn't spared her a thought since realizing Thom was missing.

"She's in her room." Wu glanced in that direction. "She's asked permission to reach out to a few of her contacts to gauge War's reaction. Santiago deferred her request until Thom was stable."

"He can track her movements and pull the plug if she attempts a double-cross." He spied on people with ease through their own equipment. Walking through the backdoor of his own tablet, he could do in his sleep. "It might be worth the risk."

"There's something else." Wu woke the screen on his phone and showed me a map. "Another body's been found." He zoomed in on the area in question. "Kapoor passed along the update. This one is the liveliest yet. It had to be restrained."

"That's who called." I had noticed him on his phone, but I

hadn't thought much about who rated an answer during an op. "How far is Redwood?"

"Twenty minutes."

"The bodies are being put into the waterways north of here," Cole said thoughtfully. "This corpse is more talkative because the taskforce is catching them faster."

"Not fast enough." Each life lost was one too many. "Do we have agents combing north along the river?"

"No." Wu cast me a withering look. "Why would we do something so obvious as hunt for a killer?"

"I've had a lot dropped on me." I huffed out a mocking laugh. "Forgive me for falling behind the curve." Heaving a great sigh, I shoved upright on Cole's lap. "It appears I've already showered." The clothes I wore were clean, and so was my skin. "Let me get dressed, and we'll go."

"Maggie bathed you." Cole followed me up when I stood. "I'll talk to Santiago and—"

"I want you to stay with Thom." I fisted his shirt. "He's back with us but . . . " I shook my head. "There's no one better than you to watch his back. Can you do this? For me?"

"For you." He covered my hand with his. "I would do much worse."

There was subtext here I wasn't grasping, a shift in his perception of me that made me warm and cold all over.

Magnificent.

That's what he called me. That's what he saw when he looked at what lurked beneath my skin.

I saw beauty in each member of the coterie, but I was vain enough to want him to find me beautiful. Full stop. That he did made my stomach do this loop-de-loop thing that made me thankful I quit eating when I did.

"I'll rouse Santiago and Portia." Cole glanced back at Thom's room. "They can help me put Miller to bed, and then I'll set Santiago to work on securing a connection for Sariah's recon. Maggie has been resting for a few hours, so she'll probably be ready to sit with him again. I'll do the same with Thom."

A peculiar sensation dragged at me, a sense of displacement that worried me more the longer I stared out the window. "How long was I out?"

"Three days." Cole palmed my nape again, and his heat radiated down my spine. "We all slept."

"Not all of us." Wu followed my line of sight. "I stood watch."

"Thank you," I rasped, "for protecting them when I couldn't."

"We're even," he assured me. "Miller saved my life. I don't forget my debts."

We parted ways then, and Cole followed me into our room. He didn't say a thing as I stripped out of my pajamas. Panties and the matching bralette Mags had layered under my clothes kept me modest, but a flush spread across my chest and up into my face the longer he watched me.

All too soon, I had the black suit on. I didn't want to leave them. I wanted to huddle together, hide in this safe place, and forget the world outside this hotel while we licked our wounds and healed. "Get an order together, and we'll pick up food while we're in town."

The coterie would wake hungry, like me, and I had decimated the groceries.

"I can do that." He tracked me, the predator in his eyes. "I'll even text with updates."

"Keep spoiling me," I warned him, "and you might never get rid of me."

"I can live with that," he said simply.

Stupid tears pricked the backs of my eyes, and I used the excuse of needing to freshen up to retreat to the bathroom. A cold washcloth to my cheeks helped get my head on straight, but I wasn't fooling anyone. Let alone myself.

Cole wanted to keep me.

Maybe that wasn't love, not as humans understood the emotion, but it was a start.

Conquest might be shadowing every move I made, but I wouldn't let her have this. I wouldn't let her have him. Never again. He was *mine*. I wanted to keep him right back. And if Conquest thought she might slip her leash, she had another think coming. I would turn that sucker into a garrote if that's what it took to keep her hands off him.

Cole had earned his happiness. He had won his peace. He deserved to love and be loved in return.

And if I had to stitch the halves of myself together to be a worthy partner for him, that's just what I'd do.

CHAPTER TWENTY-ONE

Paperwork occupied me on the trip to the morgue in Redwood. Kapoor wanted to be kept in the loop, but Wu would rather run him in circles, so that left me to file the necessary forms. I took comfort in the routine, the clack of laptop keys, and the fact even world-ending powers couldn't save you from bureaucracy.

"We're here," Wu said to snag my attention. "Are you ready?"

"Yep." I saved my files and closed my laptop. "Let's do this."

The building resembled a plain brick box from the outside, but the interior was ritzier.

Wu stopped at the curved front desk and slid one of his cards across the granite counter. The secretary scanned his credentials. Her eyes popped wide, and her mouth fell open. A tremor started in her hands when she reached for the phone, and her voice warbled when the party on the other end answered.

"M-m-mr. Wu is here to see you," she stammered. "Shall I send him in?"

We must have been given the green light. The secretary gestured toward a frosted glass door that swung open at the press
of a button. She had an entire command center up here. Nice
setup. It kept the desk manned at all times. It also made me
wonder why that was a priority and what kind of facility we had
just entered. This was no county morgue, there was too much
shine on every surface, but Wu wasn't in a sharing mood.

"Please take a seat in room one," she said haltingly. "Dr.
Franklin will be with you shortly."

Wu didn't thank her. He didn't even look at her. He was too
preoccupied for manners.

"Thanks," I told her on my way past, and she attempted a
smile that slid off her thin mouth.

The frosted door didn't wait longer than it had to before
closing behind us with a cool gust of air. The hall we entered
was sterile enough we could have eaten off the floor. Six rooms
on alternating walls stood with their doors open. From a quick
glance, I could tell they were all identical.

Wu entered room one and took one of the seats pushed
against the far wall. The chairs were mighty cozy, so I opted to
stand. Besides, there was a metal slab taking up the center of the
room, and curiosity got the better of me.

I was leaning over the side, checking out this weird hook
thing when a second door hidden in the wall swung open, and
the woman I assumed was Dr. Franklin walked in. She was a
short woman, middle-aged, with pink hair that kept falling into
her startlingly red eyes.

"Mr. Wu," she said crisply, her accent peculiar. "You
brought a guest."

"This is my partner, Luce Boudreau." He cut his eyes toward
me. "Or, as she is more formally known, Conquest."

The good doctor wobbled and went down on her knees. The

crack was audible, and I winced. She bowed, stretching her body across the floor, her fingertips almost close enough to brush the toes of my boots.

"Mistress," she breathed. "I would have prepared an offering had I known to expect you."

"I go by Luce these days," I said pointedly to Wu. "No offering required, but thank you."

Slowly, the doctor rose. Confusion lined her face, and that had me wondering exactly what kind of offering she would have given me if she was stunned I didn't want one. Gold? Jewels? Nah. Nothing so tame. I imagined only the best would do for Conquest. Probably blessed virgins or small, plump children.

Wringing her hands, she wet her lips. "Would you like to see the body?"

"Yes." I smiled like her deference didn't creep me the hell out. "That would be great."

The doctor returned to the room she had entered through, and I stared at the floor, determined not to give Wu the satisfaction of acknowledging how uncomfortable he'd made me. I almost lost the battle, but lucky for me, she returned fast.

"Here you are." She preceded a gurney wheeled in by two men who shared her coloring. The body of an elderly man was strapped to the surface. His nudity made isolating the cause of death easy. He had been attacked by an animal or—to be fair—a charun, and it had devoured his entrails. Though his lack of guts didn't seem to be slowing him down. He twitched from his toes to his eyelids. "I kept him preserved as best I could with the application of low-frequency energy pulses to keep the brain stimulated."

"He's in much better shape than the last one," I allowed.

"You've presented us with a superior specimen," Wu said over me. "Please, do pass your notes along to the other labs. What you've accomplished here is remarkable."

Her smile revealed serrated teeth. "I would be honored."

Wu rose with fluid grace. "Can we have a moment alone with the body?"

"Of course." She ushered her assistants away. "I'll return in ten minutes."

"That will be fine." He waited until the door closed before he approached the body. "Place your hand on its chest."

Eager to get this over with, I did as he instructed. On contact, the corpse sucked in a gasp it used to fuel a string of nonsense syllables that caused Wu's expression to darken until I had to lock my knees to keep from bolting. "What is he saying?"

"The message is from Death." Gold washed his eyes, and they glinted like polished coins. "She wants to parlay."

"She breached?" I snatched my hand back. "How is that possible?"

Santiago had cameras trained on the site where we entered this world and sensors in the water. Any disturbance in the area would register on his equipment. There was no way for her to have slipped in undetected. Santiago was too good for that.

"She wouldn't require an intermediary if she was here," he pointed out to me.

I walked to the antibacterial gel dispenser on the wall and pumped a liberal handful. "True."

"The corpse was reanimated and reprogrammed, both hall-marks of Death and her coterie."

"Famine left her coterie behind, but Death sent hers ahead?"

"Only one person is required to carry a message."

"That little . . . " I growled. "Sariah knew. She's known this whole time and hasn't breathed a word."

"The decision might have been a private matter between the cadre, but she would have noticed an extra body even if she wasn't privy to the reason why he was there."

"Him?"

"There's only one person she would trust so wholeheartedly." Wu gestured toward the mumbling corpse. "Janardan, her mate."

"She sent him through ahead of her." That's what he was saying. "He's already here."

"So it seems."

"Great." He must be an all-around swell guy since he was using humans as Post-it notes. Scribble his message on their brain then dump them in the water. "Do we have a location?"

"We have a general area." He pulled out his phone and started texting. "That's all we need. He's going to be watching to see if we received the coordinates. He'll make contact after we arrive and he's had time to assess the threat."

"Why water?" Santiago was aquatic. I had figured that much out on my own. So were Drosera. It wasn't stretching the imagination to picture Death as finned or scaled. "I get that it makes our job harder. Pinpointing his location via body dump site is next to impossible without the message." But there had to be more to it. "What type of charun is he?" I backtracked. "Are they?"

"He is Iniid." He didn't glance away from his screen. "Death took his form after they mated." His lips flattened. "Picture a freshwater dolphin. Imagine it having tentacles instead of flukes. Add in seven rows of serrated teeth, like sharks. That's roughly how Iniid look."

"Who thinks this stuff up?" I paced the length of the room. "Are schematics for charun pulled from some book of nightmares?"

"You have a very narrow view of the world." He put his phone away. "Have you never considered how grotesque our kind might find humans? They're largely hairless, without scales or fur, claws or proper teeth. They're flesh. Nothing more. On any other world, they would be considered prey."

I wasn't falling for his garbage. "And yet Earth was the terrene chosen as a battlefield."

He had no ready answer for that. Earth was lousy with humans. Therefore, they must hold some value. I noticed he failed to mention how the species as a whole had survived by evolving their technology. From sticks and rocks to guns and knives to nuclear weapons, humans were a clever species. Often too much so for their own good.

Dr. Franklin rejoined us, and we made goodbye noises before leaving the facility. It must be backed by the NSB to be so well funded and so open in its charunness. They weren't even playing at being human past the lobby and receptionist.

"We have another stop to make before we return to the hotel." Wu guided us deeper into town rather than out onto the highway. "I would have given you more notice, but your forced resting period made that impossible."

I resisted the urge to squirm in my seat. "Do I get details?"

"There's a clinic in Yazoo City."

"Ah." I let my gaze slide out the window as it sank in. "You're taking me for my first exam."

"Yes."

"I wish you had told me," I said softly. "I would have liked Mags to come."

"We couldn't risk the interference."

"It's not like she would have wrestled you to the ground for touching me."

But she would have given him her best disappointed teacher look, which had quelled many a tiny rebellion amongst her kindergarteners.

"I won't be touching you," he assured me. "Our top physician was flown in to do the honors."

"They're all the same." I curled in my seat, resting my cheek against the cool glass. "They all want to peel back your layers and see what makes you tick. This one might have more degrees, but that's just paper on the wall."

The weight of his stare fell on me, and his hands tightened on the steering wheel. "This was the bargain you struck."

"This is me honoring it." I shut my eyes. "Nowhere in my contract did it stipulate I had to be happy about it."

Conversation died after that, and he turned the radio to a local news station.

The steady drone lulled me to sleep, and I was grateful for the temporary escape.

The Yazoo City clinic resembled every other doc-in-a-box outfit I had ever seen. The only difference being walk-ins weren't welcome. You had to chat with someone on the intercom and get buzzed in. The lobby was empty of chairs. No family or friends were encouraged to wait. The flipside, I guess, was they must expect to shove their patients down the assembly line quickly if they didn't rate seating either.

A fresh-faced boy who looked primed for his high school graduation manned the desk, and Wu aimed us in that direction.

"Mr. Wu," he said, his voice a rolling baritone that made me do a double-take. "Ms. Boudreau." His gray eyes sparked electric blue. "We've been expecting you."

That made one of us. "How long will this take?"

"Four hours start to finish." He smiled, and the effect was that of wax melting. "You'll be in and out before you know it."

A tremor set my pinky finger twitching, so I clenched my fist. "Yeah. Sure."

"We aim to make every experience as painless and efficient as possible, so you'll anticipate your return."

Uh huh. All girls just loved having their bits fondled by strangers and devices implanted in their bodies.

"Okay, I can't even pretend to bob my head in agreement with that. I hate doctors. I hate hospitals. I hate strangers touching me. Nothing you do will minimize or change that. Let's not pretend otherwise." I let a shudder roll through my shoulders. "Less talking and more whatever-the-hell you're doing to me."

The boy's expression didn't shift. I wasn't sure it was malleable enough to form three different expressions in the span of five minutes. "Follow me, please."

He waited for me to step up beside him before leading me toward a set of double doors.

Wu offered no words of encouragement. Just leaned a hip against the desk and ducked his head to avoid making eye contact with me.

Thanks, partner.

Rixton would have at least cracked a joke about me getting felt up without dinner first. Scratch that. He never would have brought me here. No matter how many rules it broke, he would have kept me from this sterile building with its sterile walls and sterile floors and—I cut my eyes to the boy—its sterile employees.

By some miracle, if someone had twisted his arm to get us this far, he would have come with me to stand watch outside the door. One whimper of pain, and he would have shielded his eyes with one hand while he knocked the doctor out cold with his other fist.

That's what partners did for each other. We looked out for one another.

"Please, enter." The boy unlocked a door. *Unlocked.* The room was a self-contained chamber with no doorknob or window or way out except through the opening he was about to close behind me. "The doctor will be right in." He indicated a stack of white and blue fabriclike paper. "Leave your clothes on the chair. The top goes on like a vest. The blanket is for your lap."

The snick of the lock clicking into place behind him spiraled dizziness through me.

I can do this. It's an exam. I've had a billion. What's one more? Nothing.

These people weren't like the human doctors. They were well aware of who and what I was, so they ought to get the job done with minimal fanfare. As long as no one started bowing and scraping while my pants were off, I would be fine.

I stripped fast and shoved my arms into the paper top, hating how exposed my breasts felt as I reclined on the frigid table. I flicked open the paper sheet and tucked it in around me, which was pointless when the doctor would rip it aside when they got ready to ogle my wares.

"I really, really wish Maggie were here," I said to the empty room.

A static click made me wonder if I wasn't being monitored. I didn't have long to question if I had imagined the noise. A door opened in the rear of the room, admitting an older woman with silver hair and a pleasant smile. They sure did love their seamless doors around here. Maybe it was a charun thing. Or an NSB thing? Either way, it was damn creepy to never know which way to expect company to arrive.

"Ms. Boudreau, I'm Dr. Lachlan. I've been assigned to your case, so we'll be working together from here on out." She pulled a rolling stool to the end of the table and sat, giving her a prime view of my real estate. "I hope that's all right with you."

None of this was okay, but I didn't exactly have a say in the matter. "Sure."

"Today I'm going to conduct a general exam," she began. "That means I'll—"

"Been there, done that, got the pap smear." I had to force my thighs to relax when her icy fingers touched my skin. "What else will you be doing? I assume I'm here for more than a general wellness screening?"

"I'll be inserting an IUD prototype we've had luck using on charun with similar biological traits." She got down to business, and I stared at the ceiling, wishing I was anywhere other than here. "The process takes less than five minutes." I jolted at a sharp pinch. "Your sister has responded well to treatment. I don't foresee any complications for you."

Selling Famine out to the NSB might have bothered me had she not been wearing my uncle the last time I saw her. As far as I was concerned, she deserved everything she got. And if they tested all their doodads out on her before implanting them in me, all the better.

The rest of the visit passed with about as much indignity as you might expect. It wasn't horrible, but it wasn't great either. Maybe I ought to be grateful that if Cole and I ever got past first base, or even to first base, I didn't have to worry about making our duo a trio, but it was hard to think sexy thoughts with a speculum cranking my downstairs open.

"We're all done here." Dr. Lachlan patted my knee. "You can clean up and dress. A nurse will be in shortly to draw blood and take a tissue sample."

"Great." I snapped my thighs together. "Sounds like fun."

Once I was alone, I cleaned up and dressed. Walking felt . . . weird. It's not like the IUD was big or anything. She had shown the T-shaped device to me before she got started, and it was about two inches or so. The sting at insertion wasn't a picnic, but that was no reason for me to feel like I ought to be waddling.

Raised voices distracted me from being utterly ridiculous, and I strained my ears to hear.

"Unlock this door," Wu snapped on the other side. "We have to leave."

"Her exam isn't complete," the boy soothed. "We're not allowed to open the door until—"

The hinges made an unholy groan, and the door started buckling under the onslaught of his fists.

"What the actual hell?" I muttered while pulling on the rest of my clothes.

"Sir, you must stop this."

"Open the door."

"I'm not authorized to—"

Ready to rock and roll, I braced for when the door came down. God only knows what lit a fire under Wu, but if he was coming in hot, I had to be prepared to reach for the cold.

The slab of metal flew open and smacked against the far wall. Wu stood in the doorway, panting from exertion. I had never seen him so disheveled. Not even during the raid on War's nests.

"What's wrong?" I searched the hall behind him, but it stood empty.

"We have to get you out of here." He stormed in, clasped my hand, and hauled me after him. "Hurry."

"Gotta admit," I panted, "you're scaring me here. Who are we running from?"

Wu didn't slow down as he said, "My father."

CHAPTER TWENTY-TWO

———◆———

I had known for a while that Wu had daddy issues. I assumed, from the way he spoke of his father, that they were estranged. Yet somehow, in my head, that hadn't translated into us breaking into a sprint to avoid detection. Don't get me wrong. I had seen Maggie pull similar stunts when she snuck boys home or that time she smoked pot in her bedroom and didn't want her dad—whose stash she had pilfered—to smell how she had spent her afternoon. But Wu was a grown-ass man, and charun were frankly terrified of him. How much worse must his father be that he would flee from the reach of the man's shadow?

"We're going out the back." Wu set a brutal pace. "If we get separated, meet me back at the hotel."

"Is all this necessary?" A stitch was gathering in my side, and my elbow ached from the pressure of him dragging me in his wake. "Can't you guys hug it out?"

"War is an echo, a repetition of her title that's forged her into the exact same weapon that's failed to cut down Earth in all her previous incarnations. She is unoriginal. Clever, yes. Brutal, certainly. Deadly, of course. But she's unimaginative. She might have a strategic mind, but the plays in her book have been used until most players on the other teams spot them coming from a mile away."

Funny thing. No one had given me a copy of the playbook. That might come in handy. Clearly, there were cadre manuals no one was forwarding to my email. "Okay . . ."

"My father is an original. They call him Alpha. He's a prime, one of the first of our species. *The* first, if you ask him. And who can contradict what no one else was alive to argue? He's the closest thing this world will ever see to a god, and he's on his way here to check on his wayward son. He wants to meet my partner. Any interest I show to a particular person marks them as a target."

That might have been nice to know before he assigned himself as my partner.

No wonder the guards at The Hole treated him like a god. He was the son of a self-proclaimed one.

"The NSB has a god on the payroll?" They had recruited one-quarter of the apocalypse. That took balls. But a god? Why recruit from both ends of the spectrum? Had Daddy Wu refused to smite on command and gotten himself dethroned? "If that's true, then why do they need so many charun?"

Why did they need *me*?

"Have you ever wondered what happens when you deify someone?" We hit a service hallway, and he powerwalked toward the emergency exit. "Tell them they're a god often enough, and somewhere along the line, they start believing it too."

"Okay, so your dad has a big ego." *Like father, like son.* "Are you ashamed of me?" I laughed at the very idea when he'd been parading me around like a frickin' trophy. "Afraid to take me home to meet the 'rents?"

We burst outside into an employee parking lot hemmed in by trees. A limo idled a dozen feet away from us, and a chauffeur stood at parade rest beside the rear passenger side door. Three beefy guys dressed to the nines stood around the car until each point had a body guarding the vehicle. They all snapped to rigid attention when they spotted us.

"This is a minor guard." Wu sounded relieved. "Father is still inside." He ignored the lot, the road, the cars, all of it. He led me straight into the woods. "We don't have long."

"We're abandoning the car?" I glanced over my shoulder, expecting pursuit, but the men stood where we had left them. "Where are we going?"

"Luce." Wu stopped on a dime, whirled and clamped his hands on my upper arms. "Why do men embrace gods?"

"They need to believe in a higher power, that everything happens for a reason. That death isn't the end."

"They also need a figurehead to receive their prayers." His hard gaze drilled into mine. "What do you think Earth prayed for the first time the cadre appeared?"

"Salvation."

"And who do you think delivered them from evil?"

"Your father," I said, stunned.

"We don't resemble angels," he spat. "Angels resemble *us*."

"Shit." A cold rush of understanding trickled down my spine. "He'll kill me."

That's what good guys—or guys convinced they were good— did to those they viewed as the bad guys.

"You're cadre." His grip eased. "He would only see a demon from a mythology he helped create."

"What the hell, Wu?" I broke his grip and stumbled back. "This was not in the recruitment brochure."

"My father sleeps for decades at a time, and most charun will never hear of him, let alone see him." He recaptured my wrist in a brutal grip then dragged me deeper into the forest. "He roused the day you were found."

"What I'm hearing is you knew exactly what was going to happen and chose not to warn me—" a stab of true fear pierced my heart, "—or my coterie. Are they safe?"

"For now." He skidded to a stop in a clearing and started stripping down to his waist. "We're flying out. We need to be miles from here before he turns his eyes this way."

"Make with the wings." I snapped my fingers. "Let's go, go, go."

A crooked smile made his lopsided mouth more inviting than it had been all day. "I thought you were afraid of flying."

"I'm more afraid of dying and leaving the people I love behind to fend for themselves." I walked right up to him. "You and I are going to have a talk. You owe me answers—real answers—and I intend to collect."

"You're right." He bowed his head. "I thought I had more time. Father hasn't been lucid until recently, the last year or so. He's still not clear-headed. That makes him more dangerous, not less. He won't wake fully until Death breaches."

When he opened his arms, I leapt into them. I linked my hands behind his neck, wrapped my legs around his waist, and kicked him in the butt with my heel. "Giddy-up."

Wu flexed his shoulders, and three sets of golden-brown wings burst into existence. He wasted precious seconds stretching, grimacing as if the confinement wore on him, before gripping me tight and rocketing us into the sky. I leaned closer, tucking my face against his throat to keep the wind from tearing at me.

"I am sorry," he exhaled into my ear. "For all of this, but especially for him."

The raw tone from him made me squirm after our moment in Greenville.

"I get you're damaged goods. We all are." I was starting to think everyone, human or charun, carried baggage waiting to burst at the seams. "But the only way this partnership works is if we lean on each other and not pull apart at the first sign of trouble."

"Wisdom learned from your time with Rixton?"

"Yes." I grimaced to remember how we used to fight. "We were a bad match to start. He was grieving for his previous partner, and I was a rookie. We didn't try hard to find common ground. We didn't work together so much as each of us marched toward our own resolution." Remembering the moment we clicked, though. That made me ache. "Once his wife stepped in and smacked our heads together, we got over the posturing and back-biting. We became a unit. We shared our work and our lives. He was . . . one of my best friends."

"I'm not human, and neither are you. We can't have the simple relationship you enjoyed. Ours will always be more complex."

"The sexual tension thing?" As awkward as it was to admit, Wu and I sparked. Just not as brightly as Cole and I did. I never had that with Rixton. I met him as a married man, and the side of my brain that measured compatibility with guys switched off after meeting Sherry. No sane woman could see them together and think she stood a chance. And he was such a huge pain in my ass, I never got around to checking out his. "I can keep it in my pants if you can keep it in yours."

"Just not around Cole," he said, and he didn't sound bitter just . . . resigned.

"No," I answered softly, hoping I hadn't hurt him. "Not around Cole."

That mountain was in danger of being climbed the minute its ice thawed enough for me to make the trek.

Wu lapsed into silence, his focus on the journey ahead, but it grew too deafening for me.

There was too much on my mind for me to hold my tongue. "Where are we going?"

"A haven where Father would never think to look," he said with a hint of his trademark smugness returning. "He doesn't know it exists."

A place Wu had taken great pains to hide, then. "Not omniscient then?"

"Much to his eternal regret, no."

"Excellent." I squinted up at him. "Running from an all-seeing god would have sucked."

Quivers raced in trembling lines along the insides of my thighs, and my neck was cramping when our forward motion finally slowed. Lifting my head, about to ask if we had arrived, I clamped my mouth shut over a scream as the familiar sensation of freefall caused my stomach to levitate above my head. The fear of plummeting thousands of feet to splatter like a Rorschach for him to interpret later had me tightening my legs around Wu's torso until he grunted, and my arms around his throat until he coughed.

Impact jarred us both, and he eased his hands over my hips to grip my waist and set me on the ground. Well, he made a valiant effort. I hung around his neck like a pendant while he fumbled with the clasp, namely my hands, which were woven into an ironclad knot at his nape.

After he untangled us, I stood there, panting like I was the one who had flown for over an hour.

"That was not as bad as I—" Throat convulsions sneak-attacked me, and I staggered away to be sick on a square of roofing tiles that didn't deserve what I did to them. Panting through the dry heaves, I angled my head toward Wu, who had tucked away his wings. "Please tell me you're packing breath mints."

Wu pressed two sticks of peppermint gum into my palm, and I popped them in my mouth. "Thanks."

Footsteps brought my head up, and I scanned the area for their source. We had landed on a flat expanse of industrial building. A stairwell gave the wide, open space its only definition, and a slim woman with flame-orange hair and fire-bright eyes waited for us there.

"Long time, no see." The grin she shot Wu was infectious. "And you've brought a friend. Hi there. I'm Kimora. Who might you be?"

"This is Anonymous," he answered for me, but not unkindly. "We seek asylum."

"Nice to meet you, Kimora." I finger-combed the windblown hair from my eyes. "Sorry about the mess."

"That's what hosepipes are for, right?" Fire sprang to life in her palm, and she wove the tendrils between her fingers. "I picked up on your heat signatures and came to investigate. That explains why one of them was so short. You were hunched over."

"Kimora," Wu warned, his eyes taking in her display. "Don't give away your secrets for free."

"The girl was climbing you like ivy, man." Kimora huffed. "I saw you come in for a landing on the security monitors. You're telling me she doesn't know who we are?"

"All I know is Wu flipped his lid, dragged me through a forest, then flew me wherever-the-hell this is."

"Dang it." She stomped her foot. "Do *not* mention the Firestarter routine to Knox. He'll ground me for a month."

The woman was early twenties by my estimation. "Knox is your . . . ?"

"Overbearing ogre of a father."

Father. I pinned Wu with a stare that rolled off him and splatted on the asphalt below.

"We're too exposed up here." Wu searched the sky. "We should get inside before we attract attention from the sentries."

"He's right. Let's shake our tail feathers." Kimora swooped in to loop her arm through mine, but I snapped out my hand and caught her wrist. Her incandescent eyes widened. "You're wicked fast."

"Reflex," I mumbled as I released her with an apologetic smile. "I don't do touching."

"Uh-huh." Calling me on my no-touching policy, she smirked first at Wu and then me. "If you say so."

Heat marched up my nape, a thousand fire ants in tight formation, stinging all the way to my hairline.

Wu had introduced me as Anonymous. Anything I said about how the coterie was the exception would give me away. All I could do was bite my tongue and hope Wu had a damn good explanation for all this.

"Welcome to the enclave." Kimora shoved through the access door and hit the metal stairs. "Hope you're good with heights."

Nowhere she led us could be higher than the level of this roof, so I figured I had this leg of our adventure in the bag. Wu indicated I should follow her while he brought up the rear. The configuration suited me fine. Between the two of them my odds of fainting and tumbling to my doom decreased exponentially.

The air inside the building was warm enough for me to regret wearing my blazer, and that was before Kimora put me through a workout climbing down six flights of metal stairs suspended from the ceiling with chains, screws, and prayers. As the space opened around us, the sensation of descending into nothingness increased.

Curious as I was about our surroundings, I kept my eyes glued to my feet, my focus narrowed to the next step. Not until we hit the concrete floor and my knees solidified did I relax enough to appreciate what I was seeing. Though soaking in the converted living space with my own eyes didn't help me make sense of what I was looking at exactly.

Catwalks crisscrossed the ceiling, so narrow I doubted the beams were thicker than the width of my feet if I stood ankle to ankle. Beds in varying sizes hung from chains at different heights, their sheets rumpled and used. Chairs dangled in singles and doubles, with small tables affixed to their sides, creating seating areas suspended midair. An industrial kitchen, multiple bathrooms, and a laundry facility filled the bottom floor.

The sound of hushed voices carried through the cavernous building. "Who lives here?"

Wu shook his head once, and Kimora clammed up for the first time since I'd met her.

Drywall framed in a long room near the kitchen, and Wu guided me in that direction. A long table occupied its center, with molded stools tucked under the overhanging lip. Unoccupied except for a short man with a brush cut who used his prosthetic hand, a gleaming silver contraption, to thumb through a folder. He lifted a finger to acknowledge our arrival, his lips moving over the passage he was reading, then he slapped the file shut and rose.

"Well, old man, you've got yourself in a pickle I see." Knox, I assumed, clasped hands with Wu, his grin exposing a mouthful of metallic teeth. "Otherwise, you wouldn't have delivered this fair maiden into my evil clutches."

Behind us, Kimora snorted. "He was clutching her all right."

"Sly dog." Knox slapped him on the back. "I didn't know you still had it in you."

"That's what she said," Kimora snarked from behind me. Her father leveled a bored stare on her. "What? It's a classic. You don't move on past the classics."

"Ignore her." Knox pinched the bridge of his nose. "I do."

"I'm heading back to control, where me and my sense of humor are appreciated." Kimora saluted her old man then winked at me. "After I rinse off the roof, that is." On her way past Wu, she patted his shoulder. "Don't be a stranger." The smile she shot me was as warm as her hair. "I hope we meet again, Anon."

"Same," I said, and I meant it.

Kimora bolted out the door and closed it behind her, locking us in with her father.

"You have a lovely daughter," I told him just to have something polite to say.

"Do me a favor?" He stared after her. "Forget you ever saw her."

Forget I ever saw this place too. That was the wish lingering in his eyes. He regretted me being here. He wanted me gone, but the damage had already been done. Now he was visibly weighing the harm in letting me stay against what damage I might inflict if forced to leave.

Whatever his relationship to Wu, this guy was in the loop. One look at the pinched skin around his eyes, and I had no doubt he was aware of who stood before him. He must trust Wu a great deal to have allowed his daughter contact with me, and access to his home and the people I had yet to see.

"I can do that." I tried on a smile, but he wasn't buying what I was selling. "Thanks for your hospitality."

"Adam brought you here. He must have his reasons." His questioning stare begged to know what those were . . . in great detail. "This is as much his home as it is mine." I got the feeling that was a warning aimed at me, a gamble that I cared enough about Wu to protect his interests. "That said, his presence is rarely a good sign. You being here . . . That's even worse."

With nothing to say to each other, we both looked to Wu for an explanation.

"I took Luce in for her exam today," Wu began. "Cadre pheromones are drugging in the right doses, and the direction of their influence depends on the foremost emotion when they're emitted."

"He means if you're pissed, and you start throwing that around, that you can cause a riot," Knox explained to me. "We've seen it before, and it's ugly."

"You're saying the reason the coterie was so affected during the raid on War's nests was because I was throwing off sex vibes?" I stared down at my uterus like it was to blame. "What the actual hell?"

Silver lining? The Wu thing— It might have been a heat-of-the-moment confession.

Amped up hormones would also explain why he thought his manly joystick of manliness empowered him to grant me his blessing where Cole and I were concerned when—*fun fact*—our relationship was none of his business.

"The IUD will help," Wu promised. "In addition to releasing progestin to prevent pregnancy, it will also secrete minute traces of a synthetic charun hormone given to females who wish to forego their heat cycle."

"You're telling me I'm going into heat?" Legs wobbling, I sank into a chair beside Knox. "Broadcasting sex vibes was bad enough. I don't want to project an open invitation to fertilization."

"Your body is essentially human, so no. The closest you would come to a true heat is ovulation, but Conquest holds enough sway with your biology that you're throwing off mating pheromones." He hesitated over his phrasing. "There's a reason Otillians breed like rabbits. Their pheromones stimulate their partners, and they're a fertile species to begin with."

A thread of salvation occurred to me, and I grabbed that

sucker with both hands. "Does this have anything to do with how War is basically a coterie incubator?"

Knox smothered a cough with the back of his hand. "The others recruit when specific skills are needed, but those additions are often killed prior to a breach. The rest of her soldiers are usually homegrown if you catch my drift. War, in particular, tends to favor numbers over strategy when backed into a corner."

Sweet, sweet vindication swept through me, and I could have kissed Knox on the mouth.

Don't get me wrong—Cole got me all hot and bothered. But the fallout was always so humiliating.

Learning Otillian biology had been conspiring against me this whole time, kicking out pheromones to tempt Cole, to begin the cycle of strengthening my coterie by adding members the old-fashioned way, exonerated me in a way I hadn't known I craved.

Yes, I wanted him. Yes, I'm sure that was easy to smell. But this? It explained why a few dirty thoughts here or there made my coterie wrinkle their noses at me like I was a teenage boy packing a can of body spray.

"Conquest is a collector." I recalled Cole telling me that once. "None of my coterie is related."

Point in her favor. She hadn't birthed a legion to do her bidding.

"No blood ties," Knox confirmed then shared a look with Wu, who shook his head.

"What am I missing here?" Temper sparking, I flicked my glare between them. "They're each a different species, and they each come from a different world. There's no way they're connected except through me."

And Conquest hadn't used her mojo to entice them to breed an army either.

"She's piecing it together," Knox murmured out of the side of his mouth.

"Her ears aren't that poor," Wu chastised. "She can hear you."

A lightning strike of understanding zapped my skull and jumpstarted my brain.

"Cole." Sitting wasn't working for me anymore. I had to stand. I had to move. I paced the room from end to end. "He's ..." I swallowed when my voice cracked and tried again. "He's ..."

Her mate.

"Otillians mate once in their lives," Wu confirmed. "They choose their partners with care since that form is the one they will wear for the rest of their lives. Affection has little to do with it in most cases. It's a strategic decision, one of the first they make after leaving Otilla."

Losing all my steam, I sank back into my chair with a slouch. "He didn't tell me."

"Can you blame him?" Knox chortled. "You owned him. For centuries. He was given a second chance when you caught amnesia. Why the hell would he own up to being yours when he could buy himself more time while you figured it all out?"

"Knox," Wu warned.

"What?" His metal teeth flashed in a grimace. "It's the truth."

Wu cut him a flat look I had been on the receiving end of too many times from my dad. It made me wonder at their relationship.

Knox chuckled under his breath. "Why are you here, Adam?"

"Father wants to meet Luce." Now it was Wu's turn to pace. "I'm sure you can see why I thought that was a bad idea."

Knox ducked his head, unable to look at me, and Wu wasn't faring much better.

Ah. Meeting was code for execution. Or worse.

"He's not usually lucid until after Death breaches." Knox

echoed Wu's earlier sentiments. "The oldest of our kind can set alarms in their brains for lack of a better explanation. Some are triggered by the passage of time. Others get pinged by fluctuations in magic. Ascension magic is a specific occurrence. It affects the atmospheric conditions of an entire world. Odds are good he would have sensed it and risen even if he hadn't trained himself to scan for global disturbances." Knox eyed me thoughtfully. "Do you think he knows you brought her here?"

"We're not dead," Wu said dryly, "so no."

Knox chuckled, proving they shared a sense of humor.

"There's one more thing." Wu plucked at his upper lip, a sure sign the magnitude of the favor he was about to ask sat uneasy with him. "Thomas Ford has been injured. He needs a safe place to heal."

"I heard about what happened." A grimness twisted his lips. "Hell of a thing. For him or any of us."

Nausea swirled through my gut as the memory of his wing ripping free whirled in a loop through my head. "Is that a yes?"

"She'll be able to focus better if she's not worried about Thom," Wu said to sweeten the pot. "He means a lot to her."

"All right, all right," Knox grumped. "He can stay."

"Thank you." I didn't recognize my voice when I pinned Knox down with my gaze. "But be forewarned, if you hurt him—directly or indirectly through neglect—it will be the last thing you ever do."

Wu bristled. "Luce."

"No, let her get it out of her system." Knox flapped a hand at me like I was a precocious child who had done something inappropriate but amusing all the same. "It's good that she's protective of them. The others would let their injured die or kill them outright. She's invested. That's a good thing."

"Good how?" Something in his tone, in the way his mind shifted behind his eyes, had me baring my teeth. "Thom is not leverage."

"Knox," Wu snapped. All he needed was a ruler to pop our hands for misbehaving. "Whatever you're thinking—stop." He looked at me when he said, "She would tear through this building, through these people, with her bare hands to get to one of her own. That's her as she is now. Let her gain more control over her powers, and she will level this place and everyone inside to reach her people."

A calculating gleam lit Knox's eyes right up until the moment Wu crossed to him and slapped him upside the head.

"Hey," Knox spluttered. "I can't help my brain. It does its own thing, and I do mine."

I blinked at him like that might pull his comment into focus.

"What he means is," Wu explained, "I've trained him to always look for an angle. It's how the enclave has survived this long. He's not always aware he's being devious, but it's easy enough to spot if you're looking at him. He has no poker face."

The scowl that cut Knox's face made him ruthless, but truth was truth. The guy was a blunt force weapon, a solider. I was betting any diplomatic missions fell to Wu or perhaps Kimora. He was the guy you called in when playing nice didn't work.

I kept my gaze on Knox. "As long as we understand one another."

"Your people are welcome here, Luce Boudreau. The humans you claim as kin. They are family to you, not pawns, and that gives me hope Adam knows what the hell he's doing." Knox put it all out there, and for that I was grateful. It was a bigger offer than putting up a member of my coterie, who could fight for the enclave if it came down to it. He was welcoming civilians, humans. That was a bigger kindness than I expected or deserved. "Plenty of families here are mixed. Your people wouldn't be alone."

Behind my eyes, I relived the burst of light as the shotgun blasted, the spread of blood across a faded shirt as pellets chewed up Uncle Harold's stomach.

Regret was gnawing me up on the inside over Cole, over the Rixtons, over the messed-up fate I had been dealt.

"Thank you," I rasped, grateful beyond words. "I'll keep your offer in mind if things go south."

A shiver rippled the length of my spine when I sensed Wu's eyes on me.

Sometimes when he looked at me, I imagined he saw me as an urn full of ashes on his mantle. It made me wonder what my plaque would say. Maybe: *Here lies Luce Boudreau. At least she tried.*

But this . . . This was an act of kindness bigger than I would have credited him.

There was a price, there had to be, but I would pay it gladly.

"The coterie will be worried," I told Wu. "We should leave."

He took a long look around, like he was reluctant to go. "What's next on our agenda?"

"We're going after Janardan." I stood to put me closer to eye level with him. "We can't let him keep murdering humans. We also have to stop the contagion from spreading."

"That's quite a list," Wu observed. "Is that all?"

I smiled weakly. "I would also like to not die or take any of my friends with me."

Wu gestured toward the door, ready to escort me back the way we had come.

"Adam?" Knox rose with a grunt then cracked his neck. "A word?"

Taking the hint, I left the men to chat for a moment and explored the downstairs accommodations.

"Hi," a small voice said from nowhere in particular.

"Hello?" I cranked my head left then right before it dawned on me. Up. Duh. A girl around the age of six hovered above me, suspended from what appeared to be a white silk cable.

"Cheese and crackers," I squeaked, reaching for her before my brain caught up with my hands. "Get down from there."

Giggling, she released the rope and dropped into my arms, a dead weight that buckled my knees.

"You're pretty." She traced a pudgy finger over my brow, and I noticed she sported an origami ring similar to mine, this one made from a dollar bill. "Mr. Adam brought you here. Is he your friend too? Sometimes he brings me presents. One time he even let me—"

"Lira." Wu sighed the name over my shoulder. "You can't dive-bomb guests."

"Mr. Adam," she squealed, struggling against me until I passed her over to him. "I didn't show her my wings. Promise. Momma said not to, and I didn't, right?" She waited for me to nod then made grabby motions with her hands. "I used these." She puffed out her chest. "Daddy says I'm half monkey. He tried to feed me a banana for dinner." Her nose wrinkled. "I'm not a dirty old monkey. Monkeys can't fly."

The kid ought to watch *The Wizard of Oz*. Those flying monkeys would blow her mind. Or, you know, give her nightmares.

Head tipped back, Wu examined the ceiling for signs of life. "Where is your mother?"

"Washing clothes." Lira curled against his chest. "I hung my dresses up all by myself."

"That's wonderful." He squeezed her tight. "I'm very proud."

The genuine affection between them started the gears turning in my head.

"Proud means I get—" she leaned in close and whispered so loudly it carried, "—chocolate, right?"

"One piece." He pulled a shiny cube from his pocket and pressed it into her hand. "Tell your mother to blame me if she catches you."

"I won't let you get in no trouble." Kicking until he sat her on her feet, she bolted in the opposite direction of the laundry room and called over her shoulder, "Bye, Mr. Adam. Bye, Mr. Adam's friend."

As we made our exit back to the rooftop, I digested what I had seen and learned. I got the feeling the purpose of our visit was multi-layered, and I was having trouble peeling them all back to see past what he wanted to show me.

"I'll answer any questions you have, but we can't talk here. It's too dangerous for us to be spotted in the area."

That worked for me. Back on the roof, I let Wu gather me against him and fly me back to a bridge that must have been in Vicksburg. I used the time to sort through the information, and I had my questions ready when we landed. Of course, they had to wait until I finished dry heaving, which was getting old fast.

I should buy stock in Dramamine.

"How is it Lira exists?" I leaned against the railing, and he stood across from me. "Kimora is old enough she might be the result of a mating prior to the NSB sterilizing Knox, but Lira is about the age of Maggie's students. That means her mother, whatever her relationship to Knox, should have been turned in if he was playing by the rules. Unless you're actively culling the enclave as well."

That seemed doubtful given that allies expected you to do things like . . . Oh, I don't know, not kill them.

"Let's walk." Habit sent his gaze seeking all the dark corners. "Moving targets are harder to track."

We set off, and I waited on him to spill his guts. It was only fair, considering I had spilled mine twice.

"You're not asking the right question" came his answer. "Think about what you saw."

The warehouse was a massive home with all the modern amenities that catered to winged charun. Knox was the leader, and the number of mattresses indicated the place slept at least a dozen singles or doubles, so between twelve and twenty-four adults. And then there was Lira. I got the feeling where there were two illegal offspring, there must be more. The real question became why a guy like Wu, who struck me as a straight arrow, would allow the breeding to happen unrestricted and unpunished.

Culling rang with the finality of a judgment being handed down, and Knox didn't strike me as a man who had answered that call. Wu was right about one thing: Knox didn't have a poker face. He lacked the necessary acting skills to smile and back-slap a man responsible for executing his friends and family.

That left only one explanation that made any kind of sense to me. The only reason I could fathom for exposing your loved ones to imminent danger was if you trusted the other party to keep your secrets at any cost, and the price of that kind of trust was most often cemented in blood.

Only one possibility remained. "Knox is a relative of yours."

"He's my great-great-great-grandson," Wu acknowledged.

I tripped over air and almost face-planted. "The enclave is your family?"

"Yes."

"These are your friends with young children." At long last the forgotten conversation had popped into my head and filled in the blanks. "The ones you mentioned over dinner that night."

"The relationship grows more distant with each successive generation." His voice lowered to a fine rasp. "They're family,

I will always view them that way, but it's easier for them to see me as . . . a friend."

"Why on God's green earth would you expose them to me? There had to be other places we could have hidden." I whirled on him. "What if the NSB questions me? Scratch that—what if your *father* questions me? Am I supposed to lie?" I punched him in the arm. "Do you have any idea how hard you screwed me over just now? I won't be able to sit without one of those inflatable donut cushions for a week."

The mention of donuts sent my brain skittering to Rixton, and I wanted to hurl for lucky number three.

What I wouldn't give for a normal partner with normal family and normal drama. Hypocritical? Yeah. So?

"I gave you power over me." He kept his voice neutral, calm. "Power is what Conquest understands best. I wanted to speak in a language she understood. This gesture sends a clear message to her that we are allies."

"I am not Conquest," I snarled. "And I didn't ask for this."

"Surrender is the ultimate form of trust," he said, ignoring me. "My fate—the fate of my family—is now in your hands."

"You are out of your everlovin' mind." I resisted the urge to stomp his insole to make my point. "This gift horse of yours is guaranteed to kick me in the mouth."

Bad enough he was willing to risk his family by allowing mine to bunk with them . . .

Goddamn it.

Tit for freaking tat. He wanted me to defend his family if his dad came knocking, and to win me over, he had risked it all. He knew after I put eyes on them, once I knew they existed, that a haven for my family awaited, I wouldn't turn my back if they called for help. Just as he'd known Knox wouldn't turn his back on me after seeing I cared enough to protect my people.

Forget Knox. Wu was the one whose brain was always spinning.

When my phone rang, I lunged for the distraction. "Boudreau here."

"Ms. Boudreau," a woman chirped. "I'm pleased to inform you that your father is awake and asking for you."

What would I tell him when I saw him? The truth? That his best friend was locked up in a government facility? Except it really wasn't Harold Trudeau. It was Famine, my sister. That his best friend's wife had passed? That my uncle bartered his life for hers and became a monster in the bargain?

No. Lies were easier to swallow, and I was the only one who would choke on them. I had to be a good agent and tow the company line. I had to let him accept the Trudeaus were dead. Full stop. Even if Uncle Harold's body was still kicking around in The Hole, there was nothing left of his partner in there.

"Thanks," I rasped. "Tell him I'll be there as soon as I can."

CHAPTER TWENTY-THREE

———◆◎◆———

I braced my elbows on the railing of the bridge and stared down at the water swirling below us. I knew what Wu was going to say before the words popped out of his mouth, and I didn't want to hear them almost as much as I was relieved he could issue an order I had no choice but to follow.

Yes, I was a coward.

No, I didn't want to face my father.

His heart would break, and I would be the one left holding the hammer.

"You can't visit him." Wu intruded on my thoughts. "He's hidden in the system well, but today proved Father is watching all clinics and taskforce facilities."

Grateful to put off grim duties for another day, I angled my head toward him. "That's how he found us so quickly?"

"He knows protocol. He helped establish it." Wu joined me in staring into nothing. "He must be tracking me, hoping to catch you." He tossed a leaf into the air. "No one is that lucky."

I cranked my head toward him. "He can track you?"

"Not me, but my ID number. It's entered into the system every time I access a facility. The same is true for all taskforce members. The receptionists we've met have used our names to search the system for the code to plug in our arrival and departure times as well as the purpose for our visit and who we saw."

"I bet it collates surveillance footage too." Meaning the computer attached our IDs to the videos of us taken from all cameras while in the facility. In some instances, it even created files and tucked them away for later perusal. When I caught Wu starting at me, I shrugged. "Santiago was griping about it after ..." I rolled in my lips then popped them out again. "Sorry, the rest is classified. Coterie business."

I wasn't sorry.

Wu didn't even do me the courtesy of pretending to believe me. "Your poker face is worse than Knox's."

"Maggie used to say I was the worst liar." The smug grin fell off my mouth. "She used to be right."

"She's still right." He forced a smile, but it had weary edges. "How do you want to proceed?"

The coterie had to be warned about the threat from Wu's father. Meeting with Death's mate also rated a mention. Even with Wu as backup, the others would want to be there, and I wanted them with me too.

"I'll call Santiago. His line is the most secure." And he checked my phone for bugs and other infestations routinely, so it ought to be safe enough to use. "He can get in touch with the others easier than I can out in the field."

"All right." Wu swept the sky with his gaze. "Let's get moving."

We left the bridge and headed for the city park where we found a bench sheltered by the trees to cut down on our aerial visibility. I dialed up Santiago and didn't give him a chance to be an ass. "Wu and I are being hunted."

"I'm putting you on speaker."

"Are you secure?" Cole rumbled. "Do you need an extraction?"

"Yes." The sound of his voice made me flinch, and I was grateful he wasn't here to see it. "And no."

I launched into a brief explanation of who and what Wu's father was and what he wanted.

Namely, all cadre heads served up to him on a silver platter.

"That makes sense," Miller said thoughtfully. "We suspected there must be a higher power than the taskforce in control of this terrene. There would have to be for this world to stand against the cadre for so long when there are no native charun, only the descendants of past cadre coteries."

"What are you?" Portia asked. "Not to be nosy, but we need to know what we're up against."

Wu mashed his lips into a flat line.

"Google seraphim," I told them.

My new partner cast me an incredulous look that said I had ruffled his feathers with the comparison.

"What? My uncle and aunt were very active in their church." I attended bible school with the kids from their congregation each summer until I graduated. I participated in the early years then stepped up to help the frazzled adults when they were short on volunteers. "Dad and I might not have spent as many Sundays on a pew as we did on the bench of his johnboat, but I'm not totally ignorant."

"Jesus," Portia breathed.

"Not exactly."

"We figured help was coming from above," she said, "we just didn't give the charun who came before us enough credit for creating their own myth."

"What is above this terrene?" Cole demanded. "More of you? A six-winged legion?"

"Seraphim—to borrow from Luce—are royalty. So, no. There are very few of us, at least within several terrenes of Earth. This is my father's territory, and no one in their right mind would challenge him for it." Each word felt pulled from his throat. He gave as little information as he could, but it still pained him to share. He was a man of secrets, and this plan of his—using me to help end the war for good—was unraveling him. "The elite soldiers guarding the next terrene are more along the lines of archangels. The infantry itself are more angelic."

A thought occurred to me that I had to put out there. "Did your father decide anything that ascended from below Earth qualified as a demon? As evil?"

Wu cut me a wry look. "What do you think?"

"I think he set the stage so that if humans ever found out about us, they would side with him and revile us on principle." I massaged my temples. "There's no good or evil?"

"I wouldn't say that. There's good and evil within all species, within each of us, within all of us." Wu looked like he would rather be having a root canal than this conversation. "There's no heaven or hell, if that's what you mean. At least not as in a physical plane of existence accessible by the living. Earth is the midpoint of . . . everything. The only difference between my kin and yours is we had to descend to get here, while you had to climb."

Uncle Harold would have had a stroke right about now. "That explains the myth of fallen angels."

"We have fallen," he said softly. "Some of us farther than others."

"You're telling me that if the cadre managed to claim this world," Santiago said, "we'd still have to climb the distance from Earth to Otilla to reach the pinnacle?"

Massaging my forehead, I glowered at him. "There will be no world claiming."

One nutso overlord was a nutso overlord too many.

"Yes," Wu answered as if I hadn't spoken.

"Fuck that noise," Santiago growled. "I thought this was the finish line, but now you're telling me it's just another starting block?"

"We have bigger concerns than breaching a new terrene," Miller counselled after casting me an apologetic glance. At least one person was listening to my free Earth agenda. "We still have to meet with Janardan if we have any hope of figuring out what Death is up to before she breaches."

"Someone's really got to tell that guy the whole waterlogged carrier pigeon shtick isn't working for him," Portia added. "Human corpses are smelly, for one thing. They're also—"

"Living, breathing people who were murdered so he would have fresh paper for his pen," I snapped, hating I lost my temper when I never had with Mags. *She's not Maggie*, I reminded myself, but it didn't make me feel any better. Neither did snarling at Portia for placing less value on the lives of those outside our coterie, a view Conquest had no doubt encouraged. I was willing to kill charun to spare humans. How were her values any different? "We have to put a stop to his killing spree if we want to control the contagion the victims are spreading. That's one epidemic even the NSB can't kick under the rug."

Cole entered the breach blasted wide open by my temper. "What do we do with Sariah?"

"Bring her along. Leaving her unsupervised is asking for trouble." I braced for the next admission. "One more thing. I also made a new friend today. He has offered asylum for my family among his people."

"We haven't come across any *friends* during our time here who could make such an offer and uphold their end," Santiago said, and the others murmured agreement. "How certain are you that he can be trusted?"

"I met with him. I've seen his home, what he's offering." I mashed my lips together. "I trust he can do what he says."

"It's Thom's choice," Miller said.

Santiago agreed. "I don't want him out of my sight this close to the endgame but ..."

"His wounds go deeper than his wing." Maggie lowered her voice. "He's grieving."

"Any inattention on his part will get him killed," Portia finished. "We can't risk him in open battle."

The coterie had nothing to say to that. Neither did Wu. Their wings were part of their culture, their identities. Without them, they were earthbound. Crippled. Though none of them would use that word.

"Bring him," Wu decided. "We'll ask him, and if he chooses the enclave, I'll deliver him there myself."

"No." I put a hand on Wu's arm. "His pride couldn't take it if you flew him."

"I'll do it," Cole offered, regret thick in his voice. "It won't be the first time."

"I'm going to knock his ass out," Portia decided. "He's not going to know how he got there."

"Good idea," Santiago agreed. "He's got a crapton of sedatives in his med kit."

A rueful smile threatened to overtake my face. Catching a case of the warm and fuzzies after hearing a group of charun planning to drug one of their own into unconsciousness was probably wrong, but I still loved them for it all the same.

With our plan solidified, we signed off and set out for our meeting with Janardan.

*

Considering the amount of effort Janardan put into snaring my attention, I expected him to step from the bushes along the river and shout "ah ha" or "gotcha" or the charun equivalent. Other options included an ambush, the use of sniper rifles once he got us where he wanted us, or an escort of goons to ensure his safety when he approached us.

What I didn't expect, even in my wildest imaginings, was the short man who strolled the river wearing a saffron-colored robe that belonged on a monk. Sun glistened on his dark skin, including his bald scalp. His eyes were a milky silver that made me wonder about his vision, but his steps were sure. I wasn't sure what to make of him, especially after he smiled at me . . . and seemed to mean it.

"Welcome," he said, his voice as gentle as the breeze swirling off the river. "I'm pleased you received my message."

"I did," I replied carefully. "Several, in fact."

"Lovely." He remained sincere. "You saved me the effort of sending another."

"I would prefer you not murder innocents, use them as stationery, then toss them in the river like trash in the future." *Damn it.* So much for keeping my cool. "Still, your methods on Death's behalf are more peaceful than those employed by either War or Famine, so for that I am grateful."

"My apologies." He glanced between Wu and me. "I did try more orthodox approaches, but I'm afraid my touch is rather toxic to humans, and there is no one I can trust for such a task." His lips twitched. "They say dead men tell no tales, but I've found that to be untrue. They are the most faithful of all messengers."

That explained why the cause of death hadn't been apparent. Though, to be fair, the labs would have isolated any foreign toxins given time to run proper tests. This nugget of information might also explain the secondhand illness affecting humans who had contact with the corpse. It also fingered one of the aquatic helpers as being to blame for nibbling the last victim. All I could say was I hoped it didn't get sick.

Wu noticed the look and eased closer to me. "What is the purpose of this meeting?"

"Where is Nicodemus?" A frown creased his brow to find Wu at my side. "What I have to say must be heard by you both."

A fission of unease accompanied his casual use of the name I had only just learned, but I locked down the burgeoning sense of foreboding.

"I'm here." Cole strolled down the path then veered off to join me. "How are you, old friend?"

"Hold up." I whipped my head toward him. *"Old friend?"*

"This world is all we were promised and more." Janardan raised his left arm to show off the smart watch strapped to his wrist. "I have seldom beheld such wonders as the human mind conjures." He laughed at the bauble then patted it fondly. "This is the end we foresaw all those centuries ago. There are no promises to be made now. None we have any hope of keeping. I'm afraid that means the time to square old debts is upon us."

The words punched Cole, hit him low and hard, and I wasn't sure he had sucked in a breath to recover before I demanded, "What does he mean?"

"I have long been the keeper of something that belongs to you," Janardan explained. "I vowed to protect it with my life in exchange for amnesty for myself and my mate when the cadre reached this terrene."

A shocked laugh burst out of me. "What could you possibly have of mine that's worth a free pass?"

"Luce," Cole rasped, tormented, as he reached for me. His

thick fingers closed over my wrists, drawing my hands against his chest, and through them I felt him tremble. "I can explain."

"Is this explanation going to include how you failed to mention Conquest is your mate?" I actually looked around like the words might have shot from someone else's lips, but no. I tasted their residue on mine. "War told me I was owned. A mating bond—is that what she meant?"

"No."

Casting my memory back over that night, he had seemed enraged to discover another claim on me, but I had been in shock, and a lot of what I heard then evaporated between that terrible night when I lost Mags and the next morning after I fully grasped my life was no longer my own.

"Otillians own their mates," Janardan told me. "The bond is only reciprocal if their partner allows it to be so."

Cole bonded with her. That was his secret, the source of his shame. Did that mean . . . ?

Had he loved her? Before it all fell apart, had they been . . . together?

Unable to breathe, to think, I started walking. Distance. I needed distance. From him, from this, from *her*.

A mountain loomed on my periphery, and in two long strides planted itself in front of me.

"The connection we have is ours," Cole growled fiercely. "I gave her obedience, not my heart."

Stupid tears clogged my eyes until I could no longer see him. He was being so careful with me, they all were, so afraid that one wrong word might crack the shell holding Conquest hostage. "I want to believe you."

"This is all the proof I can give you." He released me and thrust his arms out in front of him. "Will it suffice?"

The angry ridges encircling his wrists were exposed. Both of them. What amazed me most was not that he was showing them to me, but that they were healing. Not just from where Lorelei had brutalized him to harvest enough rosendium for the cuffs, but deeper. He had a long way to go before his skin smoothed around the bands, and there might always be scarring, but he wasn't prying the mark of ownership from his flesh. He was surrendering to it, honoring it—honoring *me*.

And I knew in that moment I would do anything, give anything, to free him.

Cole loomed over me, a thing he did better than anyone I had ever met, and his presence comforted me as I traced the warm metal with a fingertip. "You're healing."

"Yes." He shivered beneath my touch. "I am."

"What does this mean?" A thrill zinged through me, shot with anticipation. "For us?"

"I want you, Luce." He rested his forehead against mine, and his breath filled my lungs. "Be mine."

"I think we both know that's never been the issue." I laughed softly. "Be mine too?"

The first tender brush of his lips over mine had me smelling smoke. What little brain I had left sizzled and popped beneath the gentle pressure of his mouth. The brush of his tongue against the seam of my lips asked me to open for him, and I did, groaning at his taste.

"Always." He spoke against my mouth, his taste filling my head. "For as long as you love me."

A bittersweet promise that should Conquest ever wrest away my control, that this spark died with me.

"Charun don't love," I told him, and even I heard the sadness in my voice. "Not the way humans do."

"A human heart only has so many beats." He flattened my palm against his chest. "I'm not capable of a love so small or finite. What I feel for you can't be confined to the lifespan of a century. My heart speaks the language of eternity, and the name it whispers is yours."

Unable to see past the tears veiling my eyes, I whispered, "I more than love you too."

"I was wrong about one thing," he murmured, his gaze sliding past my shoulders.

A flush warmed my nape. "We have spectators."

Now that he had mentioned it, I felt Wu's gaze boring into my spine.

"Impatient spectators," he agreed.

"Come on." I stared up at him, my heart expanding against my ribs. "Let's not keep them waiting."

I led Cole back to where Janardan stood with his bare feet in the water. I smiled in response to his broad grin when they shook hands.

"This is what I always wished for you," Janardan said. "A true mating, one dictated by hearts instead of heads."

"You dreamed bigger for me than I ever dared, Jan." Cole did some complicated back-slapping thing with him then cupped my cheek in his wide palm. "This is Luce Boudreau, my mate."

The way he growled the word *my* left me lightheaded.

I might have thought I was dreaming if I couldn't still taste him on my tongue.

"I had heard Conquest suffered a fracture." Jan examined me now that he stood much closer. "I had no idea the host was so fully formed as to be her own person."

"There's more to Luce than a simple husk," Wu said crisply. "She is a person in her own right."

Learning Cole considered us true mates was less shocking than hearing Wu stick up for me as being a Real Girl.

"I meant no offense." Jan bowed low to me. "I am honored to

meet the woman who stole the heart of a dragon." He rose and exchanged a weighted glance with Cole. "I understand now, why you hesitate."

Meshing my fingers with his, I anchored us both for what came next. "Cole?"

"I struck the bargain with Janardan centuries ago. Conquest was still enamored of me then, and her affection was genuine. She granted me a boon for good behavior with the caveat it couldn't be used against her. I asked her to grant Death and Janardan immunity from her wrath, and she laughed. She was young then, and she couldn't imagine her sisters ever betraying her, or her betraying them. She agreed, and the deal was struck. She had no idea what I bought with her favor, and I would have died before letting her discover the truth."

Yet here he stood, offering full disclosure to me. He had come here knowing the outcome, or guessing at it, and made no move to prevent this meeting from unfolding. Perhaps he saw this as inevitable. Or maybe he viewed this as atonement. I wasn't sure, and I wasn't convinced I wanted to know, but we were here now. Another truth bomb was about to drop on my head, and there was no shelter from the blast outside of his arms.

A lump formed in my throat. "What did you need to protect, even from her?"

Cole gathered my hands in his. "Our child."

The world slid out from under me, and I hit the mud on my ass. "Our ... *child?*"

He sank beside me on his knees. "Our daughter."

A fracture blazed through my skull, splitting my head wide open, and memories oozed in.

"Atru, Atru," *a breathless voice calls.* "Atru, Atru, *Atru.*"

Hidden behind the planter, sheltered by its crown of fronds, I watch the small predator flare her nostrils as she homes in on her prey. Her head jerks toward me, crimson eyes as vivid as spilled blood, and she smiles.

She will make a glorious huntress one day.

"Atru," she cries in triumph, toddling up to me. Her pudgy hands fist in my skirt. "Atru."

Unable to resist, I heft her up and settle her on my hip. "Atruhadael."

Coiling her hands in my hair, she lowers her head and yawns against my throat.

The sun hung lower when I blinked free of the vision but not by much. I had slipped down the slope of the past, but I hadn't gone under. That had to be progress, right?

Turning my head caused dried mud to flake off my neck and crumble onto Cole's shirt. He cradled me in his lap, tight against his chest, and his mighty heart drummed in my ear.

Wu sat beside us, his hand on my shoulder, his eyes on my face. Warmth spooled into me from his touch, and I might have shrugged him off if I hadn't remembered his claim of being a healer. That shined a new light on all his past acts. Any show of affection might have been an act of mercy in disguise. I didn't have much pride left for him to spare, but I was grateful all the same.

"I remember." A thickness banded my throat and made my tongue hard to operate. "Not the girl, but . . . a memory of her."

"From when you blacked out," Cole said, more confirmation than question. "You told me you saw *her*, but you didn't say who." The torment edging across his features told me he had guessed. "We were talking about Lorelei, so I couldn't be sure."

A rubber band of thought snapped in my mind, and the memory of our conversation surfaced with stinging vividness.

"She wanted a child from you." A blade of agony twisted in my heart. "You looked—" like he might consider granting her wish, "—sad."

"Our species is rare, almost unheard of this high in the terrenes. Odds are she will never have children, and that is a pity." He stroked my cheek with his thumb. "The sadness you sensed was far more selfish. I see her, her need for a child to love, and I can't help but remember what it was to witness my daughter take her first breath, to hold her in my arms."

"I thought you wanted her," I admitted weakly. "That you might want to be with one of your own kind."

"Hmm." His lips skimmed my temple. "You've glossed over an obvious detail."

Learning I had a mate, that we had a child, had kind of blown my mind to smithereens. "What?"

"You were born Otillian." Heat curled through his voice when he rumbled, "You're Convallarian now."

Black spots winked across my vision, and I dug my fingernails into his skin to keep my eyes from rolling back.

Hold on, hold on, hold on.

Wu's grip bit into my shoulder, and the flare of pain helped center me even more.

"I'm a ... a ... *dragon*?" Mouth gaping, I let him take possession of my lips. "I can fly?"

"There's only one way to find out," he teased, his adoring kisses making my head spin.

"You still have to consider—" Wu interrupted our not so private moment, "—the price of Janardan's gift."

"Amnesty for Death." I glanced over at him. "What is her usual role?"

Thom once told me she tended to work alone, the same as Conquest. But he also warned that the rules changed with each world and that the first one to learn them won.

"Death is no less brutal than her sisters," Wu confided, "but she tends to be the least vicious. Death wins in the end, with all of us. She doesn't work too hard at reaping souls when her sisters are eager to deliver them into her hands."

A caricature of a grim reaper flashed in my mind's eye. "You left your child with her?"

"There was no other choice. She couldn't travel with us, Conquest and I were the only members of her coterie then, and I refused to leave her to be raised in the ashes of my city by tutors imported from Otilla." A sigh moved through him that lifted me too. "She would have been groomed to carry on your legacy. She would have been named the next Conquest."

"It's a hereditary title?" That raised all sorts of interesting questions about my birth parents. And it made me curious why Sariah wasn't the next War. She couldn't exactly be poised for her own reign of terror if she was already tagging along after her mother.

"It can be," he allowed. "It's rare for one of the cadre to mate so soon after beginning their ascension. The pregnancy almost killed Conquest. Otillian biology adapts quickly, but she wasn't wholly converted when she discovered she was with child. She was too sick to continue, so the ascension stalled out waiting on her to recover. Afterwards, she was eager to leave, and she had no qualms about entrusting the child to her own tutors."

"How is that possible?" Human pregnancies lasted nine months. Reptilian gestation periods varied, and that was the only point of reference I had for dragons. Boa constrictors, for example, are ovoviviparous. They give birth to live young. That sounded like what Cole was describing. If that was the case, the pregnancy might have only lasted four months. That would explain why her condition progressed too rapidly for them to risk moving on, but it didn't explain the memory. "The child I saw was a toddler, two or three years old."

"Offspring are rare for my people, and our world harsh. Each birth is celebrated as a divine blessing. Our children develop at an accelerated rate—mentally and physically—until they reach sexual maturity to give them the best chance of survival. After that, their growth normalizes."

A thought struck me, and it left my ears ringing. "She's an adult."

"That changes nothing." Bittersweet regret softened his features. "She's still our child."

An adult capable of defending herself struck me as more appealing than welcoming a child into our war, but she wasn't *our* child. She belonged to Cole ... and to Conquest. I wasn't sure where that left me.

"Your bargain granted Death and her mate reprieve from Conquest." I was thinking it through. "That means Conquest can't harm them, likely me too, and neither can the coterie. Anything else?"

Cole must have already been reciting the verbiage to himself. His decisive nod came quickly.

"All right." I looked to Wu. "The enemy of my enemy is still an asshole, but it will take a power to nuke Death if this bargain goes sideways."

It was a testament to Wu's quick mind that he caught on so fast. "Father."

"Got it in one." I dusted my hands. "If this goes south, she can be his problem. We'll hand deliver her to him. I'll tie the bow myself."

A slow grin spread across his mouth. "All right." He inclined his head. "Make your bargain."

"Atruhadael." I pegged him with a look. "It means mother." I studied him. "How long have you known?"

"Until you triggered the full message," Wu said, "I couldn't be certain." He shared a look with Cole. "The news about your daughter wasn't mine to share, but I would have if he hadn't been honest with you."

The threat to his family coaxed a warning growl from Cole, but he didn't tell Wu he was in the wrong.

"My brain is a minefield." I stroked Cole's arm, soothing him, while I spoke to Wu. "We're all trying not to step on the hot spot that makes me implode. I get that. I appreciate it even, but thank you for being willing to set off a few explosions when it matters."

"That's what partners are for," he murmured, smiling when Cole renewed his rumbling.

Yep. Hormones or not, fifty percent of Wu's attraction to me was in annoying Cole.

Climbing off Cole's lap, I searched for Janardan and spotted him sitting in lotus position out in the shallow water. Wu stood as well, but he made no move to follow us. This was coterie business—no, it was *family* business. "Do the others know?"

"No." Cole exhaled softly. "I was afraid she might be discovered and used as leverage against me." His lips thinned. "I was on polite terms with the other cadre mates. Though meetings between all eight of us were rare, Janardan and I struck up a friendship." A grim smile tugged up one corner of his mouth. "Conquest tried many times to cut him from my life, she hated the competition for my affection, that I actually liked him, but she couldn't afford to alienate Death when theirs was a true mating."

How surreal. Death and Janardan. Sittin' in a tree apparently.

"Death never blabbed to Conquest?" That was the most remarkable thing to me.

"She values Janardan too highly to risk the advantage on what promised to be our final battlefield."

"Why didn't you give me a heads-up that Death might be an ally and not an enemy?"

"I prayed the bargain I struck with them would hold, but I wasn't willing to risk you if Death had a change of heart. I would rather greet her with a sword at my hip and not have to pull it than meet her empty-handed and pay the ultimate price."

When he put it like that, I couldn't fault his logic. Better safe than sorry was my motto where the cadre was concerned as well, even if it still smarted to learn there was hope of a relationship with this final sibling when it was too late to prefer for such a possibility.

"Ah." Janardan made to rise at our approach, but I indicated he could remain seated, and he nodded his thanks. "You have come to a decision?"

"First," I said, just as calmly, "I have a question for you."

"Of course." He kept emoting serenity. "Ask."

"Why now?" I had my hands full with Dad, with hunting War, with managing Sariah trapped in my inner circle, not to mention the personal whammy of learning I was a mate and now a mother-type-figure-person. "What prompted you to reach out now when you've been here as long as War? She's been plenty busy, but you've just been . . . doing what, exactly?"

"Your suspicions are well-founded," he congratulated me like I had earned a pat on the head. "None of us can afford gifts for one another unless strings are attached. I postponed contact with you after hearing of your *altered* condition. I wasn't certain you would honor our bargain, and if you didn't, then I might never see my mate again. Rather than chance it, I waited and watched until Cole's behavior toward you convinced me you were trustworthy."

"That's when you decided to use humans as messages in bottles." The bite in my words didn't go unnoticed, but they only made Janardan smile more warmly. I got the impression my humanity enchanted him. "That's when the contagion started spreading."

"Just so," he said without a hint of sarcasm.

"I will honor the terms of the original agreement." And not one clause more.

"Excellent." He cast his gaze across the river. "I must ask for one final favor."

Cole touched my arm when I started to argue. "What did you have in mind?"

"I must return to the swamp to collect your daughter. She remains in Death's care, as there was no safe way to escort her without arousing War's suspicions." Janardan locked gazes with me. "You must stabilize the breach site so that my mate and our coterie may pass through."

"I'm not sure I can do that." A ball of dread lodged in my throat, and I couldn't swallow past the implications. Death's arrival would usher in the final battle for the terrene as well as accelerate the weather phenomenon sweeping across the globe. People would die. Charun would too. The potential for catastrophic fatalities hung in the balance, and I was about to tip us over the edge for the sake of a child who belonged to the man I loved and the monster in my middle. "I don't have great control over my powers."

Cole wiped away all traces of how much my answer mattered to him. "Will you try?"

"For you." I brushed my fingers down his cheek. "Anything."

Death was coming, one way or another. At least we could control this breach. That was something. It also indebted her to me. That couldn't hurt.

Capturing my wrist, Cole pressed his lips against my knuckles. "Thank you."

"Don't thank me yet." I turned to Janardan. "The task you've given me is a second favor, a substantial undertaking, and I must ask for a boon in return." A wisp of the cold place flavored my tongue. "In exchange for stabilizing the portal and retrieving your mate and her coterie, I want you to work with—" I almost said Thom and winced, "—one of the taskforce doctors to create a cure for the contagion you unwittingly unleashed on the humans."

"I am happy to end what I began." He spread his open hands wide. "I harbor no ill will toward humans."

Pissed he could say that with a straight face and mean it, I made the diplomatic decision to keep my mouth shut on the topic. There was no use alienating a potential ally against War.

"There is also the trifling matter of Famine's coterie." Janardan had the grace to appear chagrined. "Death gave her word that she would bring them through with our people. That was the bargain struck to allow me first access to this terrene."

"We figured." I massaged my forehead. "She wouldn't have left them without a contingency plan. We assumed she would expect them to come through with Death." Hearing it firsthand still sucked. "How likely are they to come through the breach swinging?"

"The odds are low," he decided. "Without a direct order from Famine or her mate, it's unlikely they will attack without provocation."

Low was better than high. That was the only good thing to be said about his reassurances. I would have to take it and hope for the best.

"We should get moving." I squinted up at the sky. "It's dangerous to remain out in the open for so long."

"Luce," he began in a halting voice. "Do not think that because I am kind that I am merciful. Betray us, and you will live to regret your choice as many times as my wife wishes it."

"Gotcha." I sensed Cole bristle at my side. "Janardan?"

"Yes?"

"Don't think because you're Cole's buddy that I won't go dragon on your ass and eat you."

With that, we left Janardan to make his arrangements, and possibly put on dry clothes, while we saw to our own preparations.

Santiago looked ready to spit nails over the deal we'd brokered. Charun hearing at work again. Moisture smudged Portia's cheeks, and her tears reminded me of the heartbreaking loss of her own children. How that had been the catalyst for her joining Conquest. Miller didn't look at us at all. He was too busy watching Portia, in Maggie's body, leaking. Honestly, he looked too panicked by the tears for me to tell what he was thinking other than he would have traded his right arm for a box of tissues.

"I hope you've got a plan," Santiago spat. "What you've agreed to is stupid to the nth degree."

Portia rested a hand on his forearm. "I would have done the same," she rasped. "For any of my children."

His unforgiving lines softened while Miller's hardened to diamond sharpness as his gaze fixed on the point where Portia touched Santiago. Maggie surfaced, and they lowered their arm. She winked at me and then vanished beneath Portia's stronger personality.

Leaving them behind with a weight on my heart, I trudged up the path to the SUV, to Thom. Never a fan of sitting still, he fidgeted even in his sleep. He curled on his side in the front seat facing the door and the open window. I padded closer and rested my forearms in the opening to watch him rest, to assure myself he was still alive, that the Drosera hadn't taken him from me.

"You smell . . . different." He wrinkled his nose, eyes fluttering open. "Chemical."

"Probably the IUD." I stroked his hair, and his expression smoothed. "I'm still here, still me. Promise."

"Good," he murmured. "I like you."

More than anything, I wanted to haul Thom into my arms for a spine-cracking hug, but he was still too fragile. That didn't spare me from recounting Knox's offer and waiting on the verdict.

"Hmm" was all he said in response.

"I've visited the enclave and met the leader. Knox seems like a fair man, and the facility is pristine. You could rest there, heal. You would be safe."

Physically at least. Mentally, I hated he would be living among a reminder of his loss.

"That matters to you." The intonation was wrong for a question. "It would ease your burden."

"I want you with me," I admitted. "I'm selfish that way. You've got to make this decision for yourself. If you don't, I'll keep you. Probably strapped to my back so I can protect you better this time."

"I miscalculated, and I paid for it. It happens in battle." He nuzzled my palm. "You're not to blame."

"We'll have to agree to disagree."

"I'll go to the enclave," he decided. "I need to heal, and you need to forgive yourself."

Not gonna happen. I should have been there for him. No. Scratch that. I shouldn't have let him go in the first place. I should have refused to let him handle the worst infiltrations back to back. Poor leadership on my part caused this, and I would never shuck that blame. I didn't want to in case I was ever tempted to make the same mistake.

I had lost so many people I loved, and this felt like another one slipping through my fingers.

"Okay." I sniffled, wishing I could blame the runny nose on cat allergies. "Your phone was trashed, so I expect you to take one of Santiago's tablets with you. We'll get you a secure line.

I want you to check in every day. Every single day. No excuses. One missed call, and I'm coming for you."

"It's for the best." He smudged the stupid tears I'd hoped he wouldn't notice slicking my cheeks with his thumb. "I'll be fine." His lips quirked. "And if I'm not, I know you'll come for me."

"Yes." A thread of steel twined through my voice. "I will."

Conversation sapped the strength from him, and he nodded off between one halting breath and the next.

Miller must have watched my back when I was too hellbent on seeing Thom to do it for myself. His neck twitched with the need to search out Maggie, but he sidled up to me and gazed down at Thom. The ache in my heart was mirrored on his face, and his voice scraped when he asked, "Where to next?"

"Canton." A fragile tightness spread through my chest. "We're going home."

CHAPTER TWENTY-FOUR

———◆———

Cypress Swamp hadn't changed since the last time we motored through it on the White Horse airboat. The difference was Thom's absence, which throbbed like a sore tooth . . . or a broken heart. Cole had returned from transporting him to the enclave and brought a second boat to hold our overflow.

I had never seen this one. It was all matte black, and its engine ran at about one third of the volume. It screamed *stealth mode*, and it might as well have a price sticker on the bow or a receipt for payment stuffed between the cushions. I could smell the leather seats and the burnt mechanical tang of a new toy being put through its paces.

Cole, Janardan, Wu, and I took the new boat. Santiago, Portia, Miller, and Sariah took the old one.

We glided through the water, cutting a familiar path through the spotted green duckweed right up to the tree with my found day carved into its truck. This area of swamp was under constant surveillance thanks to all the night vision cameras tucked high in the mossy canopy and the sensors floating in the water. Too bad I was about to negate the need for our early warning system.

A cramp tightened my gut as we coasted to a stop. Nerves or a heightened awareness of this entry point into my world, I wasn't sure. I unstrapped and walked to the bow of the airboat. "How do we do this?"

"We go in." Cole toed off his boots and socks. His pants disappeared next and then his White Horse polo. He stood there in skintight boxer briefs and dared me with an arch of his brow. "Your turn."

I lost the shoes and socks without a flinch. Pants were more awkward but still doable. The button-down shirt was harder to part with, and it only came off because I had gotten into the habit of wearing a form-fitting silk pointelle undershirt beneath my uniform. While I could tell myself all day long there was no difference between a bikini and a matching bra and panties set, I didn't believe me. Not until my fingertips brushed the hem of my undershirt did his gaze shift from me to Wu, who leaned forward in his eagerness to examine the *rukav*.

"Maybe I'll keep the shirt." It hit my navel and offered me the thin comfort of knowing if I drowned in the swamp, my daddy wouldn't see all my assets once they fished me out for him to ID. "It's tight and thin. I don't think it will slow me down."

Wu sat back, his interest thwarted, and began examining my initials carved in the tree.

Thanks to the IUD, or perhaps our chat, his interest in me was running cooler. More professional. Just the way I liked it.

I already had my hands full with Cole. Hopefully someday I would mean that literally. I didn't need the friction my weirdo charun biology added into the mix by tossing out pheromones like candy at Canton's Christmas parade.

Having a stranger dig around in my lady bits was never going to rank high on my awesome scale, but I was starting to feel grateful to Dr. Lachlan for giving me back this slice of normalcy. Cole and I were just starting to figure things out, and it was a huge relief to know that when he wanted me, his interest was genuine.

"Be careful," Wu murmured as I wrapped my arms around my stomach. "This is a highly unorthodox mission. Conquest has never backtracked to a conquered terrene. We can't know what the repercussions might be."

As much as I wanted to ask if his father had ever tried returning home, and what had happened, I chose to exercise a smidgen of faith that if I was about to do something totally stupid that would get me killed, he would step in and shoot down my plan. Since that hadn't happened, I considered his silence as his blessing.

Cole stepped up to the edge, and I joined him, our shoulders brushing. The air vibrated around him, his anticipation stirring up my anxiety. I wanted this to go well, for his sake more than Janardan's.

"I really don't want to get eaten by an alligator," I confessed. "It seems like a bad way to go."

"I'll keep you safe," he promised. "I won't even let the crawfish nibble your toes."

"You say the sweetest things." I laughed softly. "How will I know what to do?"

"Instinct." He clasped hands with me. "Go cold. Let that guide you."

Let *her* guide me. That's what he meant. While I doubted Conquest was PTA mom material, though she might be compared to War, her memory of the child was steeped in pride and affection. I was willing to bet she would want her heir back at least as much as Cole, if not for the same reasons.

"Here goes nothing."

Sucking in oxygen until my lungs threatened to burst, I stepped out over empty air. Water licked at my heels as I was swallowed down into the belly of the swamp. I sank like a stone, and that was wrong. I should have been buoyant, but the tug in my gut tightened the lower I plummeted until my feet hit the silty bottom.

Bubbles escaped from my nose and mouth, tickling my skin as they raced for the surface. There was no point in opening my eyes. I was too far down, and the visibility was zero. I would have to do this blind.

Reaching for the cold place was instinctive, the headspace impossible to summon at will, but I had to try.

I dug deep, recalling all the glimpses I had collected into Conquest's life, and used those to bring the reluctant chill to my fingertips. Slowly, at a glacier's pace, the familiar ice swept through my chest and dulled my thoughts into comfortable numbness until I was swept along, a passenger in my own body.

Through the haze, I knelt and swept debris from a metallic circle inscribed with peculiar markings that bumped under my fingertips. Hard to tell from this angle, but I estimated it to be three times the size of a manhole cover. As I ran my hands over the raised design, a low vibration started in my bones, a welcoming resonance that linked me to this object. As if it belonged to me. As if I had every right to be here. As if it recognized my dominion over it and this place. The sensation as I located the handle wasn't the same as when Cole or Wu touched me, but it was a close relative to the feeling.

Gripping the rung as tight as I could, I heaved with all my might.

It didn't budge. Neither did I.

Weird.

Despite the effort, and the flurry of oxygen bubbles fizzing through the water, I wasn't suffocating.

Weirder.

A dull impact rocked me, and I understood that Cole had landed beside me. He existed in this same peculiar pocket where breathing water didn't drown you and gravity had taken a vacation. His fingers brushed mine where they wrapped the warm metal, and I heard him say "I've got you" in my head, as clearly as if he had whispered it in my ear.

Weirdest.

With him at my side, I cut the tether on my hesitation and submerged myself in the cold place.

Fractals of ice obscured my vision, and the bite of frost expelled from my mouth when I started chanting in the fluid language the rest of the coterie spoke with such ease. The vowels tasted sharp, the words jagged. The Otillian cut my lips on its way out. I tasted blood as it swirled through the viscous water around us.

The tithe has been paid. The thought pinged through my head, but it wasn't mine. *Take what is yours.*

Fingers and hands and arms all coordinated to wrench open the hatch. Darkness waited below, fathomless as a night sky and twice as endless. Another world slept below this one, and the temptation to crawl through creaked in my knees. Conquest was an explorer, and she was sated on that view, but I—*Luce*—was mesmerized by the peacefulness of the void.

Instinct snapped out an order to plunge my hand into the abyss, and icy fingers clasped mine on the other side. A woman with black skin and the tail of an eel swam beneath me, her clawed hand tight where our skin met. Her face was a grinning skull, a punch of white in a midnight complexion. Her ragged nails drew blood that chummed the waters around me in her desperation to climb to a higher world.

"*Death,*" I mouthed.

"*Sister,*" she spoke into my mind. "*Well met.*"

Cole's arm struck out once her head cleared the seal. His meaty fist closed over her throat and squeezed with enough pressure to cause her eyes to protrude. "*Phoebe first.*"

Phoebe.

Familiarity rode the wave of recognition that this was the first time he had spoken her name.

Phoebe.

Sweet one.

That was what he named her when Conquest couldn't be bothered to think up one, so certain her daughter would claim her title, her legacy, if she failed.

"*Nicodemus,*" she hissed through needlelike teeth. "*I see you are well.*" Reaching down into the blackness, she hauled an oblong disc beside her. "*Is this sufficient to pay our toll?*"

The egg-shaped pod floated up to us when she released its handle. Its hull appeared to be carved from charred wood as black as her eyes, and it stretched half my height.

Either Phoebe was a contortionist who traveled folded in half, or she wasn't an adult.

Grief, love, and confusion splashed across his face as he captured the handle. "*You placed her in stasis.*"

Concern for him ripped through my hard-won calm, but whatever I had expected, it hadn't been this.

"*Yes,*" Death hissed. "*There was no other way.*"

The cold place frayed around its edges, and Conquest's hold on me began unraveling. Before that happened, I needed to know, "*Where is Famine's coterie?*"

"*Below.*" Her eyes searched mine. "*I promised them safe passage.*"

"*No harm will come to them unless they move against my coterie* or me." I held her stare as she watched me closely, curiously. *"Do you need any help?"*

God that made it sound like I was inviting her to invade my world, which, I guess I was.

"I find you much changed, sister." Death tilted her head at an angle that would snap human necks. *"I look forward to exploring this new facet once my people are secure."*

Cole hauled the pod to the surface while I watched the first of many more eels zip through the water. A portion of them belonged to Famine, and I felt their ink drop eyes on me. Following his example, I kicked off the ground and swam toward the surface. The seal pulled at me, unwilling to surrender me, and when I escaped its tug, darkness bathed my eyes once again, and my lungs burned for oxygen.

A dozen heartbeats passed where I was certain I would die in the same swamp where I had been reborn.

A silken body brushed alongside mine, nudging me higher much faster than I could have propelled myself. I broke the surface gasping for air and took the hand Wu offered to pull me over the side onto the deck of the airboat. Cole had hefted the pod over his head, too focused on his task to have noticed my struggle.

Panting softly, I collapsed near him. "Did you get nudged?"

Cole shot me a questioning look as he placed his burden down gently.

"That would be me." Santiago's head broke the water, his shoulders bare and his hair slicked back from his face. "I figured you might need a hand up to the surface."

Except a hand wasn't what I'd felt. "Thank you."

"I accept monetary donations as well as payment in highly illegal gadgetry." Santiago beamed. "I accept wire transfers, or you can just pat Wu down. I'm cool either way."

The glare Wu shot Santiago belonged on a playground between two boys who didn't want to share their super cool next gen toys.

Mildly surprised, I grinned at Santiago. "Thanks for having my back."

"I was checking the ADCP and noticed you flailing. You were close to one of my lines, so I figured it would save me a future headache to bring you up before you wrecked all my hard work. You're welcome for me saving your life."

While that sounded more likely than an act of altruism on his part, I chose to be grateful all the same.

"Maybe you ought to head back down and monitor the situation." I rounded my eyes like a terrible thought had occurred to me. "Who knows how many of those Iniids will pour out of the seal? The whole pod could get tangled in your cables, and you'd be out here for *weeks* fixing it all."

Much to my amusement, Santiago clutched at the heart I wasn't convinced he had and vanished.

"That was cruel," Portia chided between snorted laughter from the other boat.

"Come on," I called back to her. "It was at least a little funny."

Behind me, Janardan had gone predator-still, his silvery eyes devouring the dark corners of the swamp.

"Every life sparks with its own energy, some brighter than others." He brought his arm up where I could see the hairs standing on end. "I'm crackling with it."

A chill seeped into my bones. An influx of energy could mean several things. None of them good when you were floating over a breach site like sitting ducks. Though his sensitivity to lifeforce might explain his connection to Death. Opposites attract and all that. "Miller, can you check the traps?"

Quick as a flash, he retrieved the laptop the coterie kept tucked in a dry compartment and got to work.

"I'm not picking up any signs of a disturbance." He tapped a few keys. "The camera feeds are normal." A few more clicks had the color draining from his face. "They're too normal." He stood in a rush, and the laptop thudded onto the deck. "We've been hacked. The feed's running on a loop."

"You said War wasn't tech-savvy," I snapped at Sariah as I scanned the area for signs of the disturbance Janardan was registering. "Are you shitting me right now?"

"What? No." Her mouth thinned at my accusation. "She must have recruited for the job."

That smacked of advanced planning when War couldn't have known about tonight without an inside man.

"Remember Janardan? Death's mate? The guy you knew about all along but didn't say boo to us?"

"That's different," she protested. "You didn't ask."

"There were other charun working with War's coterie in Alexandria," Miller reminded me, his puckered expression confession enough that he wasn't thrilled to come to her rescue. "She might be telling the truth."

"Hello?" She lifted her arms and rattled her bangles. "What choice do I have?"

Honesty wasn't a side effect of wearing the bangles, at least not without me demanding it from her, but I wasn't about to admit that if she thought otherwise. Especially not when she was already applying logic to get around telling us the whole truth.

A dozen skeletal heads floated in the waters surrounding us, summoned by Janardan's tone.

How many of them must be Death's children? And what did procreation mean for her, exactly?

I looked to the pod containing Phoebe, to my own coterie, and experienced an uncomfortable revelation.

Fertility was not an issue among the cadre. They bred like

rabbits and let their children run into snares for them. But Conquest ... She only birthed one child, a daughter, her legacy, and she left Phoebe behind on her father's terrene where she would be safe. A nod to his culture as well as hers? The rest of her coterie were recruited on different worlds, all of them outcasts or damaged in some way. She had collected her motley crew with a deliberateness that spoke of her intention to keep them. She had created what I had inherited—a found family.

The uncomfortable acknowledgement that she must have loved Cole, in her way, that she must have refused to twist the knife in his heart a second time with a second child, didn't make her any less of a monster or her crimes any more forgivable. But it did give me a new stick with which to measure her against her siblings.

The boat rose under my feet on a gentle swell that had my stomach cramping. I recognized the sensation, as if the water level in the swamp was on the rise.

"War." I met Cole's eyes as understanding flooded them. "If not her, then her coterie."

Janardan swung his head toward me. "We have no quarrel with her."

"She wants me," I confessed. "Since she can't have me, she wants me dead."

"I must locate my mate." He stood and stripped, leaving a mound of colorful fabric puddled around his ankles. "She has yet to surface and must not be caught unawares."

The water welcomed Janardan without a splash. He vanished from sight, and several of the skulls did too. For once, I was thrilled about charun taking on human aspects. We needed a way to tell the coteries apart stat.

Assuming these were emocarre and not viscarre, that is. Cohabitating with humans was fine, so long as the symbiotic contract between charun and host was spelled out for them. Parasites, however, would present an issue for me.

I should have asked, but my brain was punch-drunk on the influx of fresh information, and I was still reeling from the overload. I hoped I gave the appearance of knowing what the hell I was doing, because one look at Cole and that pod caused the world to drop out from under my feet.

I'm someone's mate.

I'm someone's mother.

Shut up, brain. Now is not the time.

It never seemed to be, but oh well. War wasn't exactly taking scheduling suggestions.

The screams didn't register at first. The species Death's coterie had emulated was too alien for me to do more than wince as brain-melting shrieks ricocheted through my skull. The blood clouding the water as it churned in a feeding frenzy was easier to recognize, and it set my heart galloping.

"Protect her," Cole barked as he touched the pod. "I'm going to check on Janardan."

"Cole—" I bit the inside of my cheek as his head disappeared. "Goddamn it."

A sleek Drosera surfaced three yards away, its eyes pinned on Cole's back.

I unsheathed the falchion and leapt in after him, no thought required.

The water slowed me down, muted my force, but not so much I couldn't shove the blade through the bottom jaw of the super gator who dared hunt him. The tip shone where it emerged through its thick skull. I shoved its twitchy corpse aside where two others nosed it with interest.

All too soon their attention shifted toward me. I slashed at them while I backpedaled. Across the way, Miller hit the water, carving through super gators, and met me halfway. He escorted me back to the stealth airboat and joined me onboard. I spun to search out the other boat and found Portia glaring a hole through his spine.

Without Santiago at her back, Miller had clearly grounded Maggie. As much as I sympathized with Portia's frustration, I agreed with the call. And not just because it protected my best friend from what prowled beneath the boats, scraping the undersides with their armored hides.

Standing on the deck made me an easy target, but I was worthless in the water. Even if I could access the dragon under my skin, she wouldn't be much help down here. This wasn't the time or the place to test the theory that I *might* be able to shift and *might* be able to hold onto my inner charun. There was too much at stake.

But Cole was down there. He hadn't come up yet. Neither had Janardan. Neither had Death.

"This rescue mission went to hell in a handbasket." I looked to Miller and Wu. "Ideas?"

"I'll secure the area around the boats until Cole and Santiago return." Miller, already soaked, kept his clothes on as he reentered the water. He stared at Portia, but I knew he saw Maggie. "Keep her safe."

"I will," I promised as the enormous snake burst from his skin. His dusky coils surfaced in the water as he swam menacing circles around us. I cranked my head toward Wu. "Are you waiting on an engraved invitation or what?"

"I'm not leaving you alone." He shrugged out of his jacket and shirt, leaving himself bare from the waist up in case we needed an emergency exit. "You can't take on all of them. Water is the natural habitat for Drosera and Iniids. We can't let them trap us out there where they hold the advantage."

Portia, Maggie, and Sariah in one boat, Wu and me in the other. Still not great odds.

"We're sitting ducks if we stay here." Wu could fly out, but not with all of us. I would strap Maggie to him if it came down to it, and Portia would have to deal. "Portia and Maggie are as vulnerable as we are without a charun form."

Portia was all human. More strength, better reflexes, but that was about it. No inner monster lurked within her. That was her job. She was Maggie's inner monster now.

And then there was the pod we had to prevent becoming a coffin.

Commotion shot our gazes to the water, and I spat every curse word I knew and some I might have invented on the spot. Thank God Dad wasn't here, or I would have been tasting soap for months.

War rose from the swamp, riding a massive Drosera sidesaddle. Its scarred sides heaved, and ravenous hunger burned in its eyes. She commanded the attention of all the gathered Iniids, and I knew what she was going to say before she opened her big, fat mouth.

Aw, hell. We were going to need a bigger handbasket.

CHAPTER TWENTY-FIVE

War had dressed for the occasion in what might have passed for a wetsuit if she had need of one. I was betting on it being a catsuit in a color that wouldn't show all the blood she planned on spilling while accentuating her curves for any male dumb enough to look at her twice while Thanases was present.

"Where is your mistress?" War cried, indignant, beseeching. "Where is Death?"

"Shit," I muttered.

"Shit," Wu agreed.

I cranked my head toward the second boat, expecting smug victory to paint Sariah's mouth, but the blood had rushed from her cheeks. For the first time in our acquaintance, she appeared young . . . and afraid. She kept the strongest emotions wiped from her face, but the tightness around her eyes told another story.

A reckoning was coming, a demand for payment equal to the loss of the nests we'd razed, and Sariah must have seen her death in her mother's eyes. She stumbled away from the edge of the deck and almost fell onto Miller's coils.

But if she hadn't outed us to War, then who betrayed us?

A good half of the skull-faced eels surfaced, hisses escaping their bony jaws that rose to manic screams. They thrashed, churning the water, and pink foam spittle gathered on their lips. The Drosera roused, a few snapping the flailing eel people in half with their spring-trap jaws.

"What the actual hell?" I murmured. "Are they all dead?"

The few not being eaten floated belly-up between us and War, who looked speculative. She had the look of someone who knew something no one else had quite figured out yet. Try as I might, I couldn't work what that expression meant, but since she wasn't calling the wrath of her coterie down on our heads, that worked for me.

Miller's broad head rose out of the water, almost startling a squeak out of me. I was ninety-nine-point-nine percent sure he was bigger now than he had been in the mall. Much bigger. Each rotation seemed to have caused him to thicken and lengthen.

Rixton would have cracked a joke about Miller being a grower, not a shower, but he wasn't here. And Wu wouldn't appreciate my gallows humor. Portia might, but it's not like I was going to call out to her. It was the kind of thing you whispered behind your hand, not shouted for all to hear.

Damn it.

Focus, Luce. Hold your shit together.

"Have you spotted Santiago or Cole?" I wiped clotted duckweed from around his eyes. "They're still down there with Death and Janardan."

The snake ribboned his tongue at me, which was no answer at all.

"Please tell me this was some type of acclimation sickness." I grimaced at the carnage. "That you guys aren't in danger from being in the water with them."

Miller studied the bodies, the feeding Drosera, and hissed in their direction.

Gotta say, it wasn't the most loquacious answer to my question.

Bubbles drew my eye behind Miller, and I leaned over the edge, fingers crossed.

The murky waters parted over Cole's head as he surfaced with Janardan held limp in his arms.

"Thank God," I breathed. "I was getting worried."

Cole spared me a soft look before indicating Janardan. "He's wounded."

"He's not the only one. Famine's coterie just kicked the bucket. All of them." I hooked my hands under Janardan's armpits, accepting his weight from Cole, straining to haul him onto the deck. Wu watched my back while I knelt beside him. "Shit to the third power. This is bad."

A Drosera had taken a bite out of him. His thigh was nothing but splintered bone and stringy meat.

Cole heaved himself up beside me and settled into a crouch, scanning the deck for the pod. The tension seeped from his shoulders when he spotted it safe and sound where he left it.

"Sorry, partner." Pivoting on my knees, I reached up and unbuckled Wu's belt. "He needs this more than you."

A scowl cut his mouth. "That's the second belt of mine you've ruined."

"You'll live. Without this, he might not." I used the leather to encircle Janardan's upper thigh, near his groin, and cinched it as tight as I dared without snapping the thick band. "How did this happen?"

Janardan hadn't gone all tentacled dolphin when he hit the water, so I had no clue if that meant he didn't want to lose his host, or if the injury was too severe for him to make the change. Though I would have expected him to revert to his natural form, not cling to this weaker one.

Odds were good that meant Iniids couldn't manufacture their own skin, or they would have started mimicking us already. No matter their designation, his coterie could shift. They would just lose their host in the process. To survive this world undetected, they would have to let go of these eel creatures regardless.

A high-pitched treatise drifted past Janardan's lips, ending on a series of clicks that made me wince.

Skull-faced bodies writhed in the water, sinking low and staying down until fountaining to the surface in the nightmarish configuration Wu had warned me about earlier.

Therapy would probably help with the mental picture. Maybe. I really ought to ask Kapoor for his guy's number. At the rate I was going, I was in for one hell of a psychotic break if I didn't get help gluing my psyche together soon.

"Join me, sister," War belted out. "Together, we can conquer this terrene as we have all that came before it. Famine's name will be our battle cry, and we will present her with this new world as a gift for her loss."

Ah. There it was. The reason she had kept her mouth shut when Famine's coterie started pushing up daisies. Or duckweed in this case. It had taken her a few minutes, but she had spun the loss into a gauntlet to throw down before Death.

"I stand with Conquest," Death screamed in her shrill voice that made my eyes water.

"You can't be serious." War drifted closer on Thanases. "She's a human sympathizer. This is not Conquest as you've known her. She thinks she's one of them. She's weak. How can you trust her?"

"Your coterie attacked Janardan without provocation. How can Death trust you? If you would kill him, what's to stop you from killing her too? Death would hardly be the first of your sisters to suffer at your hands." Cole raked his merciless gaze over War. "You set Famine up to be Conquest's first victim. You have your own agenda, as all the cadre does, but this was a malicious strike against your sisters. Death would be foolish to side with you when there's a better option."

"Peace?" War curled her lip. "That's your better option? Making nice with the humans? Bowing down to them? Hiding as all the remnants do? Pretending to be human when we're so much more? We deserve to rule, Nicodemus." Her glare sliced through me though she still spoke to him. "Grow a spine. End her while you still can. She won't allow her coterie to roam this world any more than she'll allow the charun in hiding to remain. She wants to give Earth back to the mortals." She pointed a finger at me. "She will be the death of you, all of you."

"Luce is my mate," he said, emphasizing my name. "I would be proud to die by her side."

"Remember that when she comes for your head. Fool. Love has blinded you. Such a weak, human emotion. You spent too long here, and this world has infected you. You are a disgrace to your true mate."

"I am his true mate," I snarled, the resonance in my voice multilayered as Wu's had been.

Conquest was speaking through me, I felt it, and I allowed it, knowing War respected her more than me.

Cowed by the slip in my mask, War turned her attention toward an easier target. Sariah.

"This is who you have chosen to follow?" she demanded. "This is who has won your allegiance? What of blood? What of family? What can she offer you that I have not?"

Their family dynamic made my head ache. No wonder Sariah was mommy's little sociopath.

"I am what you made me," she said, jutting out her chin. "I played the game better than you expected. That was your fault for underestimating me, not mine for fulfilling my potential."

Bubbles flurried through the water as a single laugh escaped Thanases.

Even War failed to conceal her flash of pride beneath her deepening scowl. She might be pissed, but she was also impressed.

"How did you know to come here tonight?"

Perched on one of Miller's coils, Santiago stood in a pair of skintight briefs I really wish hadn't been so white or him so proud of that fact.

"Sariah didn't tell you," he continued. "I had her farts under surveillance. You couldn't catch a whiff of her."

Portia snorted until I scowled at her, but even the reprimand didn't wipe the grin off her face.

"How did you know we were going to meet Janardan?" He paced down Miller's spine. "Scratch that. You'd be a fool not to keep tabs on him. The real question is how you knew to come here tonight."

War snapped her fingers, and a mammoth Drosera glided through the water carrying Lorelei on its back. She huddled in a ball with her arms wrapped around her knees. Her eyes cranked wide with terror when she cast them over Cole, and naked pleading sparkled in their liquid depths.

"This darling little birdie told me," she cooed. "I didn't even have to rip off her wings to make her sing."

Shock rendered Cole mute as he stared at Lorelei and then at me. "She must have followed me."

Dragons did stealth well. Better than any charun I had met so far. Hard to top invisibility.

"Go on," War coaxed. "Tell him what you wanted from this bargain."

"I didn't mean for this to happen." Fat tears spilled down her damp cheeks. "I only wantèd—"

"—for me to be unfaithful." A slow anger burned through his words. "You might stomach breaking vows to your mate, but I will not break mine."

While I didn't comprehend the mechanics of our bond, or grasp its full spectrum, or even know whether Cole could get physical with another person while we were together, I didn't care. How did the fine print matter when what he was saying amounted to *he* didn't want to be with anyone else? A vow he would never utter to Conquest, an admission he had just made—to me.

"For a child," she pleaded. "I have nothing of Convallaria. I wanted that one small piece, a remembrance, and you denied me."

"How did you imagine this playing out?" I tasted frost as the words formed. "Did you think if you got me killed he would knock you up over my cooling body?"

Fine, fine. That last bit spun out farther than I meant to throw it, but in my defense, Cole recounting how she propositioned him had fractured me enough to allow Conquest to seep through the cracks. If he had acted on her offer, and if she had shown up swollen with his child, I don't think I would have come back. At all. Ever.

I believe Conquest would have ripped me straight down the middle and made Lorelei regret having been born with ovaries. As much as she fought with me over control, over Cole, at least I was a sliver of her. Or she was a sliver of me. Our pasts and futures were so intertwined I had trouble picking the end of her from the beginning of us at times. Me, she would suffer under the illusion I was temporary. I didn't have to shout into the void to hear that answer ricochet back at me. But another woman? Another Convallarian? Touching Cole? Bearing his children?

Flickers overshadowed my vision, black spots danced in front of my eyes, and the cold place nipped at my consciousness, vicious and hungry and focused across the way.

"Your obsession with him disgusts me." War leaned forward, palms braced on Thanases. "I wish that I could blame your humanity for this disease, but the truth is Conquest was never the same once she saw him. All her desire to conquer, all that hunger for glory and thirst for power, got twisted up in her need for him."

The harder she tried to shame me, the more familiar the sensation became until I knew she had hurled these words at me, at an earlier version of me, many times. Each insult was a brick in the foundation of certainty that I was building around a theory, one I might never share with another soul, because who would believe me?

Way down deep, scraping the bottom of who I was and might be again, I had no choice but to accept the truth. Conquest loved Cole. But she hadn't been raised to know what to do with it. And she hadn't understood how to show it, how to protect it.

Instead of wooing him, she did as her training dictated. She saw, she wanted, and she took. At first the lack of reciprocation intrigued her, but over time her anger honed to cruelty, and there was no wound she could inflict on him deep enough to make him bleed as much as her heart wept each time he turned his hate-filled gaze upon her or bowed his proud head to follow her orders—no matter how depraved. His very resilience frustrated her until breaking him became an obsession she indulged at every opportunity.

Blinking free of those hazy-edged recollections, I yanked my focus back to our current predicament and away from the thin skin of memories coating the surface of my mind like pond scum.

"Cole," Lorelei pleaded, softer this time. "Please."

"You betrayed my trust." The muscles in his spine rippled. "You put my mate and my family at risk."

A sob hitched her shoulders as her reality sank in. Cole was not going to save her. She had dug her hole, and he was going to let War bury her. Despite the fact I was more interested in hating her guts than spilling them, I almost let it go. Let War remove an obstacle from my path. But that was a Conquest thing to do, and I might be picking up on her frequency more often these days, but I was still *me*.

Lorelei might not be an innocent, but I wasn't willing to let War play with her food if I could help it.

There was one more variable I had yet to pin down, and it took all I had to stop my eyes from rounding into saucers when I located her sweeping up beside War with the promise of vengeance in her eyes.

Death had yet to shuck her eel skin, the better to inch closer to her target using the minefield of corpses as camouflage. I don't know how War and Thanases missed the burning coals boring into their spines as she advanced. I felt sunburnt from here, and she was nowhere near me.

An understanding passed between Cole and me when he did the same math as me and found our missing cadre member within arm's reach of her sibling.

Behind us, Wu snapped out his wings, and all eyes shot to him.

The lust sparkling in War's eyes as she made some mental calculation had me wondering what she thought he was, *who* she thought he was, and how she could twist that information to her whims.

His distraction worked perfectly.

Death splayed a hand on Thanases's spine, casual as you please, and shoved her upper body out of the water. She perched behind War, draped one arm across her collarbones, and yanked

War back until her spine pressed against Death's chest, and then she ripped out War's throat with her claws.

On my periphery, Sariah clamped her hands around her own throat like that might staunch the flow of blood for her mother.

War's gurgled shriek roused no immediate help. Hands fastening over the wound, she couldn't slow the blood pumping down her chest. Her knees squeezed Thanases, but he didn't twitch an eyelid to zip her out of harm's way. In fact, his eyes . . . They were filming over as I watched, vacant as all things were in death.

Sariah collapsed to her knees, a keening moan dragged from the depths of her soul as comprehension dawned.

Her parents were dead. She was alone. All she had left was . . . me.

A quick scan of the surrounding area had me zeroing in on Drosera bodies floating lower in the water, bobbing among the remnants of Famine's coterie.

"She killed them," I whispered. "A half dozen Drosera, and Thanases, and she killed them."

That explained the leisurely stroll up to her sister. Death, it seemed, was an ambush predator.

I would do well to remember that.

"Traitor," War burbled. "How could you?"

"I warned you once," she said, then plunged her fist into War's chest, "that if you let your jealousy off its leash, and my mate paid the price the way Nicodemus so often has, I would kill you." A wet sound accompanied the sharp jerk of her elbow. "You forget yourself. Wars begin, and they end, but Death is eternal."

The pulpy mass of War's heart was clutched in Death's talons, and I couldn't stop staring.

"Sleep well, sister." Death took a bite as if from a ripe apple then tossed the remains into the water for her coterie to feast upon before easing back among the dead. "I pray that the bright hatred in your heart extinguishes, that you spend your eternity in peace, that you never again raise a hand or voice in anger but only know happiness."

Blood still wept down her chin when she glanced back at Lorelei, huddled in a quivering knot an arm's length away.

"Giving birth isn't a requirement for motherhood," Death intoned as the sleek tentacles belonging to her coterie breached the water around her, caressing her, and she stroked them back. "You would do well to remember that."

Tears welled in Lorelei's eyes, but she nodded then shifted on the back of her dead captor before flying away.

Death, escorted by her children, halted outside the protective ring of Miller's ever-increasing coils. He was like one of those capsules you tossed in water that expanded until the foam surprise emerged from within. Only those were finite, and this one—he was infinite.

"How fares my mate?" Her hands clutched at the water, a visible effort not to tear through Miller to reach Janardan. "I smell his blood in the water and on the air."

"He's stable," I said with more certainty than I felt. "Our healer was injured by War's coterie in battle." I gestured toward Wu. "He's done the best he can, but we need to get back to land, to one of the taskforce clinics if you want to save his life."

"The clinics are no longer safe," Wu reminded me. "Father will be monitoring them closely."

"What about Dr. Norwood?" Cole brushed his fingers down my arm. "His clinic is a half hour away if we leave now. Less than fifteen minutes if we airlift him."

"I hadn't considered him." I worried my bottom lip with my teeth. "He's trying hard to stay off the taskforce's radar, but he's going to be reluctant to leave the facility he's built." Ratty as it was on the outside, the inside was pristine and modern. He was hiding in plain sight and doing it well. "Do you still have his number?"

Santiago pivoted toward the second airboat. "I'll text him a warning we're coming in hot." He walked down Miller's spine and hopped onboard with Portia, who dug a phone out of the waterproof compartment. "We've tossed a lot of business his way over the years. He owes us this much."

"There's a doctor in town," I explained to Death before she decided that poisoning my coterie was the quickest route to her mate. "Cole can fly him there if you'll give us your permission."

"Granted." She reached out, stopping shy of Miller's sleek scales. "Please, let me see him before you go."

"Miller." I reached out and touched the back of his neck. "Give her room."

He did as I asked, and Death shot through the opening as if afraid he might close it before she got past. I offered her my hands, and her talons bit into my wrists as I hauled her onto the deck. She scooted toward him on her side, her gills flexing, and pressed her cheek against his. Their low conversation was impossible for me to decipher, but each caress telegraphed their love for one another.

After meeting the other cadre members, observing how War interacted with her mate and children, witnessing how unhinged Famine was—or had become thanks to War's machinations—I wouldn't have expected a sister of mine to have . . . heart.

"We need to move," Cole said gently. "Luce will bring you to him once you've assimilated."

Death bobbed her head then toppled over the edge into the water where she dragged in gulping breaths. Her fingers curled over the edge of the bow, crimping the metal, while she waited for Cole to shift.

After sharing a lingering glance with me, he slid from one

body into the next. His tail coiled around my ankle, squeezing tight and then releasing. Gathering Janardan against his chest, he unfurled his wings and leapt for the sky.

Movement among the bodies caught my eye. The remaining Drosera were huddling closer.

"Your mistress is dead," I told them, "and your master is too. You've got three choices as I see them. You can join us, you can turn yourselves in to the NSB, or you can die here and now."

"I'll take them," Sariah rasped. "I can control them."

A chill swept over me, a premonition that I might have done what War failed to do by making her daughter heir to her title, but I wasn't Conquest. Murder solved a lot of problems, almost as many as it created, but I had enough blood on my hands.

"Will they follow you?" Without a leader, they would look to the strongest among them. Sariah was that and then some. "Can I trust you to stand with us? Or will I have to hunt them down and kill them later?"

"I can't promise we'll fight with you." Her throat worked over a hard lump. "But we won't fight against you." Her haunted eyes swung to me then slid over to Wu. "You won't survive what's coming, Luce, but we might. If we keep our heads down."

"Thanks for the vote of confidence," I said dryly then gestured at her wrists. "The bangles stay on. For now."

"That's fair," she allowed, voice soft as a whisper.

Freed from War's legacy, Sariah had a lot of thinking to do about how she wanted to shape her future.

Assuming we all survived, I was game for letting her try to rehabilitate the coterie. But at the rate we were going, that might not be an issue.

"Take your people and go," I told her. "You've got twenty-four hours to gather the rest and go underground, or you're going on my shit list, and that means the next time I see you—or any of the Drosera—it's open season. I can't afford to have more enemies at my back, particularly ones masquerading as potential allies."

"I understand." She loosed a shrill whistle, and one of the Drosera approached. She propped her legs under her then stepped onto its back. "I'll touch base with Santiago when it's done."

"I'll be waiting with bated breath," he promised as he shot her a mocking salute.

All in all, she didn't do a bad job of saving face. And the coterie didn't put up a fuss. Eight, by my count, had survived to follow her. Some of War's best fighters had died here today, but War had others. How many I couldn't begin to guess, but I would bet money that Sariah knew each remaining nest and its contents.

Again that chill swept my spine, a foreboding that I had set into motion an unstoppable reaction, but I couldn't see my way to a better resolution. We needed the Drosera gone so we could focus on Death, her coterie, and her mate. As far as I was concerned, Sariah was doing me a favor by taking a third of the charun off my hands.

For the moment, I was counting this as a win. She still wore the bangles, and none of her coterie knew what they meant. War hadn't known to out her, or she would have demanded her release instead of speechifying about her treachery.

The silver lining here was, so long as Sariah wore the bangles, we controlled her. Through her, we controlled the remnants of War's coterie. That meant, with Death's continued cooperation, we might have just won this war in an almost bloodless coup.

I stood there, waiting for the relief to sink in, for the thought to manifest the reality, but a gnawing sensation in my gut called me a fool for thinking it would be so easy.

Massaging my temples, I put the most pressing question left to

Death. "What do you need to adopt a human form?" I gestured down my body. "Are you viscarre or emocarre?"

"I am neither." Death exhaled, a hitch in her breath. "I need a wider sampling of the humans to fashion a proper body. Give me that, and I can handle the rest." She gazed across the water at her people. "They require a . . . different . . . type of host. I will see to that as well."

Corpses.

The truth hit me with the force of a memory.

She was Death, the dead her domain, and her coterie were fashioned from corpses and given new life.

"Miller." I patted the snake to get his attention. "I need you to drive us out of here."

Between Santiago and Portia, the other airboat had a surplus of captains. This one, not so much.

"Offer them the bunkhouse," Portia called. "We can figure out someplace else to stay for a while."

Canton was home, and that made me an easy target for anyone who came looking.

"We'll need to clear out our toys." Santiago glowered. "Don't let them in my room until I get there."

"Follow us," I told Death, ignoring Santiago. "We have a safe place where your family can acclimate."

While Miller climbed on board, I went to check on Phoebe.

I sank onto the deck and rested my back against the seats. The pod was silky smooth beneath my fingers, the wood polished by time and touch. It was too large for me to haul into my lap, so I tucked it under my arm to hold it steady. A faint vibration reminding me of an egg preparing to hatch shook me, and I crossed my fingers that baby dragons didn't wake up hungry.

CHAPTER TWENTY-SIX

Though I hadn't lived at the bunkhouse long enough for it to feel like home, I did have fond memories of the week I spent there. More traumatic ones were sprinkled throughout, but that was life. This was the safest place to stash Death and her coterie, and I was happy to strengthen our bonds by showing hospitality. Even if it was odd offering them a home and support that felt more like the coterie's to give than mine.

Proving I had excellent parenting skills, I settled the pod containing Phoebe on our bed then propped a tablet on top after pulling up Netflix and tapping on a cartoon about a sponge wearing pants—I don't know. I wasn't really paying attention.

Answering my phone, and risking my day going farther downhill, held no appeal. But I couldn't afford to yank myself out of the information loop, not when the coterie was scattered. "Boudreau."

"Hi," a vaguely familiar voice breathed. "It's Jay."

"Oh, hey." I forced myself to stand still and listen. "What's up?"

"I wanted to thank you." He kept his voice low, a bare whisper. "Your friend hooked me up." Sheets rustled in the background, making me wonder if he had ducked under them. "He downloaded a portion of the video from the river onto my phone. He told me if anyone starts looking at me too hard to remind them the clip goes live if I die. He said tell them it will cause more trouble than I ever will."

That sounded like Santiago. He enjoyed the classics, and the threat of an info leak upon Lambert's death was textbook. Now I just had to hope the threat held. None of us could afford the video to go live when it would do a dead boy no good. "I'm glad he could help."

"I wasn't sure about him at first." He laughed softly. "He was so cold. Ice, man."

"He's a good guy. His people skills just suck."

"Good thing he's got you for a partner then."

The world's axis tilted a bit, and I stumbled to one side before catching my balance. "Santiago?"

"Who?" Faint static crackled on the line. "No—Special Agent Wu."

The surrealness of the moment was my only excuse for blurting, "Adam Wu helped you evade the feds?"

"Yeah." His next laugh came out sharp, like he might have done wrong by telling me. "You didn't know?"

"I have to go," I said when no other answer formed. "Keep a low profile. Call if you need us."

"Yeah." He sounded uncertain rather than jubilant. "I'll do that."

After ending the call, I dialed Santiago to save myself a trip up to his room. The curses drifting down as he packed his life into boxes weren't all that welcoming. "I thought you were working on the Lambert situation."

"I am," he bit out in response. "I ought to have him squared away tomorrow. That soon enough?"

"No need." I turned the situation over in my head. "Wu fixed the situation."

A snarl ripped from his throat. "If you think for one minute that he's better than—"

"It's worse than that." I rubbed my forehead. "He did it behind my back."

Asking how he did it when Santiago had scrubbed the video was a waste of breath.

"Either he's a double agent," he said flatly, "or he hasn't given up on getting in your pants."

The joke deserved a laugh, but I was in short supply. Wu was a double agent.

He worked for the NSB, and he worked against his father. He was already risking his neck for the charun his father wanted exterminated. Picturing Wu extending his neck a bit further on the chopping block to protect humanity from the charun too? The crazy thing was—I could see it.

I had no idea what it meant, but then again maybe I did. The enclave was a mixed community. Knox told me that much. Maybe Wu wasn't as stuck in the *human are cattle* mindset as he let me believe. The real mystery was why he would keep it from me. I would applaud him, and he knew that.

A sick feeling curled through my gut that forced me to acknowledge he hadn't likely sought credit for his good deed because Lambert might still be taken out. He must not want my thanks to taste like ash later.

"Luce."

Ending my chat with Santiago, I met my partner on the deck near the patio set. "What's up?"

"I just spoke with Kapoor." A phone dangled from his finger-tips. "The Hole is ... gone."

"What do you mean *gone*? It was a massive military instilla-tion staffed with hundreds of people. Those don't just vanish." A shiver of unease swept through me when Wu didn't answer. "Are we talking explosives?" Collapsing a network of tunnels and manmade caves was about the only way I could see them containing charun if a breakout was imminent. "Or ... ?"

"He killed them all," Wu said slowly, tasting the shock I heard so clearly. "The guards weren't told to evacuate. There was no warning. Father collapsed the entire prison on top of them. Rescue teams have been dispatched, but they'll find bodies if there's anything left at all."

"Why would he ... ?" My heart smacked against my ribs in a hard thud. "Famine."

All those people crushed to end a single life. All that blood spilled to send us a message.

Uncle Harold, what was left of him, was truly gone. He could never be laid to rest with Aunt Nancy now.

Famine had cost him and his family so much already, and the tally kept rising.

"She's dead," he rasped, his voice hollow. "There's no way she survived the blast."

"War knew." I finally understood the look. There had been no remorse, only calculation. "When Famine's coterie died, she realized Famine had too. That's why War used her name as a call to arms." I wet my lips and braced my heart for his answer. "Will my people die if I'm killed?"

"The coterie will survive you. They're not born of your essence or dependent upon your oversight." His voice rang hollow. "Famine's coterie should have outlived her. Only Death, as far as I know, must remain near her offspring to sustain them.

However, I can't recall a coterie entering without their mistress. Perhaps that made the difference. They might not have been able to acclimate without her."

A creeping suspicion gripped me, but I didn't want to voice it just yet.

"We're all that's left. There's only the two of us." Shock blasted through me as I grasped what that meant. "What if Death agrees to surrender? What if I do too? This can end here, now, today."

"Father has declared war on the cadre." Wu rested his hand against my cheek, his gaze roving over my face like he wanted to memorize every detail. "Hunting you, killing Famine. This time is different, and he senses it. He's not going to take chances. Neither of you are safe. None of your people are safe."

"This is the cycle you meant for me to break." Insight sparked my nerves alight, like his prolonged touch had shocked awake some forgotten corner of my brain. "This is the war you wanted ended. It was never about me or my sisters. This is about your father."

A surprised laugh caught in my throat that bordered on maniacal.

Played.

We had all been played.

There was no struggle to master this terrene. There was war with a fallen god. Earth was simply the chosen battlefield.

"That's why you've allowed the cycle of ascension to continue for so long when you could have simply slaughtered cadre as they breached once you located the seal. You can beat us, but you can't defeat him."

"Earth needs a champion." His hand fell, tightening into a fist on the way down to his side. "I wanted it to be you."

"Sorry, Wu, but this is for your own good." I drew back my

arm and slapped the taste out of his mouth. "Did that do it, or do you need another one?"

A bright red handprint marred his pale cheek, and his eyes crackled with shocked fury. "That was sufficient."

"Good." I stood taller. "I have family here. Human and charun. This changes nothing for me. I'm fighting. I have no choice. I have to protect my people." I stuck out my hand. "The only question is— Are you still in this?"

For a fraction of a second, he stared at my outstretched arm, and I watched calculations being tabulated behind his eyes. "Yes." He blinked them away, and we shook on a new partnership. "I'm with you."

"Then we need to rally all the allies we can beg, borrow, or steal." I puffed out my cheeks and anchored my hands on my hips. "Can you do me a favor?"

"I can try," he said with less bravado than usual.

"Find Ezra for me."

Wu recoiled like I'd slapped him. Again. "What?"

"We have enough skeletons jumping out of closets as it is. It's time for me to do some spring cleaning of my own." I chewed the inside of my cheek. At this rate, I was going to gnaw right through. "Ezra is powerful. He might be an asset." I shrugged. "Even if he's not, I owe the coterie the truth." What few scraps I had to offer. "War told me I was owned. I want to know if it's him. I need answers before another surprise jumps up and bites me on the ass."

The pipe dream of meeting up with their maybe-Otillian agent had evaporated around the time Janardan came into the picture. As invested as I was in Conquest's past, her history, it was ancient history. What I needed now, more than to sate my curiosity, were answers relevant to *me*, to this moment in time, to my future. Ezra, whatever terrene he hailed from, whoever he was, had those.

"Are you sure?" He plucked at his lip, staring at the space between his feet. "This is what you want?"

"I'm compromised." Tartness flavored my laughter. "On more than one front." I scrubbed my face with my palms like it might help wake my brain. "Someone altered me between the time I arrived and when my coterie breached. I came out wrong. That's what everyone keeps telling me. How did it happen? Why me and no one else? I'm different, and there's got to be a reason for that. There's another player in this game, one who has yet to reveal their agenda, and my money is on it being him."

Thankfully, I could eliminate one person from the suspect pool. Wu's fruit loop of a father couldn't be the one holding my leash. He would have strangled me with it by now.

"All right." Wu lowered his hand then tucked them both in his pockets. "I'll give you what you want."

"Thank you." Searching the NSB database while his father had us in his sights would be next to impossible, but he could always ask Santiago to lend him an extra set of hands. "I appreciate you doing this for me."

"You should go." He started walking toward the parking lot. "Cole is waiting for you."

As much as I hated to pile things on his plate, it needed saying. "We might need Deland Bruster too."

Wu pinched the bridge of his nose, and one of his eyelids twitched. "You want Bruster to evaluate Ezra?"

The man saw into other people's souls. What he glimpsed in Ezra's might save us all.

"I know it will cost." Probably more than I could afford to give. "Tell him to give me a ballpark."

His arm dropped like dead weight, his fingers limp as noodles. "As you wish."

Wu took one of the White Horse SUVs. I'm not sure where

he got the keys, but it's not like the coterie hid them. Letting him drive one felt like painting a bull's eye on his back, but he'd made the call. He knew what he was doing. That was more than I could say for the rest of us. Maybe while he was out driving around he would rescue my laptop. Then again, it had been left alone with his father and his goons. Better write it off as a loss. Maybe Santiago could hook me up with one of his billion tablets in the meantime.

An otherworldly quiet had descended on the bunkhouse while Wu and I had our chat, and I was glad for it. It would make what came next that much easier. And more dangerous. For me.

Santiago had gone ahead in a rental van packed with his gear. Portia had followed in another rental stuffed with clothes and supplies for the rest of us. Miller drove a third padded with blankets to cradle the pod on his way to rendezvous with us at the clinic. That left me to play chauffeur for Death.

Finding her was simple. She was the only Iniid to have embraced a human appearance.

"You ready to go?" I studied the body she crafted and wondered if she had gotten impatient to see Janardan and copied an actress from whatever movie had popped up on the tablet Santiago left her for research purposes. Her face was familiar, too familiar, down to the mole riding high on her upper right cheek. "We'll talk about impersonating famous actresses later."

A slight crinkle to her brow was the only indication Death was confused by the reference.

The fact her coterie didn't blink at her accompanying me without a guard didn't surprise me given she could kill with a touch. Nothing like impending doom to make conversation awkward.

After we got strapped in the SUV, I got down to business. Better to die in the backwoods where the vehicle would slide off the shoulder of a dirt road if she took offense than to wait until we hit traffic. I wasn't going to risk innocents getting hurt if I could help it. I had to handle this with delicacy.

I cut my eyes toward her. "You killed Famine's coterie."

Smooth as a baby's behind, Boudreau. No wonder Rixton had preferred interviewing our subjects solo.

"I did," she said, voice solemn.

At least she hadn't tried to lie. This was already going better than expected. "Why?"

"I gave Famine my word I would bring them to this world, and I did. She didn't ask what would become of them once we arrived. That was her mistake."

A shiver swept down my arms. "You killed them for the hell of it?"

"No." A smile twitched on her lips. "I killed them because they conspired against me."

"They weren't happy Famine left them behind."

"No, they were not." Her gaze turned distant. "I lost three children to their petty jealousy, but a vow with Death is binding. I had to bring the remainder through as promised, or there would have been consequences." She didn't elaborate on those. "Beyond that, I was under no further obligation to them, and I exacted my vengeance."

Call me crazy, but Death seemed big on vengeance.

There was only time for one last question before we arrived. "Is my coterie in danger from you?"

She reflected on her answer. "Not at present."

Chuckling at her frankness, I asked, "Will you give me a heads-up when that changes?"

"You'll know." Her smile flashed rows of serrated teeth. "I won't leave you wondering."

"Oh good." I tightened my hands on the wheel. "That's . . . comforting."

The white moving van waited for us in the lot, and I nodded to Miller on my way past.

The hole-in-the-wall clinic was exactly as I remembered it—or didn't remember it—from the night of the accident when I took the first dose of my new reality. Dr. Norwood hadn't changed either. He was still a middle-aged man with thinning hair, except perspective filled in the blanks about his charun ancestry. Hindsight told me the rest. This was a practice meant to help charun stay off the NSB's radar. I just hadn't realized it at the time.

"Ah, Ms. Boudreau." His frazzled smile was explained by the mountainous shadow in the room behind him. "Such a pleasure to see you again. I trust you've been feeling well?"

"I've got no complaints." I indicated the woman at my side. "This is Death. She's here to see her mate."

"It's a pleasure to meet you," he said, paling. "Janardan will make a full recovery. While I'm not overly familiar with Iniid biology, I suspect he will regenerate the leg given time."

The slightest hitch in Death's breath exposed how much the news meant to her. "Thank you."

While Dr. Norwood led her into the room where he had treated me months ago, I waited on Cole to extricate himself. He did so, closing the door behind him before joining me in the dusty waiting room.

Though he rested his hand on my cheek, he slid his gaze past my shoulder. "Where is Phoebe?"

I tried to ignore the pinch in my chest, but I mostly failed. Phoebe was a complication. I wasn't sure how she would fit with us, with me, and that left me jittery. Cole adored her, that much was obvious, so I would have to embrace and adapt. Two things I excelled at these days.

"The pod is locked in the van with Miller standing guard. I

wasn't sure if she was cognizant of her surroundings, but I left a tablet with her playing cartoons just in case."

"Thank you." The warmth in his gaze tangled my heart-strings. "Your kindness can't be easy."

Phoebe was proof of his relationship with Conquest, and that hurt. But she was just a kid. I couldn't hold that against her. Even if it hurt. "However this shakes out, none of it is her fault."

"We got lucky tonight." He slid his palm down my neck and across my shoulder before walking into me. "Things could have gone so much worse." His lips brushed my temple. "How are you coping?"

"With matehood, dragonhood, or motherhood?" I snorted then sobered. "It's a lot to absorb, but I'll manage. I have you to help me."

"Always."

The tight expression he wore gave me a twinge, and I dug deep. Really deep. Way deep.

"I know better than anyone that blood is the least of what makes a family." I squeezed his hand. "I'm going to try. That's the best I can promise you." His expression relaxed a fraction, and I was glad I had made the effort. "When will she wake?"

"The effects will wear off within a few days after separating her from Death's influence."

"Why did they keep her in stasis? Surely lugging the pod around raised questions."

"The others would have noticed her if she'd been allowed to mingle with the coteries. They had to isolate her to protect her. They told the others the pod was critical to Death's rebirth cycle for the coterie to avoid questions."

"Sleeping Beauty," I murmured. "They let her sleep away the time like a fairy tale princess."

"Yes." He sounded conflicted. "I'm grateful for the chance to raise her, at least in part, but we won't know what we're dealing with until she wakes."

Worrying my bottom lip between my teeth, I had to ask, "Can you deal if a maternal bond doesn't spark?"

"Your relationship with Phoebe is yours to define. I will support whatever feels most natural to you." His arms formed a warm cage around me, like I might escape if he let go. He really ought to know better by now. "I'm sorry I kept this from you."

"I understand why you did. You had no way of knowing if you could trust me. I even get why you didn't tell the coterie. You did the exact thing my dad would have done, so I can't hold it against you." I relaxed into his strength. "With that in mind, I have a confession to make, and I hope you'll show me the same consideration."

With a tight nod, Cole guided me outside where we took a short walk that allowed him to keep an eye on the van while giving us privacy. Aware how precious time was to us now, I kept my confession brief while explaining when Ezra entered my life and my suspicions about the bond War had identified.

"This Ezra called you every year on your birthday?" Cole scratched his jaw. "That's the only contact you had with him? You never met him? You only ever heard his voice?"

"Yes." I cut him a sideways look. "Does that matter?"

"Bonds work in myriad ways." He hesitated. "Their effectiveness relies on proximity or a talisman." He lifted his wrist, and the rosy metal band there glinted. "Conquest implanted us with a part of herself. She's the only person who can break the bond, and she can exert her will through it."

Hardly breaking news, but I regretted the reminder of the control I wielded over them.

"Less powerful charun have built coteries using their ability to mesmerize, but that requires daily contact. Voice works, but touch is best. Psychic connections fade without regular feedback, and so would any bond requiring blood or sacrifice to reaffirm it."

A purest flame of white-hot fury ignited in me. "You're saying Ezra gave me an implant to control me."

"Assuming Ezra is responsible, yes. That seems most likely." Cole slowed his pace. "The calls might have been maintenance, checking to ensure you were still susceptible to him."

"You mean the episodes might not have been a thing he saved me from, but conditioning. Inflict enough pain that my eyes crossed, that I was so desperate I would take any help to make it stop, then dial me up and heal me with a magic phone call." I thought about it. "It would reassure him I was still under his thumb while stockpiling my goodwill and preserving his anonymity."

"I wish we had known," he said, and I understood he saw it as a failure that someone had gotten to me first, that they had kept a bead on me all that time while my coterie was unawares.

"I kept it to myself at first. Any one of you might have been Ezra, and I wasn't sure what he might want if he revealed himself. I thought it was smarter to wait him out, let him come to me. But he didn't." I scuffed the soles of my shoes. "Later, I wanted to tell you, all of you, but I kept thinking I would gain access to the NSB's database soon. I could pin him down, figure him out, and then present the problem and the solution."

"That's not how this works." His fingers tightened around mine. "You're not a liability, Luce."

"You haven't seen me around my birthday." I laughed hoarsely. "I come apart at the seams, Cole. It ain't pretty." I shut my eyes for a heartbeat. "I wanted to believe that being with the coterie might be enough, like all I needed to get my head on straight again was contact with my own kind, but I can't be sure. None of us can be sure what Ezra was doing for me—to me—all those years."

We reached the farthest point where we could keep the van in sight then paused together.

"All this time we were planning for the wrong war." Cole's breath tickled my cheek. "I hope Wu finds us answers." A giddy flutter accompanied the word *us*, a thrill that we were in this together by his choice. "We need the whole truth about his father. We have to know what we're up against, and we must be certain of his loyalties."

I quelled the knee-jerk response to defend my partner. "You think he might turn on us?"

"He could have pitched saving the world to you ten different ways, and you would have jumped on any of them. It's who you are, it's what you do. But he chose to go with the version we would most easily accept, the one we anticipated. He didn't warn you about his father until he was cornered. He didn't do a lot of things that would have proven his allegiance to a shared cause." Cole shook his head. "I believe he wants this to end. I'm just concerned what acceptable losses look like to him after all this time."

"Collateral damage," I agreed, understanding what he meant. "That's us, all right."

"His Utopia will be built upon the bones of all the cadres who came before this one." He released me. "We have to be careful, or he'll add ours to the pile."

As much as I wanted to defend Wu, say he wouldn't use us like that, I didn't know him well enough to swear that was true. He had opened himself up, shared his home and family with me, but he hadn't done it out of the goodness of his heart. He saw an opportunity, and he took it.

"We have to get Dad away from the taskforce clinic." Until I spoke the words, I didn't realize I how long I had been holding them in. I could have raised the issue with Wu at any time, but

I had kept my mouth shut. Relocating Dad meant facing him, and it was easier being a coward, but it was time to woman-up. "The issue is where do we put him? The enclave is a solid option. I'm not hypocritical enough to say it's good enough for Thom but not Dad."

Cole read me with ease. "But you aren't sure if you can trust Wu to protect them."

The usefulness of the information Wu had entrusted to me hinged on finding a receptive listener willing to bargain. From what I could tell, his dad wasn't the chatty type. And I doubted he would deal with me. That meant Wu's secrets, while damning under other circumstances, might not be worth the oxygen he used to share them. There was no leverage there, and I wouldn't use innocents in that way. I couldn't if I wanted to stay in the saddle on my high horse. Falling off meant I was just as underhanded as Conquest.

"Thom is their guest, for now," I admitted, "but Knox already views him as an insurance policy."

Cole picked up on my meaning. "You're worried Knox might sacrifice them to spare his family."

"I'm more worried Wu might let him." All his careful plans were crumbling, and I didn't want my people getting smooshed in the process. "Where do we go from here?"

"We let Santiago live his prepper dreams. He purchased safehouses and cached supplies for the coterie all over the country." A shrug rolled through his massive shoulders. "We fall off the grid for a while, get our affairs in order."

The fine print, as I read it, was get *my* affairs in order. Set up long-term care for Dad and arrange protection for the Rixtons, things I might not be around much longer to guarantee.

"We'll gather intel and rally our allies," Cole continued, "and then we'll make our move."

"I wish things were different," I whispered more to myself than to him. "I wish we could just live."

"I've had different," he murmured back. "I'll take this life—take you—over that any day."

And when his lips brushed mine, sealing the vow, I believed him.

EPILOGUE

———◦◉◦———

Ensconced in his high-rise apartment, a glass and steel work of art that pierced the clouds, Adam dialed up Kapoor, filling the seconds between hitting send and the call being answered with the myriad ways he had fucked up his operation. Underestimating his father had bitten him on the ass too many times to count in his youth, but he liked to think he had long ago accepted the hard truth his father was capable of anything.

Anything, yes, but he still hadn't expected The Hole.

No war was won without casualties.

Two hundred inmates. Three dozen civilians. Over three hundred guards. All gone.

And it was his fault. His careless words had ended in an execution . . . and in mass murder.

"What fresh fuckery do you have for me?" Kapoor rasped. "I'm goddamn finished with today."

"Luce wants to meet Ezra." Adam kept it blunt. "She wants to hold him accountable and turn him to her cause."

"I don't have enough fingers to count off the reasons why that's a bad idea, but damn if I have a better one." Kapoor shut a door, probably to his office, to give them privacy. "Adam, this has gone on too long. You've got to come clean with her, or we're going to lose her."

"She's mated," he said softly. "They have a child."

"Half of that you already knew." Kapoor wasn't pulling punches, probably why Adam called him in the first place. "The kid changes nothing." Bitterness weighted his words. "You have to focus on Conquest, or Luce, or whatever the hell you sleep better calling her at night. We need her to seal the breach, or the Otillians will just keep coming. Earth is already on the brink. We can't keep taking in charun refugees while pretending they don't exist. This needs to end. She can do that for us."

"Farhan," he allowed himself the brief intimacy of acknowledging their friendship. "She'll die."

"There's only one way to plug a hole between worlds, and she's it." He sighed. "We're never going to get another chance like this one. There will never be another Conquest willing to sacrifice herself for the sake of this world. Either Luce Boudreau dies, or we all do."

Adam disconnected without saying goodbye and padded into his library. A portrait hung over the fireplace, a reproduction of a reproduction of a reproduction. The original was in a climate-controlled storage unit safe from the ravages of time in a way his human wife had not been.

What he recalled of her was not a flesh and blood woman, but the sweep of paint on canvas. He had memorized each brushstroke, absorbed each detail with rapt fascination, until it all blurred in his mind.

Marrying her had been forbidden, mating her biologically impossible.

Humans simply lacked the depth of soul required to forge a bond that weathered eternity.

Love was not enough. That wasn't the first lesson he learned, nor the hardest, but it left an impression.

Adam should have died with her. She should have lived with him. But neither of those things happened.

His kind mated only once in their very long lives.

He had mated twice.

First, he gave away his heart, and then he gave away his soul.

Luce wasn't the only one condemned by his scheming. Adam had finally succeeded in what he failed to do all those centuries ago. Adam had damned himself too.

Kapoor listened to the dead air and sighed. Wu was fraying under the strain. He'd been holding together fine until his father got involved ahead of schedule. Then again, maybe it would have always gone this route. Maybe his old man really was divine, and they had all been doomed from the start.

A pulse of energy swept through the room like a spring breeze, and Kapoor shut his eyes and prayed to any gods who might hear. But the trouble with living in the shadow of fear cast by one was you didn't have much faith that any others might be roused to lend a hand.

Heart slamming against his chest, he watched as the knob turned, and the door swung open. The man who entered his office was tall and lean, dressed in pressed jeans and a white button-down shirt. His shoes were brown loafers, and they matched his belt. Looking higher than his collar—that was the problem.

Ezra was the most beautiful person Kapoor had ever seen. You had to look and then look again to be certain you were seeing what you thought you saw. Sometimes even that wasn't enough. He was compelling, emitting his own gravitational pull that had Kapoor rising from his chair to greet what amounted to certain death.

The would-be god just smiled, benevolent, used to the attention he commanded from either sex.

Square jaw, bladed cheekbones, aquiline nose. He was the whole package. The curtain of wavy blond hair that brushed his wide shoulders didn't hurt things either. His eyes, though. That's what trapped you if you were dumb enough to meet his gaze.

As it turned out, Kapoor wasn't half as smart as he thought. "To what do I owe the pleasure?"

Just the word—*pleasure*—and the throaty rasp that passed for his voice left Ezra chuckling.

"I need to have a word with my son." He strolled over and shook the hand Kapoor didn't remember extending. "I was told you could make that happen."

The touch of skin on skin was electric, and Kapoor shuddered from the wash of power across his nerves. "Adam doesn't report to me, but I'm sure I can locate him." The oxygen punched from his lungs when he severed the contact, a small death that reminded him how alive Ezra could make you feel. "He was out in the field last I heard, so it will take a few days."

"A few days," Ezra mused. "Are we going to pretend you didn't end a call with him before I arrived?"

Only his mastery in the art of lying, a job requirement with the NSB, saved him from stumbling.

"Big difference between answering a call and arranging for a meeting between the two of you." He flicked his hand toward the mountain of paperwork on his desk. "Adam heard about The Hole. He was calling in to confirm the casualties."

"Famine is dead. I snapped her neck before the charge detonated." He stared at Kapoor and let his inner monster slip its leash. Just a bit. "The cadre must be eliminated. They are foul creatures bent on destruction. They are not pets to be fed and watered and kept in cages."

"We had hoped to develop more effective weapons to use during the next ascension by allowing scientists access to a live specimen."

The way things were going, there would be plenty more to come.

Goddamn, he was tired of the subterfuge. How Wu survived playing both teams this long mystified him.

"Otillian biology makes the creation of effective weaponry impossible." He steepled his fingers. "They're too altered when they arrive to be taken down by anything but brute force. The standard protocols don't apply."

Since Kapoor's best chance at survival was keeping his mouth shut, that's what he did.

"I'm aware of my son's perversions." The monster in Ezra wet its lips when it looked at him. "I have made the same mistake as so many parents before me. Indulgence. The time for such leniency has passed." He tucked it back out of sight. "I want you to arrange a meeting with my son, and I expect Luce Boudreau to be in attendance."

Ezra didn't lower himself to explaining what would happen to Kapoor if his demands weren't met.

"I'll get right on that." Kapoor's hand trembled when he reached for a pen. "Where can I reach you?"

"There's a converted warehouse in Summit, near Lake Bevin." A smile tugged at his lips, and the effect almost struck Kapoor dumb. "I'm going to pay the inhabitants a visit."

The enclave.

The fucker knew about the enclave.

"Leave the address with me." Kapoor kept his expression blank, his soul dark. "I'll be in touch."

"See that you are." Ezra pivoted on his heel. "I am not your god, but I'm not without my wrath."

Whatever magic had strung Kapoor upright during his conversation with Ezra got cut once the door closed. Knees buckling, he collapsed in a limp heap, his tailbone driving into the hardwood floor. Hidden behind his desk, panting like he'd just run a marathon—or for his life—he dialed Wu. "We've got a problem."

Talk about the understatement of the century.